An entire phalanx of Nova Cat warriors lined the Hall of the Nova Cat's Clan Council Chamber. Not only Khan Jacali Nostra and saKhan Niko West, along with Oathmaster Kanaye, but also a bevy of Bloodnamed warriors, from the two on-world Galaxy commanders down through a dozen Star colonels and even a Star captain or two. The leathers of their ceremonial outfits created a wash of blackness—liquid void sloshing against the bottom steps of the tiered council chamber, swallowing almost the entire bottom circle and the Khan's dais.

Against this mighty display of Nova Cat power, a single, diminutive female entered the chamber.

Against the black army below, Katana's outfit stood out in bright, vibrant colors, as though disdainful at such lack of originality. Black, loose pants tucked into red, knee-high boots, overlaid with a pristine white jacket, trimmed in orange down the front and on arms and cuffs, with a red belt woven into the jacket, a dragon etched into the belt buckle. The red piping on the pants and a slash of red on the shoulders denoted her status as a MechWarrior. Even at this distance, her high collar could be seen displaying the logo any warrior here recognized as belonging to a *tai-shu*.

With great will, Kisho finally pulled eyes away from her serene face and searched in vain above her, waiting for the rest of her troops to arrive. She took almost a half minute to sedately move down the entire length of steps in between the various tiered, circular benches, before coming to rest on the last step, as though afraid to step down to the bottom floor and its ocean of darkness.

DARK AGE

HERETIC'S FAITH

A BATTLETECH™ NOVEL

Randall N. Bills

A ROC BOOK

ROC

Published by New American Library, a division of
Penguin Group (USA) Inc., 375 Hudson Street,
New York, New York 10014, USA
Penguin Group (Canada), 90 Eglinton Avenue East, Suite 700, Toronto,
Ontario M4P 2Y3, Canada (a division of Pearson Penguin Canada Inc.)
Penguin Books Ltd., 80 Strand, London WC2R 0RL, England
Penguin Ireland, 25 St. Stephen's Green, Dublin 2,
Ireland (a division of Penguin Books Ltd.)
Penguin Group (Australia), 250 Camberwell Road, Camberwell, Victoria 3124,
Australia (a division of Pearson Australia Group Pty. Ltd.)
Penguin Books India Pvt. Ltd., 11 Community Centre, Panchsheel Park,
New Delhi - 110 017, India
Penguin Group (NZ), cnr Airborne and Rosedale Roads, Albany,
Auckland 1310, New Zealand (a division of Pearson New Zealand Ltd.)
Penguin Books (South Africa) (Pty.) Ltd., 24 Sturdee Avenue,
Rosebank, Johannesburg 2196, South Africa

Penguin Books Ltd., Registered Offices:
80 Strand, London WC2R 0RL, England

First published by Roc, an imprint of New American Library,
a division of Penguin Group (USA) Inc.

First Printing, August 2005
10 9 8 7 6 5 4 3 2 1

To all my nieces and nephews, who bring such joy to all our lives: Amy, BreeAnn, Brian, Brooklynn, Cody, Devon, Dylan, Emily, Eric, Hannah, Hunter, Jeramy, Jessica, Jordan, Kelsey, Kristy, Kylie, Meghan, Seanne, and Shannie. Never be afraid to seize your dreams, but remember to include the Savior in them.

Acknowledgments

To my first readers for always catching those extra bits: Herb Beas, David McCulloch, Mike Miller, Jeff Morgan, and Oystein Tvedten.

To Loren (and of course Heather) for always lending a helping hand, whether for writing this novel, writing the next one, or the one after that.

To Sharon Turner Mulvihill, for almost ten years of friendship, a helping hand to improve my storytelling abilities and for helping draw out the true story in this novel.

To my magnificent children Bryn Kevin, Ryana Nikol and Kenyon Aleksandr: when I fail to live up to the example of my father, thank you for your hugs of forgiveness; I love you.

To my wife . . . my supporter . . . my best friend: it all would be blackness without you.

REPUBLIC OF THE SPHERE

AD SECURITAS PER UNITAS · REPUBLIC OF THE SPHERE

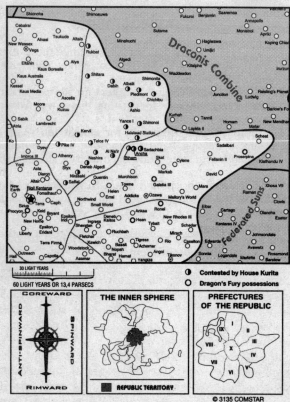

30 LIGHT YEARS

60 LIGHT YEARS OR 13,4 PARSECS

◐ Contested by House Kurita
○ Dragon's Fury possessions

COREWARD
SPINWARD
ANTI-SPINWARD
RIMWARD

THE INNER SPHERE

■ REPUBLIC TERRITORY

PREFECTURES OF THE REPUBLIC

© 3135 COMSTAR
CARTOGRAPHIC CORPS

Prologue

Zane Plateau, Tengoku Mountain
Nova Cat Reservation, Irece
Irece Prefecture, Draconis Combine
5 November 3135

The ancient volcanic mountain pressed against his consciousness, until Kisho dug his nails into wind-whipped palms to stay present. His raspy, torn flesh hardly resembled human skin.

The mountain was a living entity with roots sunk to the white-hot magma flows of rock-blood at the center of Irece and a white-cold, snow-hooded cap that pierced the atmosphere itself, towering in its inhuman arrogance to 9.7 kilometers above sea level. The small, snapping flames of the fire just out of reach seemed beyond insignificant—a penlight to the endless darkness of interstellar void.

A susurration wafted flames like a gentle fan, snapping sparks into the air—a small, burnt sienna kaleidoscope spinning and singing away on the wind—and prickling flesh along the exposed arms and legs of his ceremonial leathers, while gently ruffling his hair.

> *Flames grant sight*
> *To eyes wide shut*
> *Visions unfold*
> *Purified in soul*

Need to cut my hair. If he concentrated hard enough on such mundane minutiae, he could ignore Kanaye's almost inaudible recitations of ancient script. Could ignore the gentle wind that felt like the sleeping breath of the gargantuan mountain, waiting to be awakened, startled up from slumber to a frenzy of hate and heat and destruction as it spewed forth violence to sweep away all before its path.

He shivered, though not with cold. The purifying bath an hour past in the icy springwater hadn't even raised goose bumps. Yet he almost leaned forward with palms outstretched to the fire, but caught himself before violating the ceremony.

What is the matter? Too close for comfort? Too close to what they try so hard to awaken within you?

His stomach rumbled. Kisho closed his eyes—locking interior blast doors, sealing off such thoughts down deep—shamed at having been distracted so easily by the hunger pangs of fast snapping at his stomach like razor-caws to fresh kill. He breathed deeply—the burning scrub tree branches of the rite (found, never cut) filled with hints of dark cinnamon and freshness eons in the making—and tried to set aside all consciousness. Tried to merge into the moment, to be one with the mountain that could not possibly feel his presence, much less care about the puny humans perched so precariously on its hardened, patchy skin.

He'll be done soon. This idea usually snapped him into a light trance, but this time it failed. Regardless of the reprimanding look from Kanaye (*he always knew!*), Kisho floundered like a fish out of water, flopping wetly from one side to another, frantic to find the cool reassurance of the watery depths of trance, but knowing Death would strike with his steely scythe before he might plunge back to safety.

Or in my case, the scythe of Kanaye's disappointment.

Kisho just managed to keep the sigh of his own discontent within. *They'll be starting the feasting soon.* Tables would be laden with fresh fruits grown in the agro-domes (denying Irece its rightful due of winter's barren lands); meats from cattle, lambs, pigs, and even horse; an abundant flow of liquor (even warriors will douse themselves into oblivion this night); sweetmeats, rolls, sugar cakes and more. The air would be filled with smiles and good cheers to celebrate the Exodus of the Great General centuries ago.

What, three hundred and fifty years ago? He quickly ran the math and corrected. *No, three hundred and fifty-one. Three and a half centuries ago and now we are back, different and yet the same. And we Clans celebrate this great event as though we journeyed the depths of space to the Clan homeworlds, leaving a dying Star League to destroy itself; as though we colonized those hellish, barren rocks; as though we survived the horrific wars that killed millions and lived through the reforging of the very bedrock of human society from the ground up into a new warrior society: one that returned to the Inner Sphere to conquer . . . and failed. And now we Nova Cats live on our reservations in the Draconis Combine, beholden to oaths of fealty sworn to House Kurita, having defected from the Clans once we saw the writing on the wall. Having followed the visions that caused our brother Clans to fall on us and kill us by the millions. Until now I sit on this mountain, cold and hungry from fasting, wondering when Kanaye will awaken and proclaim his visions that will lead us down some new path. Some new path that must lead us to a better tomorrow. Because, by the Founder, the Clans have been corrupted. And if we do not—*

"Kisho."

His eyes snapped open, meandering thoughts sundered like a laser punching through 'Mech armor. He immediately averted his eyes, bowing deeply in his sitting position. He held it for several moments in an attempt to recover, then raised his eyes to Kanaye's.

Knowing eyes burst like halogens across him, stripping away all pretense. Shame and anger mixed liberally. But Kisho kept his aplomb, as he had trained himself for long years to do, in spite of Kanaye's best attempts to slip past his defenses.

"Oathmaster." The word hung on the precipice between them, shredded in the wind. Their eyes locked in a probing stare.

The wind began to gain strength, as though the battle of wills had begun to disturb the sleeping mountain. The fire giant adjusted in his repose, dreams troubled. Liquid shadows ran across Kanaye's features, conveying an otherworldly feel. Kisho could not shake the feeling that Kanaye was an incarnation of the spirit of the nova cat, a corporeal manifestation from some spirit world. A world to which Kisho would never have access.

Right. He shook himself out of it. *Spirit world!*

Kisho's lips quirked ever so slightly, though he hoped he managed to keep most of his reaction covered. Yet something sparked within Kanaye's age-old eyes and he nodded imperceptibly.

What did you see, old man? He knew better than to ask—the mountain would cough up a straight answer before Kanaye would.

"What do you see?" Kanaye uncannily echoed.

My stupidity. He breathed in the scent of burning wood and that hint of dark cinnamon once more, playing for time. He finally responded, without raising his eyes. "I see young bloods from a dozen tribes, their anxious eyes failing to shield burning desires." He fell easily into the game, executing his flimsy reflection of the old man's true abilities.

"Ah . . . the trip to humanity's cradle. And what did you learn?"

"Learn?" *Nothing.* "I do not know. But I know the universe is falling back to war. War has already started and will only escalate. That regardless of the long decades of Stone's peace, with the continued loss of rapid interstellar communication and without Stone himself, his cult of personality is fragmenting quicker than the homeworld Clans during the Wars of Reaving."

A log shifted, snapping loudly and disgorging a shower of sparks that momentarily lit the immediate region, before whipping away on the now steadily blowing wind. As the Clans were stripped down and torn away so brutally during that time.

"All from the Founder till now, slowly ground down and ripped away."

"All?" Kanaye rejoined, his soft voice smothering the anger of Kisho's words.

Kisho raised arrogant eyes to impassive ones. *"Aff."*

"Neg."

"What?"

"Why did the Founder create us?"

I am not a five-year-old crèchekin, old man! Arrogant eyes locked with cool ones and the silence stretched, while the wind played fits with the small fire. Finally, as the silence became unbearable, Kisho answered, the weaker one as always. "To return and establish the Star League. To save the thousands of

Inner Sphere worlds from themselves and the Great Houses that rule them. *Quiaff?*"

"*Aff.*" Silence once more descended.

Kisho knew how to play this game, had fine-tuned his participation over the years, acting the role of something he didn't feel. The well-played game used to give him a feeling of self-satisfied conquest. But lately, the hollow ring of his participation had begun to make him weary. And with his weariness came anger and impatience.

Wishing to bring this round to a conclusion, he broke the silence for a second time. "But we failed. There is no Star League and the Clans are half their original numbers. And those of us here . . . are half what we were."

"*Aff.*" Kanaye's lips barely moved and the now dying flames of the fire cast his features further into darkness.

I can never read you in the fullness of noon, much less now, old man. Frustration gnawed, warring with hunger pains. "Then how is all not lost?"

"Because there is always tomorrow."

Kisho opened his lips for a hot retort, then swallowed, knowing only more riddles would ensue. He forced himself to take several deep breaths of the crisp air. Then he centered, despite the situation. He thought through several permutations of what the old man might be saying.

Kisho finally responded, under control once again, his voice a match for the best prophetic tone Kanaye could offer. "The Star League can be founded tomorrow and we have achieved our goal."

The flames flickered down to coals, lambent crimson casting no real visibility, heightening the mystical feel to the entire encounter.

"I have a vision," Kanaye finally responded.

Of course you do. The harshest of inner silence met Kisho's sarcasm. He struggled to keep his body from telegraphing his sense of defeat.

"The Dragon has taken flight."

Kisho jolted imperceptibly. *That is your vision?! Of course the Dragon's taken flight!* His memories of the long trip to Terra came rushing back. He saw the funeral of Victor Steiner-Davion and the plethora of old and young bloods, all scheming to use the event to their own best advantage, and the assault of the Benjamin Warlord on The Republic—an assault the coordinator disavowed. *Surely he isn't referring to the warlord. Then what?*

His facial features slackened momentarily, as he drew lightly upon his years of training—modeling and scenarios running through his mind, the shape of his perceptions forming and reforming in cycling permutations. In a flash, he realized there could only be one person fitting that description. He came back to the present, his face resuming its usual arrogant cast.

"Katana Tormark."

"Aff."

Kisho leaned forward as though to capture the meager heat of the dying coals and ran it through slowly. "You refer to the information passed to our Watch by the Order of the Five Pillars, *quiaff*?"

"Aff."

"How can you mean Katana when she has had her wings cut?"

"She has?"

"Scooped from battlefields in The Republic by the heir to the Dragon and even now in route to Black Luthien? Considering she just killed a warlord and took worlds in the Dragon's name without his sanction . . . House Kurita has never been known for its kindness. A dank cell, or a parting of her head, *quiaff*?"

"Neg." The single word fell softly, but behind it Kanaye's eyes thrust straight through Kisho.

A challenge, old man? Kisho's more frequently surfacing anger overcame the shame at his growing disrespect. This time he drew fully on all the years of his training—going deeper while still keeping the lid firmly shut on the pervading fears he kept at bay— and his face fell into the blank expression of deep mystic trance. He took the tidbits of information and began to plug them in and rearrange, mind spiraling through dark space and across the reach of infinity until a pattern slowly emerged. One so delicate and gossamerlike, it might rend if touched. Instead, he fed it additional bits of information, allowing them to fall where they might on the framework, until the shape solidified, the outlines becoming clear and sharp. He slowly withdrew, his face sloughing the deep trance and returning to humanity's facade.

"A vision," Kanaye intoned.

Right. Sure, old man. A vision. "The Dragon will name her warlord," was Kisho's only response.

The old man nodded slowly, as though a prize pet had just performed a unique trick.

Kisho's anger burned hot at the perceived condescension, but not hot enough to flame away the truth. It *was* but a trick, not a vision. *Never a vision.*

And yet Kisho also felt the old satisfaction at having emerged victorious for another round.

"And?" the old man continued.

"To replace the fallen Sakamoto."

"Neg."

Satisfaction flamed away as though a ship lost to an out-of-control reentry to atmosphere and Kisho cast about, but found nothing else within. As ever. The growing silence became an invisible partner, sitting at the campfire as though to scold them both for their strained relationship.

This time it was the old man who finally spoke. "Dieron."

Kisho reared back as though struck. He wasn't able to sense the thread. *Seems I only ever fail around the old man. Someday, old man. Someday.*

"And?" Kanaye pushed.

Kisho swallowed, hating the incessantness of the old man and knowing he had no choice but to continue in his role. He forged on with this new tidbit. "The Dragon will offer her warlordship of Dieron. She will accept, and be wedded to House Kurita. But we of all people know the harsh mistress that is the Dragon." He prided himself on the fact that no bitterness crept into his voice.

"Aff."

Kisho continued, his confidence building again. "No additional aid will be forthcoming. Either she expands her conquest and fully becomes the warlord of the paper Dieron Military District, or she dies unborn, unable to break out of her egg. A stillborn not worthy of the Dragon's succor."

"Aff."

Kisho nodded, still troubled by the encounter, but intrigued, despite himself, by this new turn of events. He raised his eyes once more to the ancient face. To the face he'd seen from his earliest memories.

To the face of the old man . . . his mentor.

1

Bivouac near New Anaheim
Copenwald, Halstead Station
Dieron Military District, Draconis Combine
1 February 3136

Duchess Katana Tormark held the hard-edged, enameled metal in the cusp of twin palms. The small, cherry-red rectangle, overlaid with an apple-green *katakana* "five" numeral, seemed surreal and out of place in her small, calloused hands, the fingertips and palm pads hardened under years of handling a katana, or the joysticks of a BattleMech.

Not handling this. Never this.

For an irrational minute, she desperately needed to scratch a nail across the surface, confident the hardened enamel would turn out to be acrylic paint, tearing and flaking away. Proving a forgery.

Proving me a forgery.

Katana licked her lips, tasting her own nervousness.

She shifted slightly, her usually bound hair cascading around her shoulders, whispering across a linen shirt, open at the throat to show chocolate-brown skin and whipcord strong muscles. The squeak of hard rubber on tile brought her awareness to the chair she occupied, the table, the room. Eyes so dark they appeared jet-black slowly rose to take in the other occupants of her private command quarters. Unashamed of her obvious trepidations over the rank insignia, she laid it down at the edge of the holographic table gingerly, as though afraid the weight of it would shatter the metal.

From one breath to the next, it sat coiled like a red-and-green snake, poised to strike, kill, and swallow any who dared think their arrogance strong enough to wear it. Ready to decimate any who believed their power was large enough to bear the burden of being a warlord of the Draconis Combine, sworn to their liege lord, Coordinator Vincent Kurita.

You are who you will be. The words of the Old Master percolated and slowly swept away nagging self-doubts. A small smile played across her lips, as she truly focused on the here and now. The past, after all, stayed for no one, regardless of her aspirations, or the towering heights to which she suddenly found herself clinging.

"What do you have?" Katana finally spoke, a soft contralto that filled the room easily.

Just to her left, *Chu-sa* Andre Crawford's emerald-green eyes held hers for a moment. He nodded, leaned forward to tap lightly at one of the holographic table's interfaces, drawing up information he'd obviously prepared beforehand. The room's lights automatically dimmed as a laser-generated, three-dimensional display sprouted.

Human-occupied space (discounting the home Clans, which Katana did regularly) spread out from Terra in a roughly thousand-light-year radius, encompassing more than two thousand inhabited worlds and many hundreds more of colonies lost to the harshness of their environs or the endless wars over centuries. Her eyes danced around the color-coded display, recognition as instantaneous as the contours of her own body reflected in a mirror: House Davion's giant yellow, the green sliver of House Liao, the shattered realms of House Marik's purple, House Steiner's blue, the hodgepodge of the Clans and, of course, the ochre of The Republic of the Sphere and the red of House Kurita.

Now focused, her eyes centered on The Republic of the Sphere and its two hundred and fifty worlds in the vicinity of Terra. Where she'd grown up. Where she'd owed fealty and served in the military for years. She took a small breath . . . where she'd broken those oaths and followed a new master.

Switching to the coreward, spinward region of The Republic, in its Prefecture III, a blood flower bloomed, its deadly petals reaching and soaking up worlds for House Kurita, red smearing down from the Dragon to cover The Republic in blood.

I have done this. She contemplated this thought, but could find no pride, malice, or despair. It also didn't matter that similar incursions of Liao dark green and bright Jade Falcon green occupied two other sections of The Republic. It simply was.

Andre hit a final keystroke and leaned back, as though the display could substitute for any amount of words. And it did.

Highlighted were those worlds previously a part of The Republic but now encompassed within the blood flower of House Kurita. Sakamoto might have included even more, but she was a realist and sporadic fighting on a world meant it was not yet secured. Silence enveloped the room as though they all stood in the presence of some deity of light, worshiping at an altar and hoping they might understand what the hell they were looking at.

Twenty worlds.

The tension in the room rose as Katana fell into the image, absorbing every detail. No matter how many times she'd studied the map and the events leading to this place, it still seemed as though the pieces did not fit together. As though some of the pieces were missing.

Or had some pieces been substituted—they look right, but are really fake? *Yeah, that feels right.* She surreptitiously stole a quick glance at the rank insignia of *tai-shu* and tore her eyes away as it seemed to wink at her in the lowered light.

She sniffed at her flight of fancies and caught the heavy whiff of the ubiquitous diesel fumes that seemed to clog the nasal passages in barbed needles and block out the sun. This was the price of placing her temporary headquarters so close to DeValt Industries and their IndustrialMech manufacturing.

"Behold, the mighty Dieron Military District." As though a bomb detonated within a shoji house, the voice sliced through tension like shrapnel through rice paper walls, causing most at the table to jerk visibly. Dark, suspicious eyes swept towards the opposite end of the table.

The young, Oriental-looking man almost seemed a boy, with clear, smooth features, bright eyes, and short, well-manicured hair. But the full lips were not turned up in the half smirk of a joke, but turned down with a cynicism well beyond his years. His eyes were not bright with vigor and hope, but with delight at the potential to cause pain. And while the others in the room wore a uniform, the young man wore a simple jumpsuit, at total odds with the military surroundings.

Katana slowly shook her head. *Of all the strange paths I have taken, you are the strangest.* Her eyes danced down the cuffs of the jumpsuit, taking in the young man's yakuza tattoos peeking out like runes of power and authority, demanding they put up with him, regardless of his uncharacteristic attitude. Despite herself, she appreciated the stab of the man's wit, regardless of his lack of decorum. Before she could help herself, she chuckled, sarcasm rich in her timbre.

"Leave it to you to state the obvious."

"I live to serve," Lance Shimazu responded, then boomed a laugh that echoed through the room.

She stared daggers at the man, knowing he dismissed all those present, eyes only for her; after all, only the oyabun matters in the end. *I'll be damned if I tell you to shut up.* She wouldn't ask and even if she had, he wouldn't respond. Such was the relationship.

Several dark chuckles finally joined hers around the room.

"You live to be a pain in the ass, you mean," Viki Drexel said from Katana's immediate right. Katana glanced in her direction to see her cute features squeezed into a grimace of obvious distaste. After Drexel's forays into the Combine to secure aid from the House Kurita's criminal underground yakuza—leading to the very presence of this boy-man in their midst—she'd become one of Katana's most trusted agents, despite her obvious first calling as a MechWarrior. A woman to go to when you needed something done on the black side.

But it was one thing to accomplish your mission. And another for the yakuza to demand that a sarcastic pain in the ass sit as a liaison at your command table.

"Isn't that the same thing, Driki?" he rejoined, without even turning his head.

An obvious smile on Parks' face to Drexel's right—Katana even caught a smile on Crawford's before he concealed it—puffed up Drexel as though she were a blowfish trying to scare away predators. Though Katana managed to keep her own face impassive, she couldn't help the inner smile. Shimazu found out about Drexel's playful use of an anagram when she went under cover—Dixie Lever—and had goaded her with it ever since, considered it beyond naive and a mistake a first year SAFE agent wouldn't make.

"Should we not stay on the subject we are here to discuss?" Wahab Fusilli said from Drexel's right.

"I thought we *were* discussing it," Shimazu responded. "After all, we're here to protect the mighty Dieron Military District. Great and mighty shall Katana reign over innumerable worlds—"

"Shut up," Katana interrupted, laser-sharp and cracking, forgetting her previous decision. For once, he actually acquiesced, leaning back as though he could care less one way or another. *Why do you care? Why does your* gumi *consider this deal so important they would assign a liaison? And why someone like* you? She shuffled those questions around for a moment and then filed them away, content to deal with that struggle on a future field of combat. Right now, an urgent battle was unfolding.

"As our illustrious liaison has so succinctly put it, behold the mighty Dieron Military District. Twenty worlds. And if I don't want the other warlords to hand me my own head, or laugh me right out of court, I better not only keep these worlds, but expand. And, by the way, perhaps even take the military district's namesake."

"Um, boss," Parks dropped in. "That ain't gonna

happen with what we have. Unless our new commander and chief handed over a pocket regiment or
two you didn't tell us about."

Katana noticed the frown of disapproval from
Wahab Fusilli over such familiarity concerning their
new liege lord, but dismissed it. The man could be
such a stiff at times, honor or no.

"No, no regiments here."

"Then, um, I'm assuming you've got a plan."

"Well, one or two, but I want to see what you've
all got for me. You *are* my command staff, after all."
Lighter tones of real laughter chimed together, washing away (at least momentarily) the tension and weariness so prevalent since her return from Black
Luthien and the sudden thrusting of her and her military command into a limelight they had never
imagined.

"So, what do we have?" Katana said. She looked
pointedly at Shimazu.

He shrugged casually, then leaned forward slightly,
as though he intended to stay in the conversation for
but a moment. "You will not be getting any more
reinforcements from my quarter. Not in the near
future."

"Well, isn't that just peachy," Drexel pounced.

"Driki, unlike some, we have bigger responsibilities.
And other concerns to deal with."

She blushed at the name she so despised, but forged
a rapid response. "You mean you're dealing with the
fallout of supporting us in the first place. Some of the
other *gumi* oyabuns don't agree with Matsuro Kami-
kuro's ideas of how best to serve the Dragon?"

The man casually shrugged, as though discussing the
difficulty of trying to decide between a white or red
tie for a meeting. Katana winced at the idea of what

that might mean, of how many family members and innocents would die in such an underworld war.

"None of the other warlords will support you," Wahab Fusilli spoke next, his controlled tones a mellow counterpoint to Drexel's.

Katana cranked a pencil-thin eyebrow way up, until Fusilli conceded, with a soft dip of his head.

"At least, that is what my contacts say."

"And when will they support me?"

"Realistically?"

"Of course."

"Likely never, though you might win a temporary alliance with whomever they find to replace Sakamoto."

"I'd think the man, or woman," Parks interjected and conceded with a nod towards Katana, "would want Katana's head on a platter. She's effectively stolen twenty worlds from him."

"And taken on the almost impossible task of securing them and expanding to a large enough defensive perimeter of worlds that a hard strike by The Republic out of Prefecture X, or a hard push by House Davion through the almost collapsed Prefecture III into our rear echelon, won't cut off our own supply lines and leave us speaking French, walking around in silly spurs, and waving a sunburst before you can turn around," Fusilli spouted in an uncharacteristic rush. "I'm thinking whoever the new warlord will be, he's oh so glad Katana has stepped up onto that particular chopping block. As for the rest, well,"—he shrugged—"they're confident you'll fail, so they've no need to spend too much time contemplating your soon-to-come death."

Stunned silence met Fusilli's comments, as much for their stark, brutal truthfulness as for the light, uncharacteristic wit nudged between words. *Was the man getting a sense of humor?* She stared hard at Fusilli, as he switched impassive features away from the stung Parks to her. *No, couldn't be.*

"And what are the chances of The Republic striking at us before we're ready to strike at them?" she asked, ignoring Fusilli's comments about the other warlords. One fight at a time.

"Next to nonexistent, which is the only good news," Crawford jumped into the conversation, his red hair jouncing as he suddenly leaned forward. "After the havoc of internal groups, the Liao invasion, the strikes of the Jade Falcons and the hammer Sakamato delivered, The Republic appears to have collapsed." He quickly tapped on the keyboard, highlighting the worlds of Northwind and New Canton. "In late October, the last coherent regiments of The Republic in both these regions pulled back to both those worlds. Now, we all thought they'd push forward. I mean, the Northwind world allows them to come at us from any direction and New Canton might as well have Liao as a moon. But the latest report dropped off by a merchant junket coming from New Canton says there's not hide nor hair to be found of Republic forces and, as we all know, Northwind has simply gone off the radar—no one's come in or gone out, that we can tell."

"For that matter," Fusilli responded, "seems nothing is going in and out of what was Prefecture X."

"Are you saying that The Republic has given up on everything but Prefecture X?" Katana said. She looked at Fusilli and then Crawford, but their blank looks likely mirrored her own. *What is the new exarch up to? What is The Republic doing?* She flexed her hands, as though preparing to heft her namesake. "So, we can hit Dieron now?"

"Ah, I didn't say that," Crawford said, lifting his

palms to warn her off. "They are likely not in any position to strike us, but we can't really strike them either. Let's not forget what happened to the Sword of Light unit that decided to capture all the glory while you were off on Luthien."

She grimaced at such a waste, while the others contemplated the apparent massacre of almost an entire battalion of troops.

"And there is the pesky issue of such worlds as Athenry, Styx, and Saffel that still need to be secured."

"And if you strike The Republic—I mean truly strike into Prefecture X with force, not the ridiculous raid by the Steel Wolves on Terra—you might just unleash something powerful," Fusilli interjected.

All eyes turned his direction. "A Republic reprisal? Something more than what happened to the Sworders?" Katana asked.

The man shrugged slim shoulders, easily deflecting their intensity. "Perhaps. Or, seeing The Republic so close to a true collapse, other still-sleeping powers might surge forward to grab the prize of Terra."

"Fedrats?"

"Perhaps. But neither the Bear nor the Wolf sleep lightly. In grasping for the prize of Dieron, you don't want to unleash the beasts that'll run us down before we're prepared to deal with them."

All eyes shifted back to the holographic map, and the factions that, to their limited knowledge with such slow interstellar communications, were not yet joined in the general war sweeping through the Inner Sphere.

"So they won't strike at us, but we don't have the forces to strike at them, and if we don't strike at them, then no other faction will see the need to keep us from possibly handing Terra to the Dragon. Does that about sum it up? An impasse?"

Five heads nodded in unison.

"Which means you die." Shimazu's voice once more exploded in the small command office, pulling eyes like filings to loadstone.

The blatant confirmation of her thoughts didn't lessen her desire to be rid of the man. She sighed heavily. "Exactly."

"What?" Parks asked, the obvious confusion in his voice spilling liberally across his features.

"The Dragon is testing me. And to sit still is death."

"The other warlords will eat her alive," Drexel jumped in, quickly grasping the situation. "Even if the Dragon doesn't first."

"I can't sit still. I *must* act." She clenched a fist on the table, hating those words worse than anything else in her life.

"But we already covered all the bases," Parks said, earnest eyes suddenly widening. "Mercenaries? That's not what you're thinking, is it? 'Cause I got to tell you, that way leads right to hell. Sure, grab some lu-crewarriors for the easy assignments, but for trying to secure the rest of the worlds in Prefecture II and prep for taking Dieron . . . no way."

Katana finally calmed enough to respond, having already come up with the answer some time ago. She'd hoped her advisors might find a way out for her. But it was not to be. She glanced around the room, meeting each pair of eyes, letting the leader within calm their fears. As you taught me, Old Master. After all, she *knew* what she was doing. Right.

"Spill it," Drexel finally broke out, bringing a smile to Katana's lips.

I wonder if I'll need to pull them all back down a rung or two when I'm really *a warlord.* The thought troubled and saddened her all at once. Her eyes again found the metal rank insignia, dark and latent, perched as a raptor on the table, waiting for her to unleash it.

"Nova Cats," she finally said. A *nekakami* spirit warrior would've been heard across wet grass at a hundred meters for the depth of silence that swallowed the room. Amazement, incredulity, absolute confusion: a myriad of emotions twisted features equally.

"God dammit!" Shimazu practically shouted. He laughed and banged the table and laughed, until Katana was on the verge of taking her blade to the idiot. "Goddamn, Katana. That's eggs, woman. Giant, iron-cast, 'Mech-sized eggs. I love it."

"Will they play?" Fusilli recovered first, a strange look actually twisting his features slightly.

"I don't know," she managed, overcoming her continued dismay at the yakuza's blunt, boisterous style. "But I've got to try."

"You?" Crawford said.

"Don't even start," she cut him off with a slash of her hand. She was *not* looking forward to the confrontation with the Old Master, and wouldn't have it here with her own command staff. "If we have any chance of bargaining a force from Clan Nova Cat, it can only be me. Honor for honor."

Though Crawford stood on the verge of opening his mouth, he finally leaned back, discontented but willing to accept that Katana could not be swayed from her course.

"When will you leave?" Drexel asked.

"As soon as possible. To the depths of House Kurita is a trip. I'll be back as quickly as I can."

There seemed nothing else to say. She slowly rose, accepted salutes, and moved out of the room and down the hall towards her quarters, where she'd grab her already prepped bag and immediately head for the DropPort, where a DropShip and a select crew already waited.

Their previous meetings had been filled with securing the worlds they currently held. They knew what needed doing. Now she must once more throw herself into Fate's hands and hope like hell she survived. As the noise from her talking command staff finally fell away, she had a sinking feeling all the backlog of karma she was generating would see her reborn as a Capellan in her next life.

2

Ways of Seeing Park, Barcella
Nova Cat Reservation, Irece
Irece Prefecture, Draconis Combine
15 March 3136

The air stank of expectancy.

As though not just the room, but the whole world held its breath. As though the entire Milky Way galaxy paused in its furious thousand kilometers per second hurl through the vacuum of endless space; the entire known universe paused in its endless destructions to pay tribute to these births. After all, the universe, regardless of all its obliterations, represented the pinnacle of birth and new life and creation. For with each collapsed star, destroyed planet and annihilated solar system, a new star spun into existence, a world coalesced, a cooling planet spawned alien flora and fauna.

And some tin cans spit out life.

Kisho shifted uncomfortably on the tatami platform, overly aware of how many long hours of preparation for the rite were infused into this moment. The taut muscles of his neck almost creaked audibly and his jaw clenched against the sharp pain. He surreptitiously worked his head in a small circle to relieve the pinched nerve.

Serves me right for skipping tai chi this morning. The thought didn't bring relief. Trying to shake off such sacrilegious distractions, he concentrated once more and slipped into a light trance, while the room exploded in activity over the birthing, a babble of voices breaking the pause and sending the universe back on its endless spiral into the unknown. A cascade of noise Kisho took in with no immediate awareness of individuals, content in allowing the din to wash away his disdain for the whole process.

Please.

"Canisters one through fifty report optimization. Decanting commencing."

"Thirty more work chits and I can earn passage off the reservation."

"For the whole month? Where did you get the extra work chits?"

"No, I worked a deal for two weeks."

"Canisters fifty-one through one hundred report optimization. Decanting commencing."

"Have you seen the new 'Mech. The *Wendigo*? It is awe-inspiring."

"No. But, Jib—you know him, the technician casteman I introduced last Homecoming Day? Jib said he worked on part of it and he could not resist talking about it. I hope to see it someday."

"Hold. Canisters three and nineteen and sixty-seven report abnormalities."

"Status review?"

"Have you heard? We're going to war?"

"War, really? That cannot be right."

"Stop your contractions."

"Confirmed. Unknown contagions introduced during final cycling to optimization."

"The Dragon gone to war?"

"I spoke with her and I do not believe you. The council will never agree to our pairing. How dare we ask?! *Savashri*."

"Percentage of deformity error?"

"Point oh-three-nine."

"No, I don't think the Dragon's gone to war."

"Stop your contractions!"

"*Stravag*. The Dragon *has* gone to war. And you know we will go as well. After the downsizings, they will have to contract us, *quiaff*?"

"Terminate."

"*Aff.*"

"*Aff.*"

The constant, soft purr of machinery hitched for a moment (did the others even notice?), and three lives snuffed away, their potential taken at the minuscule chance of missed perfection.

Is it so simple?

Kisho slowly opened his eyes to take in a birthing chamber few, even within the scientist caste, ever saw. The Mystic Chamber. Buried so deep within the bowels of the genetic repository—at the bottom center of the entire Mystic complex—Kisho's first impression on visiting the room was that it sat on the bedrock of the continental shelf.

Despite the ongoing shuffling of bodies moving in between the hundred steel canisters—each container an explosion of multihued wiring, and the bank of

machinery coating each wall in technological fungus—
his mind's eye transported him outside, to an overhead
view of this most sacred of grounds.

The Ways of Seeing Park. In the wars following
their Abjurment from the Clans—the Ghost Bear–
Combine war, the second Ghost Bear–Combine war,
and even in the depths of the horror known as the
Jihad—though so much of Barcella lay wasted, not a
leaf or a mortared stone was damaged here. Others
saw it as good fortune. The Nova Cats, with their visions and portents, saw something entirely different.
Despite all they suffered, all the lands given to them
and then stolen back by the Dragon, despite all the
deaths and hardships, this was their land. Their sacred
ground. Here, despite every blockade thrown up
against them, they prospered and survived.

Do I believe that? The thought floated up from the
depths. Doubter and blasphemer that he was, Kisho
ignored it, content for now to allow his inner eye to
roam across this holy of holies.

The Ways of Seeing Park stretched for long kilometers in every direction, with a mammoth, hand-built
wall of stone towering around the entire perimeter.
Near the only entrance, the Circle of Equals glade
waited for such important trials as the annual Oathmaster Grand Melee.

Off the back of the glade and filling most of the
park, a rugged, natural woodland ran untamed and
uncut, where several packs of nova cats thrived.
They'd adapted well to Irece. Thriving colonies of
nova cats existed on all the continents as well, but the
cats within this sanctuary were viewed as a level
above.

Finally, Kisho's inner eye moved to take in the
mammoth genetic repository, sitting some five hundred meters from the Circle of Equals. The Neo-

Gothic, circular building thrust to the sky, with flying buttresses, vaulted roof, and triforium. The glossy black edifice—a combination of native stone and nanostructured ceramics—seemed to swallow the bright morning light, pulling in energy as though to power the sacred events performed within. Rising almost three hundred meters into the air, the piercing structure represented the defiance of the Nova Cat Clan, its ability to rise above it all.

Around the base of the cathedral, as though children protected under raptor's wings, twelve house-sized chapels nestled, their limestone walls works of art. Ornate friezes depicted the glorious lives of each Bloodname warrior deserving of such honor and the House Blood Heritage. Each chapel contained repositories for the DNA of every member of a given Bloodname House, living or dead.

As though it were a peregrine catching site of prey, his inner vision suddenly swooped low, through the gargantuan doors, and then wafted down endless tunnels, moving ever deeper, ever quieter, ever more still, until Kisho opened his eyes wide to the here and now.

"Mystic, we have ninety-seven confirmed decantings." Kisho's new eyes found the green-suited speaker—his head and face mostly covered with protective gear, but strong, blue eyes spoke competence and arrogance in equal measure. A true Clansman.

The other dozen people in the room paused in their work, looking at him. Long minutes must have passed. He glanced down and his stomach muscles began to cramp in their usual fashion. *Must it always be this way? Cannot I perform a rite just once without this?* He took a slow, deep breath and recommitted himself to his role. *Let the games continue.*

Kisho slowly unfolded, careful to hide the weakness of his pained muscles. *Idiot! No missing tai chi!* At the head of the room, his ceremonial black, leather-suited form stood out in the sterile whiteness and soft greens like a blazing antiflame—a void. Like the cathedral itself, in the Peace Park. *A statement of what we are.*

His eyes roved over the room, taking in the mystic sibko of newly born potential—double the normal warrior sibko size. After all, most would never see adolescence, much less become mystics. So maximization was required. And if this were not bad enough, the year interval between each new sibko—to incorporate what had been learned into tweaking genes and subtly massaging training to ensure full potential—was cut down by a third. Because the Oathmaster knew war was coming months ago, and he ordered a new mystic sibko over a half year ahead of schedule, in defiance of tradition. *To replace the losses that will surely come, old man? Regardless of the decade and a half it will take before they will be of any use? Do you see so far, old man? Is war so inevitable? Will it grind on inexorably?*

Does the First Mystic's blood cry out at such rape? At our splicing and dicing of the blood-soul over and over and over? Kisho's teeth bit into his tongue until sweet copper quenched the shaking threatening to tear free of his iron grip.

Must it always be like this? A soft sigh whispered between lips compressed into a flat line, before they quirked into their usual arrogant twist. *Yes. It must.*

From Blood of the One
Mystics to steer, to guide—spirit
Past, Present, Future to seize

His voice carried strongly in the chamber, setting up a slight echo, reverberating in countersynch to the *shush-shush* of machinery, before falling away. All bowed low, while Kisho stepped lightly down off the tatami platform and moved languidly towards the first canister. He glanced through the ferroglass and saw a decanter, with gray eyes. Always gray.

With a hiss and pop of equalizing pressure, an unseen scientist released the hatch, and the wet newborn drew in its first breath, after an automatic body-response of a cough to clear the lungs of fluid. The astringent smell of birthing-fluid chemicals assailed his nose and coated his tongue with vileness. Yet, despite his disquiet, intelligent eyes stared at Kisho, as though the spirit within already knew its meaning. Already knew its life's purpose and acceptance shrouded him like the armored carapace of battle armor to his trooper.

Kisho managed to resist clenching his fists in jealousy.

With strength he did not feel, he firmly placed his right palm upon the child's forehead and closed his eyes. Within, spirit muscles screamed with an agony of yearning and need. Searching, pummeling the depths of darkness, demanding. Something. Anything.

"Ken'ichi." He spoke softly. "Strong one." The name effervesced upon his lips, but brought no comfort. It came from within, not without. Never from another source. Only from himself. Never the burning vision handed to him as to who these sacks of flesh would be, what names they would be allowed to bear once they passed their Trial of Mysticism.

He moved on to the next canister as the same sounds precipitated the opening of the top hatch and an identical ceremony unfolded. And so on. And so on. And so on. A ceremony as empty for Kisho as the three failed canisters, already flushed clean of failure.

But how do I flush myself clean of failure?

Eyes itched as he moved on to the next child.

Interlude I

Japan, Terra
Prefecture X
The Republic of the Sphere
27 April 3135

Kisho slowly walked along the banks of a stream, un-caring of its name but appreciative of its subtle gur-gling and the peace in its incessant dedication. Another cherry blossom undulated down an invisible current, before easing into the water without a ripple; it joined a dozen other white and pink blossoms, already on their journey downstream to destruction.

"Such a waste."

"Why do you say that?"

Kisho sucked in a lungful of oversweet air as he

quickly found the voice that startled him. Eyes narrowed taking in the beautiful woman across and up the small stream a dozen paces. After a moment, he remembered himself and inclined his head. "I beg your pardon, Kurita Yori-san. You startled me."

Her features warred between annoyance and mild pleasure as she wended around a small sapling, coming closer—graceful in an unconscious way—before she responded. "Then that debt is discharged."

"Debt?" he responded.

"Over you startling me at our previous encounter."

As ever, in place of the displeasure he should feel—regardless of the mildness of the rebuke—only . . . kinship . . . seemed available to him. Though they could not help but interact on the DropShip during the long transit from the Combine into Republic space, it should not have been enough to cement such a feeling of closeness—a companionship he would never feel for Tanaka, though they were raised and trained together.

"However, Mystic, it behooves you to stop using that name. I am Yori Sakamoto."

And, of course, there it was.

Another cherry blossom spun into view, the beauty of its delicateness and purity an accent to Yori's slim form and perfect features. Kisho opened his mind but found no desire for coupling. Instead, he felt an honest closeness, as though they were sibkin. And in a way, they were.

Both outcasts for the blood that flowed in their veins.

"What is a name? Does it change who we are?" With a sudden desire to feel the cool, clean grass in his fingers, Kisho eased into a sitting position, feet a scant meter from the edge of the stream. His fingers immediately tweezed out the fibrous-textured plants, their flat blades calling to be rolled into forms, as though he were a child trying to occupy time.

She expertly stepped over the small stream, the hem of her demure kimono not even rippling in the hop, and paused before joining him on the ground. "The last time we met, you told me I could be anyone." Her soft voice almost seemed an orchestrated counterpoint to the gentle bubble of water and the sighing of the winds through the cherry trees.

Kisho pointedly glanced around and she nodded in resignation towards where her trailing guards were hid. He nodded in response, as though the very presence of those guards cemented the words he spoke. "No, you cannot be."

"What?" She said, taken aback, a frown beginning to mar her smooth forehead. "Yes, you did."

"*Neg*, Yori-san. I said you could be anyone you wanted to be." As he spoke, he slowly began to strip the grass, folding the various-sized blades without conscious thought, while his mind wandered across seldom-trod paths.

He thought of their last meeting, when he had shockingly found himself baring his soul to the scion of a House that just might be trying to destroy his Clan. *How is it I reveal more to an almost perfect stranger than any other?* Why he would do so hammered at him like depleted uranium autocannon rounds spewing from an enemy 'Mech.

"And what's the difference?"

He looked up sharply from his folding, his eyes punctuating his point. "You cannot be someone you do not desire to be."

"But how do I know what I desire to be? Perhaps tomorrow I'll want to be a geisha." The slight coloring to her face spoke of the crudeness of her words and yet the determination in her eyes belied the apparent soft facade.

There is muscle in you. Strength. But strength enough for what is to come? "And perhaps tomorrow," he responded, "I will desire to be a Dark Casteman, selling my services to the highest bidder like a *stravag* mercenary."

She tilted her head, eyes holding his, before she responded. "No, I don't think I could ever see such desire in you."

"Nor I a geisha in you."

She contemplated this as another two blossoms floated down, one settling peacefully into her lap as though it belonged there. Finally nodded, albeit grudgingly.

"We can only truly *be* what we desire to be," he continued. "And who we are, regardless of how much we rage against it, defines what those desires will be."

"That sounds like mystic talk."

He shook his head angrily, then smoothed it away as though he were pouring it into the stream. "I told you, we observe. And I observe this. The desire within us, that is what defines what we can be. You can go and do the things a geisha does, but you will never *be* a geisha. Blood calls."

She turned away slightly, breathed, "Hated blood."

He nodded, understanding of his own previous actions surrounding Yori beginning to crystallize. *It is not simply that she is an outcast as I. But she is not within my universe. She stands on the outside looking in. And, in her, I can possibly find a slight reflection of myself.* The admission hurt. He needed no one.

But perhaps no one within the Clan. Aff, that might be it.

"*Aff,* Yori-san. Hated blood. But despised or not,

it will out in the end." He said it with a resolution he did not feel.

Yori turned back to him once more, her strength radiant. "And your blood, what does it call you to do?"

He shrugged, as though to dislodge a feather, when it felt as though the whole of Tengoku Mountain rested upon his shoulders. "It calls me to be a mystic."

A small smile creased her lips. "I know little enough about you Nova Cats, much less you mystics."

He contemplated ignoring her, but once more found kinship calling—a rare moment when he might crack his own facade and, for a dozen heartbeats, allow another to feel part of his burden. "We are outcasts within our own caste."

She nodded, face falling into a mask of intent listening. But whether a charade or not, it only eased his tongue further.

"And yet the greatest of our numbers is the Oathmaster of all the Clan. Protector of our traditions and advisor and vision seeker for the Khan."

"I thought, among the Nova Cats, the Oathmaster position was fought over every year. A Circle of Equals and a Circle of Law."

He nodded absently, fingers continuing their work with the grass, slowly staining his fingertips, while he responded. "Forum of Law. *Aff.* But none have defeated our current Oathmaster in long, long years. His vision is too powerful, his knowledge of The Remembrance and our traditions absolute." *Is that not so, old man?*

"And what of you? Is that your calling?"

He shuddered slightly, as some unnamed fear stirred nightmares and his fingers shook momentarily. "I do not know."

"Then what do mystics do? Aid the Oathmaster?

Do you walk among your warrior caste or civilians, making sure they maintain a dedication to Nova Cat traditions? That sounds like the reinforcement of loyalty the Internal Security Force has used in the Combine in the past."

"In a way, but nothing so large, so harsh, as that. We are assigned to detachments of warriors when appropriate, to provide council, to provide vision"—he managed to say it without a single hitch in his voice—"so they can emerge victorious in battle. In a way, we are the silent protectors of Clan Nova Cat. Or at least that is what is supposed to occur." This time some emotion did stain his voice with an ugly tone.

"If you mystics are so powerful, why do you appear to be so few? You should walk among the civilian caste and every other warrior should be a mystic."

She had allowed his comment about what was supposed to occur to pass. He glanced directly at her for the first time in his recitation to see that it was no accident that she consciously steered away from what he obviously did not want to talk about. He nodded slightly to acknowledge. "We have no interaction with the lower caste," he continued, slightly disturbed and confused that she might think them worthy of needing interaction with a mystic. "As for 'every other warrior,' our numbers are very few because the training is . . . difficult."

She arched a delicate eyebrow as another cherry blossom passed into and out of his line of sight. He took a deep breath and for a moment thought cherries rested on his tongue.

"Isn't all Clan training harsh? I thought few warriors managed to graduate from a sibko, passing their Trial of Position."

"*Aff.* But mystics train almost exclusively along mystic lines, until our Trial of Mysticism, when we turn thirteen." Once more, restless demons stirred at his direct invocation of training, but he forged on. "If we succeed, then we not only continue our mystic training but we also go through a crash course of warrior training. Then, when we turn eighteen, we must also pass a Trial of Position, along with every other warrior in Clan Nova Cat."

She contemplated him and for a moment fury sparked as he anticipated an outpouring of much-hated pity. Instead, he saw only a sense of yearning to understand. To accept.

"And they hate you for it. Hate you for being so much more than they?"

For that, and for other things. He contemplated revealing the final aspect of his training that so disarmed most warriors, but realized that would be going too far. *"Aff,"* was all he finally said. *And so often we hate ourselves.*

"And that is where your blood calls you? But the last time we walked along a river, you told me you did not believe in these visions you must use to protect your Clan."

"Aff." His stomach tightened.

"And."

"Blood will out."

Her head sunk down, until her chin rested against her chest. "And my blood?" she whispered.

"You can only be what your blood wants you to be."

"You are saying we have no choice."

He hesitated before answering, and glanced down to see what his hands had subconsciously wrought. His face went blank as he tried to grasp the meaning of the crude yet discernable crane made of grass in the palm of his hand. Dozens of different paths wove and skated around and through, as he strove for an understanding . . . that he could not find.

"Kisho," a soft voice interrupted and he zoomed out, features softening back to humanity, to find Yori, a disturbed expression molding a harsh frown onto her face. "What happened?"

He shrugged off his lapse, presenting her with his creation. She glanced down and a brilliant smile smoothed away the clouds of doubt and fear. "A crane! From grass. I did not know you knew origami."

He smiled slightly. "I do not."

She pursed her lips, both pleased and puzzled, before looking at the crane once more, the earnest joy at his creation warming the small glade they occupied.

"You keep it, Yori-san."

"What? I can't."

"I must insist."

She gave him a mock frown. "And if I do not?"

"Then I will refer to you as Kurita Yori-san everywhere we go."

She winced and he almost regretted his statement. Almost. But Warlord Toranaga Matsuhara would use her blood, as the old man used his. She, like he, could only run so far from who she was. Even when you knew you could not possibly be what your blood demanded, you went through the motions. Because that was what was expected.

What was needed.

"Then I see no option but to accept your gift. But in return you *must* stop using that name."

He nodded, handed over the crane, then stood. "I have been in contemplation too long. The Oathmaster is expecting me." He bowed his head, and abruptly spoke words unused to his lips. "Thank you." As he turned to leave, she spoke again.

"Kisho, you distracted me. You said 'What a waste.' Why did you say that?"

He stopped, glancing back. "Is it not obvious? The cherry blossoms become what they are meant to be, falling from the trees. And they are beautiful in their dedication as they find the water and follow the course laid before them. But in the end, they simply follow those who have come before, all to their destruction." He turned away before she could respond.

As will we.

3

Unity Palace, Imperial City
Luthien, Kagoshima Prefecture
Pesht Military District, Draconis Combine
15 May 3136

Coal black eyes cut the room to ribbons as surely as laser fire, certainly with more hatred.

Ramadeep Bhatia paced within the small confines of his office, a mere shadow of the size of his appointed quarters in the Internal Security Force headquarters of New Samarkand. However, despite the strength of the ISF position on that world, it remained too far from the halls of power to be truly useful. Yet Ramadeep knew it remained a bolt-hole, a place of refuge, should the Dragon be roused to turn on its guardian. Until then, the halls of Unity Palace, despite the dangers, would remain his home.

Another circuit brought him back to his desk like a wolf to its kill, where he collapsed in exasperation, the chair creaking loudly despite its expense. He brushed calloused palms roughly across his face as though to scour away the malaise of sleep deprivation and the paralysis of anger. *Concentrate!*

Sucking in a huge breath, he tasted a hint of jasmine and freshly trimmed bamboo. Despite the despised sweetness in the air, the tension abruptly drained from him, water sloughing off the wolf, leaving him refreshed and even invigorated. *Must the Peacock insist on his jasmine and bamboo in every hall?*

He leaned forward slightly, resting his palms on the desk, taking in the four holodiscs before him. Four separate possibilities; four separate potentials; four separate outcomes. Any of them desirable, any of them able to raise his star more. *You may have learned a thing or two from me on how to play the game, Peacock, but your extravagant vanities will be your downfall in the end.*

He reached forward and casually raised one holodisc, and began spinning it through his fingers, as though it were an oversized coin, while his right hand touched small studs inset in the rim of the table. A small holoprojection blossomed before him—bust of a nondescript man, with the classical slanted eyes of the Japanese of the Combine, short-cut black hair, black eyes, slightly sallow complexion as though too long in an office cubicle, or hailing from a world where the sun never shines. A man to lose in a crowd or to overlook as you looked right at him. The perfect spy.

We have confirmation of movement. The target departed weeks ago, destination unknown. However, considering the target's last such foray, assumptions can be made. Will continue for confirmation of destination.

And that was it. It took weeks for the man to discover the bitch was off-world—his replacement was already in route—and then four weeks to arrive on Luthien so as not to arouse suspicion by coming through a command route (damn the downed HPG net!) and he'd been sitting on it for a week, slowly fomenting plans. *Where have you gone, geisha?* His pet name for the she-bitch always brought a smile to his face; he ignored the whispers within of the she-bitch comparison to his wolf. Eight weeks. He tapped another stud and the holoprojection message swapped out for a map of the Inner Sphere, centered on the Combine and The Republic. With deft finger movements he spun up quick schematics, overlaying jump routes and possible paths.

The first grid, in bright indigo, used the traditional JumpShip routes, with star systems and their recharge times determining how far she might have traveled in that time. Another grid, in a glowing crimson, outlined the expanded territory she might reach, based upon her possible use of known space stations where she might barter/steal a quick charge. Finally, a dark forest green grid added in the potential based upon known JumpShip merchant routes. He knew the last was completely suspect, as most of the charts were months out of date. And with the loss of rapid communications, a merchant ship could've been commandeered by a new, upstart warlord looking to secede, attacked and destroyed by pirates, or simply stranded due to a blown helium seal, and it would be long weeks, if not months, before anyone knew about it.

And if you put together a command circuit, you'd be anywhere by now, eh, geisha? His dark eyes scoured the intertwining lines of possibilities and slowly discarded things one by one. *No. You may have risen kilometers above your station, geisha, but no way do you have the resources for a command circuit. The Peacock?* He leaned back and gazed up at a Spartan ceiling unseeing, as he contemplated several possibilities, then flipped them away as well. *No, the Peacock doesn't have the resources either, not with the damage done by the fool Sakamoto and now with the other warlords agitating. . . . Not to mention, I would know.*

Ramadeep's eyes once more pierced the skein of the holomap, slicing away prospects too remote, trying to untangle the mess. His eyes finally began to itch and he blinked rapidly to wet them, realizing he'd been staring far too long. *I'll not untangle this today. Nor tomorrow. But it will untangle. You have to surface somewhere. And where could you possibly go for more help? The yakuza helped you once. They're unlikely to be so generous next time. Where?*

An ache intruded and he glanced at his left hand, realizing he still spun the holodisc. He sighed in exasperation and carefully placed the disc back into its row, and massaged the tired muscles with his right hand, while his mind bounced from one disc to the next.

He slowly began to smile, stretching muscles unused to such facial movements. *You're just now beginning to truly understand the albatross the Peacock threw around your neck. And despite your allegiance to Vincent Kurita, his Peacockness will cast you aside as easily as one of his once-used, ten-thousand-K-bill robes if you fail him. You've got to build your District and you've got nothing to build it with.*

Ramadeep slowly reached into his desk, pulled out four separate holodisc envelopes, preprepared with appropriate addresses. With exquisite care, he packaged each, sealed them, and then stacked them on the edge of his desk. They would go to wolf pups learning at the knee of the alpha male.

And you'll soon learn who that is, geisha. He tapped

another stud, calling for his aide to send the dispatches out by JumpShip to far star systems and their waiting agents.

Yes, geisha. You'll soon learn.

4

Despite Kisho's anxiety, as he entered the hall his mouth slowly opened wide, eyes dilating until the pupils swallowed the whites in surprise.

An entire phalanx of Nova Cat warriors filled the Hall of the Nova Cat's Clan Council Chamber. Not only Khan Jacali Nostra and saKhan Niko West, along with Oathmaster Kanaye, but a bevy of Bloodnamed warriors, from the two on-world Galaxy commanders down through a dozen Star colonels and even a Star captain or two. Though not a true Clan Council discussion, requiring a quorum of Bloodnamed warriors, Khan Nostra nevertheless made the decision to meet the strong delegation from Katana Tormark with an equally strong show of force. The leathers of their ceremonial outfits created a wash of blackness—liquid void sloshing against the bottom steps of the tiered council chamber, swallowing almost the entire bottom circle and the Khan's dais.

Against this mighty display of Nova Cat power, a single, diminutive female entered the chamber, eliciting a similar chagrined reaction from nearly every warrior present.

Against the black army below, Katana's outfit stood out in bright, vibrant colors, as though disdainful at such lack of originality. Black, loose pants tucked into red, knee-high boots, overlaid with a pristine white jacket, trimmed in orange down the front and on arms and cuffs, with a red belt woven into the jacket, a dragon etched into the belt buckle. The red piping on the pants and a slash of red on the shoulders denoted her status as a MechWarrior. Even at this distance, her high collar could be seen displaying the logo any warrior here recognized as belonging to a *tai-shu*. After *Warlord* Kiyomori Minamoto's partially successful attempt to forcefully integrate the Nova Cats into the Combine, no Nova Cat from the highest warrior to the lowliest born labor casteman would fail to recognize *that* rank insignia.

With great will, Kisho finally pulled eyes away from her serene face (as though she were attending a simple tea ceremony?!) and searched in vain above her, waiting for the rest of her troops to arrive. She took almost a half minute to sedately move down the entire length of steps in between the various tiered, circular benches, before coming to rest on the last step, as though afraid to step down to the bottom floor and its ocean of darkness.

Kisho gave up waiting for the small army of Kuritans that would never arrive and took in her presence once more. She openly looked around at each warrior.

As their eyes connected for a moment, an almost electrical charge bounced through Kisho, sending the hair on his arms and the back of his neck erect, the puff of spines of a startled nova cat.

No, not fear. Not that one. Simply waiting. For what?

The minutes stretched, until warriors actually grew restless. Waiting for an introduction? Despite the Nova Cats' long association with the Combine, old traditions died hard. *We wait for you to announce your arrival, as you wait for us to announce yours.*

A warlord would always conjure images of death and destruction for any Clansman, and her arrival precipitated Kisho's departure into a larger world he knew might destroy him. And yet he decided on the spot he liked Katana, though he couldn't exactly put a finger on why.

Perhaps it is your humor? A smile pulled at his lips, amused at his own sarcasm about the heavy aura of solemnity. He casually took in the Oathmaster, wondering if the old man could read his flippant thoughts. But, if possible, Kanaye's face bore even more serenity than Katana's. *Nothing will upset that still pond, eh, old man?*

"*Tai-shu* Katana Tormark," Jacali called out, her permanently hoarse voice still booming in the chamber. "We bid you welcome to the Nova Cat domain."

Kisho almost winced at the hostility, though Katana weathered it without the blink of an eye. She bowed deeply, in Combine fashion, before responding.

"Khan Nostra, saKhan West, Oathmaster Kanaye," she began, specifically looking at each individual as she named them, "gathered Nova Cat warriors, I bask in your skills and honor, and bid you welcome from the Dragon."

Kisho shifted slightly, absentmindedly laying a light

hand against the cool stone chamber wall as he bumped it. *Done your homework. What else have you done?*

"I have traveled a great distance and am most grateful you granted me permission to step upon your domain and travel within."

He couldn't help the smile that slid fully onto his face at the usual subtlety of Combine speech. It had taken Clanners decades to learn that nuance and some still refused to learn. *As though we could truly stop you without bringing down the wrath of the Dragon.*

A new thought intruded. *But why did* you *come, Katana?* She was a newly minted warlord, and surely Warlord Saito would have been anxious to try to negotiate Nova Cat troops away from their worlds. Soft and decadent Saito of Pesht might be, but if given the right chance he would throttle a weak child if it increased his power.

His mind spun down that line of reasoning as the two fierce warriors, the khan and the warlord locked eyes, the energy of their wills practically coalescing within the confines of the chamber. Finally, as though Katana were conceding a point, she broke the silence, bringing a slight smile to Jacali's lips.

As Katana began speaking, Kisho glanced once more at his khan and realized that once more Katana had scored the point in that exchange. She had handed the khan the upper hand in exchange for previously forcing her to submit by speaking first at the start of this encounter.

A fierce warrior and talented politician—skills needed by a khan who must stalk the prairies of the Bloodname Council Chamber and the young cats looking to take her place, while watching for the shadow of dragon wings above—but Kisho wondered if she were up to such subtleties. *Are you up to keeping me away from the future I cannot bear?*

Perhaps it made no difference in the end, but by such acts the will could be softened, the mind massaged into just the right course when needed.

"Per our agreement before planet fall, I have presented myself before this council to negotiate a contract. By this council and the khans and oathmaster in attendance, we shall not leave without an accord."

Silence greeted her words, and Kisho's eyes roved the chamber before resting with Jacali's. Katana had done her homework—she must have studied over the months it took her to get here—but she'd not gotten it all down. This was no quorum council meeting, nor did they have to reach an accord based upon the negotiations made before she made atmospheric interface. How many times had trials taken before the council not been resolved? How many reverted to the field of battle? It could happen here all too easily, depending on his khan's animosity to this warlord who dared to present herself directly into the teeth of the cat. Could there be any doubt who would emerge victorious? At least that would put a stop to the disastrous future of Kisho going to war. Then again, Katana had spent the last two years carving out a realm at constant war . . . perhaps not so clear-cut.

"Seyla," Jacali finally spoke, immediately eliciting a chorus of replies from the gathered warriors, and Kisho exhaled softly. He had been unknowingly holding his breath.

"What are you bargaining for?"

"A troop of Nova Cat warriors to once more fight alongside the Dragon against our enemies."

"I suppose a Star of Nova Cat warriors would be

more than willing to bid for the right to join your quest."

Kisho canted his head at the slight crease that furrowed Katana's forehead over his khan's dissemblance. *Ah, so you are not impervious.*

"Though I know a Star of Nova Cat warriors would be the equal of any Dragon lance and would be much appreciated among my troops, I believe a more substantial force is needed if we are to achieve victory."

Kisho caught Jacali's smile out of the corner of his eye at the choice of Katana's words, and clenched muscles along his shoulders slowly began to relax. *She's up to this bargaining.*

"Then, *tai-shu,* speak plainly. What have you come to bid for?"

"Two Galaxies." Her words swallowed the small noises in the chamber, dropping it into shocked stillness.

A hoarse, booming sound abruptly swept through the room, startling Kisho. All eyes pulled towards Jacali and the strange sound emanating there. Then Kisho understood. Laughter. The damage done to her face and throat after a Trial for the Khanship left her permanently marked in voice and face. Yet Kisho realized he'd never heard his khan laugh. He shuddered, hoping to never hear such a disturbing sound again.

"I did not realize a *tai-shu* was allowed such humor, *quiaff?*"

"*Neg*, Khan Nostra. There is no humor to be found in this situation."

Jacali continued her wheezing sounds, though her eyes were hard as malachite spikes. "Then perhaps you misunderstood our Touman's organization, *Tai-shu* Tormark. After all, you have not had any previous dealings with our Clan."

"I have dealt with the Spirit Cats."

Jacali waved her hand, as though dismissing a small irritant. "They are misguided and misled. Kittens who have lost their way and need to be brought home." She paused, stopped the horrible sound, then spoke in a soft whisper, which scoured like sandpaper along nerve endings. "They are no more Nova Cats . . . than, say, the Dragon's Fury are Kuritans."

Kisho nodded once again, giving Katana credit, despite his wishes that she be sent back to her troops gored by Nova Cat claws. Not an emotion marred her features, but something hard and burning swam in the depths of her dark eyes. *I know the hatred of decades burns within, my Khan, but are we awaking a dragon?*

"The Dragon is already at war, and I march to war as its loyal liege," Katana began, all civility stripped from her voice, the bared blade of her namesake. "As vassals of the Combine, you are required to provide a force to fight alongside the Dragon as well. An agreement you cannot abrogate if you wish to maintain your semiautonomous rule . . . on your remaining reservations."

A low, almost subsonic noise rippled through the chamber as every Nova Cat warrior growled at such a blatant threat. Though enough removed from the mainstream of Clan indoctrination to have a more unique view on the relationship between House Kurita and the Nova Cat Clan, even Kisho found his hackles raised and his lips peeled in a harsh grimace. After a moment, he slowly smoothed the snarl from his face.

You play us, Katana. Your first path began to fail, so you move to the next with new tactics. Her eyes found his somehow and some expression briefly peeked through her impervious facade. *Are you surprised by my apparent lack of anger? You should've seen me a moment ago.* He actually smiled, eliciting a further expression he couldn't grasp, as she continued to survey the gathered throng as though contemptuous of Khan Nostra's ability to make a singular decision without consulting the body of attending warriors.

That will only enrage the khan more. He glanced at Jacali, then once more to Katana. *Which is the point, of course. But why? Why are you here? Why confront us directly with such shared enmity? To throw us off guard?*

"You go too far," Jacali ground out.

"I simply remind you of oaths and the consequences of breaking them."

"I need no reminder of oaths, or of who broke what oaths and agreements between our people, *tai-shu!*"

"Then two Galaxies."

"*Savashri.* That is ludicrous and you know it. It would be impossible to strip such a sizable force from our holdings. You would leave us nothing to defend our reservations from our enemies."

Katana nodded at the implications in that statement. "Fine. Then a Galaxy should not be too much trouble, *quiaff*?"

Jacali opened her mouth to respond, then sealed her lips, actually closing her eyes as well. After a moment, she slowly reopened them.

That is right, my khan. Regain control of your hatred or Katana might just steal away half our Touman . . . and me with it.

"Katana," a new voice intruded, pulling eyes towards the Oathmaster.

"Yes, Oathmaster," she said, some modicum of civility reentering her voice.

"I do not mean to interrupt this meeting, but I would ask a favor," the old man responded, a grandfather asking a favor from a cookie-carrying Girl Scout. "It has proven extremely difficult to negotiate with

Warlord Saito. You obviously were able to secure permission to travel freely across his domain and speak with us about securing a contract for our troops. As I am looking to travel into the Combine myself, any help would be most appreciated."

Most were still looking at Kanaye, but Kisho still tried to watch Katana and Jacali simultaneously. Otherwise, he would have missed the chagrined look that etched Katana's features for a heartbeat before vanishing. *What the . . .* Then he noticed a look wash Jacali's features as well, as she immediately broke in, as though the old man had never spoken. *Ah, old man. You play them both; knocking Katana off guard, while providing our khan with a way to save face. Always the game, eh, old man?*

"You have cut down to a Galaxy from your original bid. But what will you offer to us in return? A year's worth of production from one of your 'Mech manufacturing centers? Ten years' worth of foodstuff exports? And to ship so far? Through two different warlords' territories? Then again, if you could negotiate the right to come into another warlord's territory and contract *his* troops, then that should be no problem, *quiaff*?"

"*Aff*," Katana responded strongly. Yet he detected a slight hitch in her voice. *What is it?* His previous questions slowly rose up and his face began to blank as he reached for clues and a sense of what had occurred blossomed. *Can it be . . .*

"Then you will not mind if I send a fast courier to Luthien to verify with Warlord Saito?"

"Of course not."

Kisho slowly nodded. Despite her acumen on this battlefield, the slight hesitation in her response answered as plainly as a ghost bear on a black beach.

Jacali, sensing the imminent kill and looking to toss

the corpse aside after stripping away the meat and cracking bones for the marrow, pounced. "I believe I will. After all, the Inner Sphere has long proven to the Clans that war is a long game, which can swallow years as well as decades. What are a few weeks, *qui-aff*? You are more than welcome to stay as our guest."

Katana Tormark slowly looked around the hall, as though searching for answers that did not exist, then centered once more on Khan Nostra and apparently came to some decision. With exquisite care—obviously, so as not to alarm any in the chamber—Katana reached beneath her jacket and extracted a small bamboo tube. Squaring her shoulders, she left the final step and passed into the sea of blackness, holding up the tube. Like startled crows, the closest warriors actually veered slightly away, before returning to their original stoic positions.

"Before you send the message, Khan Nostra, perhaps you might care to glance at what I would use to secure the contract of a Galaxy of Nova Cat troops, to use at my discretion."

As though preening, confident of her victory over Katana—after all, despite the Oathmaster's predictions, she'd proven unworthy and could be discarded—she waved her hand and motioned Katana closer. The black-clad warriors closest to the dais slowly parted, allowing the *tai-shu* to move right up to the base of the small, raised platform, where she passed the tube into Jacali's hands.

Jacali casually pulled the corked end and withdrew a small sheaf of rice paper, which, even at this distance, Kisho could tell were sealed with numerous colorful sigils.

With an air of humoring a country bumpkin, Jacali casually leafed through the sheets. The air of victory gradually drained away as Khan Nostra's expression passed from pleased to startled to utter shock. Her wide-eyed, open-mouthed appearance stripped the khan of any semblance of power and authority and left her almost breathless.

"This cannot be," she finally spoke, the words hardly reaching Kisho's ears.

"It can and it is. You can, when the time is appropriate, threaten to forward that document on to the coordinator himself, should I prove unwilling to fulfill my own oaths as sworn therein. Should the need arise," she finished casually, her tone and face a stunning counterpoint to the khan's bereft expression.

Jacali slowly looked up from her sheet into Katana's eyes, then swiveled them towards Kanaye, shock and despair at defeat painfully planted large on her features, but also some hidden hope swimming in stunned eyes. Kanaye slowly nodded in return and Kisho gritted his teeth until stars exploded from the pain.

Again. How by the Founder did you do that? How did you know? Katana's won?! What is on those papers? As myriad thoughts whirled madly within, one overriding concern sliced down through everything with its urgency.

I am going to war. And that war will destroy me.

= 5 =

Santin, Comitatus-*class* JumpShip, Zenith Jump Point
Arkab, Buckminster Prefecture
Benjamin Military District, Draconis Combine
17 July 3136

*"Y*ou coddle him." Tanaka spoke harshly, standing at ease on the gravity deck.

Hisa—sitting down, her eyes still almost met the standing Tanaka's—responded softly. "You think."

"Aff. And you know you do."

She shrugged as though it could be interpreted many different ways, while waiting a moment to respond until a group of warriors passed their position, their voices a hubbub she ignored. "Do we not all need such now and then?"

He stared daggers at her, as though she had just blasphemed the First Mystic. *"Neg."*

She continued to look at him serenely, until he broke eye contact first. *I have my nightmares, but I live with them, as you never will, Tanaka.* She sighed, a sadness welling that he might be so haunted and unable to deal appropriately with it.

Like Kisho.

"He must be strong. If we are going to survive this war. He must be strong."

"As you are, *quiaff?*"

His head whipped back, hard gray eyes even harder, as he tried to pull out some meaning from her words.

She wielded her serene smile as though it were shield against his attacks. *When you truly accept what we are, Tanaka, no other mystic will read you. Have you ever read me?* Her eyes almost spoke the challenge.

"Aff," he finally responded to her first question, taking her comments at face value, despite his obvious discomfort at his inability to read her.

She swallowed and realized she would like another drink. But not just yet, though. One more attempt to bridge the gap. "Tanaka, he is strong. He would not be on this ship if he was not, *quiaff?*"

"Aff. But there is something there. Something that has always bothered me, since . . ." His voice trailed off, his discomfort broadcast like radiating heat.

You would be horrified to know how well I read you, Tanaka. "Since the ro—" She paused, then continued, "Since our earliest training?" Accepting she might be, but she held no wish to unnecessarily disturb her own demons.

Tanaka nodded, unwilling to respond verbally.

"We all have burdens to bear," she said. "It makes us what we are—especially us. Kisho is a *mystic*. He will do what we both will do. Help to ensure the success of our mission."

"And the war."

"Of course. And the war as well."

His hot eyes found hers again, pinning her into her seat as though with a scalpel. "Is that a vision?"

She did not flinch before responding. "I have seen a vision of what will happen."

He nodded, then turned away to fall into his own contemplations as his face blanked.

I have seen a vision of what will happen. But it is just one of many. As ever, the dissembling of a mystic, even among ourselves.

She leaned back, feeling the falseness of the neo-leather seat and wondering if it might apply to some of her visions. *I have seen visions of you, Kisho, and I hope for all our sakes that I am wrong . . . and right.*

The crowd actually jostled for position in front of the main viewport. One hapless technician lost his handgrip in the microgravity and began to slowly tumble towards the overhead bulkhead.

Stupid stravag *lower castemen. They have never seen space? Just endless emptiness.* Kisho shook his head in disgust—breathing shallowly to keep their inferior stink from his lungs—and moved silently past and out of the primary viewing cabin.

As if they have not seen the exact same thing through five jumps this trip alone: a burning ball of gas several hundred million kilometers directly below the aft of the JumpShip, where it sat above the plane of the ecliptic, its station-keeping drive already emitting a steady, small burn to counteract the slow draw of the star's gravity, even at this distance. The kilometer-wide solar sail, painfully slow in its deployment—a product of its microns-thin structure— flowering to the energy it voraciously swallowed from the class K4 star; trickling energy at a safe rate into the Kearny-Fuchida drive; spearing through the core of the entire six-hundred-and-eighty-meter-

length ship; until enough storage energy could be released, tearing the very bedrock of existence apart, folding space and hurling them thirty light-years distant.

He did not get sick. He did not have transit disorientation syndrome. Absolutely not. But he preferred to avoid talking to anyone for as long as possible after each jump, which tore a body from the weave of reality and then reassembled it in the subjective blink of an eye. All he needed to do was not open his mouth for about ten minutes and it would be fine. Of course it would.

Stupid stravag *lower castemen.*

Entering the passageway, he began to gingerly make his way towards the vessel's only gravity deck. *Should have been on the gravity deck when we made the jump. Just wanted a first-time view of the Arkab system. Just to give a nod of respect to the amazing Azami troops who have cross-trained with our warriors. Like us, they are honorable warriors the Combine couldn't subdue, and so House Kurita instead levied regiments for its use . . . just like they did with us. Had to be there . . . should have been on the grav deck.*

As he made his way down corridors, several Lancers' warriors passed his position, each nodding respectfully, making a circular finger gesture pressed to the chest. But the long years of training at the old man's knee held true and his eyes automatically registered and cataloged each minuscule reaction as the warriors under his counsel slipped by. From the way their hands moved, to the pulse at their necks, to the rise and fall of their chests, to the dilation of pupils: a checklist, which, when compared to the framework of thoughts within, added up to one of the best polygraph tests available . . . and all without the other person even aware of the scrutiny. It took a lifetime to master (he was far, far from perfect!) and not all could master it. But for those who could . . . the Lancers, who disliked mystics, effectively lying about their respectful greeting, stood out like images painted in glowing smears across infrared goggles at night.

Many rumors swam through the warrior caste, murmurs of this ability, but none voiced it, despite the unease the warriors felt. After all, it could not possibly be true, *quiaff*? But it was. After all, this technique was verifiable. He had tested the results numerous times and knew the truth of it. Unlike visions and portents and so much else. . . .

Though no sarcastic smile ever graced his lips, Kisho nevertheless acknowledged each show of respect (lie or no lie), filing away such information for the future. *Just one more burden you placed on me, old man,* quiaff? *One more.*

Reaching the exterior of the gravity deck, he waited for an open tram, then boarded with several others (they packed in, but never once touched him) and the car slowly accelerated to match the spin of the grav deck—he always hated how long the tram took, regardless of the knowledge that not even veteran spacers could handle zooming between microgravity and half gravity at any appreciable rate—where it mated to a hatch and disgorged the occupants.

"saOathmaster," a voice pounced almost the instant he left the hatchway, nova cat to its prey.

He turned towards the voice, only mildly disconcerted to have run into Tivia so quickly.

"Yes, Star Colonel Rosse?"

"Have you reviewed the personnel codexes?"

"I am currently in the process, Star Colonel." *Trying to second-guess me?* His pulse quickened at her presumption, though her eyes managed to keep any true irritant from sparking into outrage. Her deep, almost indigo eyes seemed catlike, as though she had had genetic implants from a nova cat; for a moment he thought he saw vertical slits and the flash of glowing luminescence from the lighting coming down from the central hub.

"Okay, okay," she said, swinging her head slightly, sending brunette, shoulder-length hair swinging. Her too-large nose even wrinkled, as though trying to avoid a smell.

Trying to avoid me?

"There are several Elstars in the Lancers." Her tone of voice spoke her discomfort and Kisho smiled slightly. *Ah, that is it. Or maybe both.*

A different permutation of the genetic breeding program himself, Kisho held no reservations over the still relatively new philosophy entrenching itself within the warrior castes of such Clans as Jade Falcon, Wolf, and even the Ghost Bears, and now starting to appear among the Nova Cats. A philosophy originating within the Scientist caste (if word from the Watch could be believed, the *Falcon* caste, of all places), which believed it had been wrong to allow the Elemental, MechWarrior, and aerospace pilot phenotypes to remain unchanged for centuries. That just as the breeding program mixed new genes to create the next greater generation of warriors, phenotypes should be massaged as well, experimenting, ever looking to create the epitome of the warrior caste.

As for the Elstars (a phrase Kisho believed the old man coined: elite ristars), they could look . . . very different, each Clan moving its warriors down different paths, from pasty skin and emaciated, to squat and broad, and so on. The percentage of Elstars to the general warrior caste was still minuscule; they were only used for the most important missions. But their superior abilities and their burgeoning alien looks threatened so many warriors.

As do we mystics. And at least it is only the flesh of Elstars the Clans rape, and not the mind and soul as well. "They will be evaluated as any other warrior," he finally responded coldly.

"Do not be offended, Mystic. Simply my job to make sure you know all my men and women. *Quiaff?*" She canted her head, her last statement almost a challenge.

Once more Kisho's irritation flamed out under her assaulting stare. *'Mech class-weapons have stares like that, Star Colonel. She knows?* He almost jerked, as though someone spoke softly in his ear. Before he could catch himself, he actually glanced to the right, as though expecting to find someone. He glanced back and found his neck muscles bunching at the smile twisting her lips and lighting her eyes. *How can the game be slipping away so easily? After all these years?*

"TDS."

"Neg!"

"Sorry," she said, hands raised, though no apology tinted her voice.

"A strange echo. Thought I heard something."

"Aff. A strange echo." He tried to avoid her eyes and finally glanced away, as though looking for someone. He ignored the fact that hearing voices was often a symptom of TDS, and she knew it.

"Well, I will leave you, though I hope to see your report on my personnel before we jump. The Republic is all too close, regardless of how many weeks remain before we meet battle."

"Aff, Star Colonel. You will have it."

She nodded her head, those too-knowing eyes once more prying under flesh and tumbling every twig and rock hiding secrets within. She turned away and gracefully leapt onto a ladder mounted on the unmoving bulkhead, which immediately carried her away as the grav deck continued to spiral.

You would make a good reader, Star Colonel. Are you a Moly? He chuckled darkly at the idea of her developing latent abilities, before the obviousness of her comments washed coldness along skin, raising goose bumps. *She knows you do not believe and does not care, provided you do your job.* He shook his head slowly. *But how can I do my job, if I do not believe?* The conundrum was painful.

He reached down to a small pocket on the thigh of his single suit and retrieved a small energy bar as he began making his way towards his favorite place, an out-of-the-way set of chairs and a table. As the spicy nuts and meaty fruits of Irece filled his mouth with memories, he easily moved among crowds of Nova Cats, a shadow hiding in the shadows and moving effortlessly without detection. Mystics, after all, were outcasts, but he made it a fine art.

"Kisho," a delicate voice intruded. Stomach muscles began to unclench as he slowed to a stop and focused, then redoubled in intensity at the pair moving up to stand within arm's reach.

A more strange match he could not imagine. Tall and thin, almost to the point of gangly, Hisa's thin cheeks, bland eyes, and lackluster hair assured him no MechWarrior would ever mount her likeness on a flatvid in their cockpit. Hisa stood, as usual, slightly hunched, as if expecting a strong breeze at any moment and preparing to shield against it.

Her companion, short and stocky (not fat, all muscle), with dark complexion, overly large eyes, and unique, among the Mystics, fiery red hair—an almost unheard-of case of the genefather's genes overpowering those of the First Mystic—Tanaka did not simply stand. Instead, he seemed to meld into his current position, his feet sealing to the ground, so a punch of a BattleMech's fist would not dislodge him, even in the half gravity.

"Kisho," Tanaka said, the clipped, deep voice a perfect match for the solid body. They both bowed slightly, then formed the circular finger gesture pressed to the chest.

He bowed in return and calmly returned the sign of respect for a mystic, while frantically throwing himself into a first-stage trance in an effort to distance his fluttering spirit from his body. They would find no truths betrayed by his physical form.

"I see you still cannot accept the weakness within. You will never master it, if you will not accept." Tanaka spoke, dark eyes all too knowing.

Savashri. Does everyone know? Hiding anger and trepidation was one thing. A blatant lie about wanting to be on hand to view the Arkab system as some type of honor to Azami warriors was another thing altogether, when it came to Tanaka, whose vision for truth-telling went beyond even Kisho's excellent forms. No, better to say nothing at all.

Twin eyes lunged and parried as though they were bared blades, Tanaka looking to batter down doors he could almost perceive; Kisho, in a defensive stance, throwing up a whirling screen of scintillating gray.

After several long heartbeats (a lifetime under his scrutiny!) Tanaka simply turned and walked away. As though the hatch in a cockpit popped following a horribly overheating battle, Kisho sucked in the stale, regurgitated air of the JumpShip as though it were the sweetest mountain air on Irece, redolent of evergreens and the heavy moisture of coming rain.

"He would not push so hard, if you did not keep yourself apart," a voice caressed his ears. Kisho glanced away from the retreating back, only slightly ashamed to be imagining PPC bolts stripping flesh and vaporizing bone. "We outcasts must stand together, *quiaff*?" A smile in the voice.

"He has no right to push at all!"

"Of course not. Shall we actually sit down?" she responded, her voice devoid of any recriminations as she walked the half dozen paces to his favorite spot—a set of utilitarian chairs surrounding a small desk, all secured to the floor in case of a gravity deck malfunction. Well away from any other location, it afforded a refuge in plain sight.

For just a moment he chose not to follow, sure that he heard accusations in her tone. Yet something about her drew him reluctantly to her side, where he deliberately took a seat. The neoleather gave little and the hard backrest reminded him of an interrogation chair. No creature comforts. *The Clan way,* quiaff? He kept the sarcastic smile from his lips with no small effort—having lost first trance with the departure of Tanaka—and wiggled into the seat in a vain effort to find a more comfortable position.

"How are your dreams?"

His head whipped towards her like a targeting reticule to an enemy target. "What?"

"Your dreams? How are they?"

"They are my own."

Her bland, brown eyes held his face with a completely different sensation then Tanaka's. Where his demanded absolute obedience without question, hers seemed to beckon, to show him her own soul and invite him to do the same. Slightly akin to Yori, he contemplated, thinking of their meeting almost a year gone, but not nearly so serene, not so accepting. He glanced away, almost ashamed to peer through another's spirit windows. He shivered despite the warmth of the deck. *How can you bare yourself so easily? Akin to standing naked in front of your peers . . . but a thousand times worse. Ten thousand.*

"Of course. Simply a conversational piece. You have proven difficult to know, Kisho."

Because I do not wish to know you, or anyone. Too late, he knew the partial lie, even to himself, might be betrayed to Hisa's eyes. Despite their bland and soft appearance, the old man would not have chosen her unless she were a mystic of unparalleled abilities. A mystic, very different than Tanaka in her approach, and yet identical to him in every way that mattered.

She believed.

His stomach began to cramp once more as the yawning hole tore further within him. A gaping wound across which no hand might reach.

"You must have a headache."

He came out of his growing despair with some difficulty, confused at her odd observation. His eyes widened slightly to find her hand outstretched to him. *Are you reading my mind? Do you have the old man's power?* For a tick in time, he almost believed, could almost see the knowledge written within her liquid vision. Then he came to his senses. More trickery.

I know your tricks, Hisa. They hammered them through me as well. They will not work on me.

Nevertheless, he laid his hand gently within hers, drawing away attention from the knowledge of her motives. She began to gently massage his hand, particularly seeking out the pressure point in between the thumb and index finger, back towards the palm. A sudden pressure and he gasped with the sharp pain. Yet, as usual, the pain brought a relief, a lessening of the headache he did not know he had. As though it

were a cold compress drawing off the heat of an infected wound, the pressure fell away from his temples,
down his arm and out.

He took in her eyes once more and wondered if she
drew the pain to herself. Such a fool. *A little release
of pain and you immediately fall back to your
indoctrination.*

"Sometimes it can be such a little thing. Just a hand
to hold and a gentle massage to release the pain
within."

*Ah, you do it so well. Tanaka has nothing on you,
Hisa. And yet I am pulled to you. Your pheromones
work overtime to synch our heartbeats and raise my
own endorphins to a level where I cannot think, but
want you.*

"And sometimes it takes more, Hisa, *quiaff?*"

"*Aff.*"

He canted his head at the world of possibilities in
her statement.

6

The sound of forged steel sliding from a boiled-leather sheath hissed like burning sap in the guttering darkness.

Breath loud in his ears, he let the cross-hatched, smooth leather wrap of the hilt and its familiar weight bring reassurance. Shadows gyrated and leapt across moss-strewn stone, as frigid wind wafted down endless corridors, sending sputtering torches into gasps of agony and raising goose bumps. His harness creaked slightly as he shifted leather-shod feet across the pitted, ancient stone, trying to find a dry bit of ground. The comforting presence of a companion at his back calmed a fluttering heart, allowing him to unlimber stiff joints and prepare for the coming battle.

As though it were a tide of physical water, *something* ebbed into the room, under the iron-bound wooden door, washing across the filthy floor, pushing detritus of unimaginable ages aside as it engulfed his feet. He choked off a scream, as the fear beat within, fanned by billows from warm coals to a white-hot forge threatening to consume everything. Numerous scars across arms, hands, and chest ached as muscles bunched, tendons stretched, and skin pulled taunt until the battle marks stood out rigid and harsh as the day they were born, like a dollmaker stretching satin to the breaking point to make a closing stitching.

"It comes. Ware," he said, voice horribly harsh and stiff with restrained terror, a mouse squeak in a giant's domain. When no response came, he turned, only to find an empty room. The hint of the companion's presence was already fading.

He opened his mouth to yell the companion's name and abruptly couldn't remember. Couldn't remember where the person came from, or even what the companion looked like. Could only remember the pain of betrayal like a hot, cauterizing blade.

A sound. Nothing truly coherent, more felt than heard, slipped underneath the iron-bound wooden door. He spun back around, his finely tuned balance off so he slipped on wet stone, almost crashing to the ground. Despite previous knowledge, his eyes moved to the leather hinges; they were moldy and half eaten by rats. A determined child could force his way in, much less the thing stalking him. The thing coming with burning eyes, and teeth and claws and strength, from endless darkness. Coming to take away all he knew.

All he had built across a lifetime.

Knuckles cracked and color drained from flesh as the sound materialized, undulating closer to the door. His heavy breathing spiked, at first covering the sound. Despite his resolve, he took a hesitant step back. Then another. One more, as the crescendo of the thing's movement overcame the volume of his body's betrayals.

A small puff of white shot underneath the door,

followed by a sound he did not recognize. He jerked his head upwards as stinking droplets fell from a stalactite of some mucus, splashing onto his bare shoulder through the top opening in the leather chest armor, hitting his head with their incessant beat, fingers of doom to his skull. He bumped into the wall with a painful crack to his elbow, just as another puff underneath the door billowed, and this time the knowledge burned through. He tried to find strength in his grip on his blade, but numb fingers refused to move.

Snuffling. The nightmare taking his measure, assuring it tracked down its prey. Its exhaled breath in the frigid room raised bumps that turned white and hard as an armadillo shell. Fear dilated his pupils and locked his arms, arms long accustomed to facing battle with sweeping blows. A roar thrashed the air, booming against the door, sending a shower of ancient stone flakes and droplets raining across the room, as though a small dervish coalesced.

He almost vomited as his stomach clenched until his vision ran red. The door exploded inward with a sound to shatter eardrums, and crimson eyes and mouth stretched wide, launching into the room to rend and destroy and kill and kill and kill. . . .

Spirit Cat Encampment
Addicks, Prefecture III
The Republic of the Sphere
29 July 3136

. . . Galaxy Commander Kev Rosse flopped off of his cot and hit the dirt floor and vomited. Bile splashed his hands with warm, sloshing liquid and he vomited again. And again. The stench filling his nostrils, while muscles racked under the horror of the nightmare and a headache exploded pinpricks of flashing light under tightly lashed eyelids. As the dry heaves began, he wished he were dead.

A lifetime later, stomach so empty it felt shrunk in size and tongue swollen until he almost gagged, Kev Rosse gingerly rolled onto his side, then slowly, ever so slowly, over again. Then, centimeters at a time, he maneuvered into a crawling position, from which he managed to get to the edge of his tent and poke his head outside.

The pressure on his forehead immediately began to ease under the ministration of Addicks' local night breeze, the usual cold wind now a blessed balm to aching muscles and a tortured soul.

By the Founder! In the darkness of the new moon, he could see almost nothing, beyond the fitful flame of a torch almost four hundred meters distant. It burned at the entrance to the cavern system where his force stowed most of its equipment—even held room for three 'Mechs. Nevertheless, the stench of his guts still encrusted his fingers in stickiness and the nightmare coated his knowledge of the most powerful vision he had ever experienced.

I must speak with Davik. Clumsily wiping his hands through tufts of local shore grass, he levered to his knees and finally to his feet. Wiping bile from his mouth onto a sleeve, he wove as though drunk, trying to regain control of his body while zeroing in on Davik's tent. The cold night air now seemed less of a relief, raising goose bumps on his flesh. The memory of his dream hitched his breathing and invaded reality. He glanced upwards, as though afraid to see a crimson rent stretching the sky, but only found blackness. The minuscule oases of lights that were the stars seemed to disappear against the sheer magnitude of such dark-

ness. Imagined snuffling across his neck sent him running, though staggering was the best he could manage.

"Davik!" he almost yelled as he collapsed through
the tent opening, falling onto hard-packed dirt and
scraping his left palm free of flesh.

"Wha . . ." a confused, muffled voice answered.
Scrabbling sounds and movement in the darkness almost ripped free a scream, before a small light pushed
back the night with its steady, man-made solidity.

"Kev . . . Galaxy Commander . . . what the . . .
you . . ." The voice trailed off as the old man shuffled
into the light to peer down at him with shadowed eyes.
The man, at least into his sixties, with a flowing beard,
and a face filled with the crags and clefts of flesh only
a lifetime of experiences can gouge, gracefully bent to
one knee despite the hour and abrupt awakening. He
brought up the length of his own robes and began to
wipe away vomit from Kev's hands.

He stared, unseeing and dull-eyed, ignoring the
sting of stomach acid on the torn flesh of his palm,
for almost a minute as Davik continued his ministrations as though he was the lowliest casteman. The ev-
eryday act pulled at Kev's anxieties and fears until
they bubbled to the surface, burst, and were carried
away on the soft wind ruffling the tent flaps.

Finally Galaxy Commander Kev Rosse stilled Davik's
hands with his own, and then settled into a more appropriate sitting position, legs crossed. Shock, pain, and
now shame warred within him at the way he had arrived. Kev waited to be sure his voice would not betray
him, then spoke. "Visionmaster, I request *surkai.*"

"You've no need to ask for forgiveness," Davik
said, the smile plain in his voice, if hidden in the
giant beard.

"Your contractions?" Kev said, responding to Davik's levity.

"Don't hurt anyone, least of all you. Kills me how we can throw ourselves into the way of autocannons shells and PPC streams and yet can be terrified of simple words."

"It is not that simple."

The man stood, pulled a small folding chair to him, and settled down, ignoring the stains on the edge of his robe from the vomit. Kev almost blanched as he saw it.

Seeing his look, Davik glanced down, then waved his hand in a gesture of dismissal. "I hope you don't mind if I sit on a stool. You young people can cross your legs in the dirt all you want, but beyond the length of my beard, I should get something for living so long."

"What you should get, Visionmaster, is a little more respect for Clan ways." They shared a smile.

"Now, that vision?" he continued, the non sequitur catching Kev off balance and causing his fear to surge.

"Um."

"Speak up. Unlike you young'uns, I need sleep."

The casualness of tone pushed darkness back into its corner and unstopped his tongue. In halting steps, Kev unlimbered the vision. Each word reawoke the visceral sensations of the nightmare and the sure knowledge of impending doom. Finally, as his words died out, he realized he'd start vomiting again if he didn't wash away the stomach acids still coating his tongue.

As though reading his mind, Davik thrust a bottle into his hands and reseated himself. *When did he stand?* Kev shifted position and took several mouthfuls, which he leaned back and spit out the tent flap after sloshing. Finally, he reseated himself, relieving aching muscles, and took several long, slow swallows. Then a deep breath calmed his jangled nerves.

"What did you see?" Visionmaster Davik said.

He responded without looking up, his hands caressing the plastic water bottle, eyes elsewhere. "Our doom."

"Are you sure?"

"One is never sure."

"Exactly."

"But it was there."

"Of course. What else?"

"A monster. Something hunting for us."

"For us?"

"No, not just us, me," Kev said, closing eyes, gritting teeth. "Me."

"Who could it be?"

Laughter barked into the tent, spilling into the night. "Anybody," he finally responded, pictures moving against his closed eyelids as he named them. "The Republic. Bannson and his *stravag* Raiders. Campbell and her Highlanders, though she has been busy trying to put out every brush fire in The Republic. Swordsworn. Fury?" He shrugged his shoulders, found an itch on his arm from drying vomit that Davik had missed. "We have a history that predates us, but if they come, they will come. An upstart? Anyone."

"What else?"

He opened his eyes and unhinged his jaw, popping it twice as he ransacked his memory of the vision before responding. "No. Nothing else. My doom. The doom of the Spirit Cats. Something. Someone. Someone hunting us."

"And the companion?"

Kev jerked as though struck by feedback from a neurohelmet during an ammo explosion. "The companion."

"Someone we trust. Someone you trust. Betrayer."

"Betrayer? But who?"

"So someone comes and someone will betray."

Kev slowly lowered his head until his chin rested against his chest, the shirt smooth against his stubble-filled chin. "Not much."

"Of course not. It never is. But it is enough, *quiaff?*"

At the man's deliberate use of a Clanism, Kev raised his head and met the man's eyes. They both smiled as Kev Rosse nodded. *I have not come this far in leading my Spirit Cats in their quest for safety to be undone now. I have a warning and what comes, will come and I will be ready.*

"*Aff.*"

7

The first time in microgravity caused no end of problems. Yet their mutual comfort in the act led to the development of new tactics and numerous repeats. By week's end, such difficulties were vanquished and they stood (or laid, in this case—in near zero-g, "lying" was absolutely relative) on the field of battle, victorious.

And what victory. Droplets of sweat retaining their cohesion spun in slow, orbiting arcs, an accretion disk of hard work and spent pleasures. The air stank of musk and dedication.

He stretched like a cat finishing its feast—tendons and muscles popping luxuriously—and settling in to bask in the sunlight warming a patch of carpet. "Can you keep this up?" he finally said, words almost too large for the small berth.

Laughter slipped into the room, slow and warm. "I believe, Kisho, the question should be can *you* keep it up, *quiaff*?"

His laughter, though not totally devoid of edge, joined hers. "*Aff*, Hisa. *Aff*." Reaching hands out towards the bulkhead, he grasped a ring and slowly reoriented, to find Hisa—as could be managed in such tight confines—in the process of taking a nearly moistureless sponge bath. "I see you enjoy your sandpaper baths."

"And I see you have been listening to lower castemen again."

He stiffened, tongue wrapping around a retort, then stalled. *Not Hisa. Tanaka. Tivia. But not Hisa.*

"I do not offend," she said, stowing away her personal gear. "I simply prefer to wash, or in this case scrape, away the past before moving to the future." She barely flexed her legs and swam with effortless grace across the short distance.

"You need to teach me that."

"What?" she said, reaching out her own arms, which outreached his by almost four centimeters, to stop forward movement a hand's breadth from his chest.

His eyes never once strayed to her body, despite the nudity. She would never be beautiful, or even pretty. Too much bone, not enough skin; he knew *male* Spheroids with larger breasts. But something in her eyes. Something in the openness of her face, in the way she smiled. And over the last few weeks, two things had become apparent as they coupled and talked, as crèche do (or are supposed to do—he had kept himself from such companionship for so long).

That she allowed a vulnerability in looking past her shields, a vulnerability that dwarfed the mere physicality of her nudity. And more stunning, such vulnerability came not in weakness. No, in strength. A strength that towered above anything he had ever known.

"Tanaka says that," he finally responded.

"What?"

Gray eyes met gray and he kept silent until she finally spoke, hair floating around like lazy seaweed fronds in a slow ocean current. "That you spend too much time listening to the lower castemen?" she asked.

"Aff."

She shrugged, began caressing his chest. "He pushes you. That is all."

"Pushes me. That is an understatement."

"He pushes everyone, including me. Including himself. Is that not our way?"

I do not believe you. He pushes no one as he does me. But he conveniently ignored part of her comment. *"Aff."*

Her hands began further ministrations. "What do you think of the coming war?"

"What?" Confusion painted his voice.

"I thought my question plain. Do I need to stop?" she said, pulling her hands away.

"Neg," he said, anger replacing confusion, despite the twinkle in her eye. What did one have to do with the other?

"Perhaps I should tell Tanaka I have found your Achilles' heel. He has been at you for weeks and yet nothing. We mystics have to stick together."

It took every ounce of willpower not to react. Of course they would talk about him during their own coupling. Once more, gray eyes challenged.

"No, I think not," Hisa finally said without taking her steady gaze from his. "After all, what is the best victory but one achieved alone?"

He sighed. So it was to be the game. Was she always the mystic? She was sending him mixed signals. *Very well. If it is to be the game, with the endless riddles and conundrums, then you must lose. I have mastered it far longer than you might possibly imagine. Mastered it in a way you could not understand.*

"You surprised me with your change of subject," he finally responded, content to play the game with a subject change of his own. "Tanaka. War. What next? Which warlord will replace Sakamoto? It might have already occurred."

She resumed with a sniff. "I do not care which warlord replaces Sakamoto. That is not the warlord that matters."

"And Warlord Tormark should?" His own hands began caressing her body in return. "Saito should have been the only warlord our Clan must deal with."

"Not this again." Her sigh practically sang through the Spartan room, with its single fold-down cot and small desk, both bolted to the floor. She moved close, her hands expanding their movements.

Kisho's anger rose a notch. "Yes, this again. Why are we traveling to The Republic? Why are we going to a war that has nothing to do with us?"

"You have been at this since we departed. Should it matter? War is war and we are Clansmen. We have not fought in such a war in far too long." Her breath quickened as well.

"I look forward as much as any warrior to the coming battles. But the *battles*. Not the war of politics. We mystics are supposed to think of such differences."

She shrugged, as though discounting that entire argument. "Because we swore oaths. The Dragon roars and we respond." Once again, a change of subject.

"But is it the right Dragon?" he shot back immediately, as they began to lock synch their ministrations.

"Why should that matter?"

"Because it should. What honor will this gain the Nova Cats? Do we follow blindly?"

"I do not know, Kisho. Do we?"

He almost blanched, grateful his body's current occupation would mask nearly any reaction. So many times in the last few weeks, as he began to know her, as he began to understand her in a way they never had all during the crèche years and even afterwards, as they began to assume their responsibilities, he asked the question. Does she know? For so many long years following his Trial of Mysticism—that perfect moment, that one instant of savage understanding and clarity, when he realized he had passed the test, somehow, yet had no vision, that he had won through trickery of mind techniques and not the pure sight demanded of the mystic he would never be—he perfected a facade to cover his inadequacy. Turned it all into a challenge, part of the game.

The Game. A game starting to unravel.

"Yes. We do. We move blindly. Ordered by those who think they know a better path. By superiors who think they know better and yet do not."

"That is almost cowardice talk from a Clansman. Almost traitorous talk." She increased the rhythm.

Such words would have led to a Trial of Grievance on the spot from any other person. Yet he knew she pushed him, just like Tanaka. Yet, unlike Tanaka, her soft approach revealed far more than his savage frontal assaults ever would.

"Is it cowardice to question? To demand to know if our leaders know the path they follow?" The words were spoken before he could call them back. These words were not a blatant declaration of his lack of faith, but as close as he had ever come to speaking his shame out loud to anyone within his Clan. Fear, a small, constant pulse since the Trial of Mysticism, gouged painfully across his soul, the notch at a height never before encountered. A screen, torn away by his own hand, fluttered slowly to the ground. Eyes wide, his breath sped well beyond what their coupling ever produced. *What have I done?!*

Gentle arms drew him close, until their faces almost touched, eyes locked in a gaze far more intimate than their bodies, as she finished pulling them together and began the slow movements needed to keep from spiraling out of control in microgravity.

The pain within diminished as Hisa did not immediately cast him away in disgust. For, though couched in talk of Katana and wars, her eyes said she knew of what they spoke. Her legs and arms wrapping his in bony flesh as she increased the rhythm.

"You have not spoken of your nightmares."

Words cavorted within him, demanding an outlet. Demanding to answer that stab. Yet they were sealed as he gazed into the windows straight to her soul. Because if he opened his mouth, he knew there would be no lying to her about his dreams, and he'd lowered enough barriers this day.

The rhythm began to reach a fevered pitch and endorphins spiked throughout his body, sending heat flashes and sparking pinpricks of bliss along his skin. A sad smile curved her lips as they reached towards the end. And he knew. Not sadness for his lack of faith or that he would not answer. No, as though the words etched themselves in fire across his sweat-slicked skin, her sadness sprung from his inability to simply share with her. To rest, even for a moment, from the mountain on his back and take her helping hand.

He could find no words for any response, as their bodies answered a basic genetic need and they exploded together in rapture and all thoughts finally fell away.

8

Yellow light, harsh and bright, spilt across the *Santin* as it materialized in the Lambrecht system, eddies from the emergence already sweeping away in every direction. The stabbing luminosity found portholes and viewports, mercilessly raking photons across unprotected eyes, illuminating darkened quarters

Warning klaxons pealed down corridors, clarion calls to battle.

"What?!" Kisho mumbled incoherently, roused from slumber, the klaxons hammer to a headache only partially vanquished. Opening eyes to slits, Kisho almost screamed as the sunlight pierced straight through, white-hot shivs skewering his eyes and penetrating straight to the brain. Kisho shivered, the image of a spitting and hissing cortex on a superheated armor plate looming large. Like a dogged sphynx raptor, the headache slipped quicksilver fibers back into gray matter, threatening to set off the mind-numbing pain once more. He squeezed his eyes shut and turned away from the microsized viewport, hand automatically slapping full darkening of the aperture. For a moment the bed beckoned, as though it were the glory of a Bloodname all mystics were forever denied. A haggard breath pulled in the stink of sick flesh and the claustrophobic confines of the berth abruptly threatened to squeeze him until he popped like an infected wound.

Gingerly he moved off the fold-down cot, careful to make sure his mag-slips adhered fully, then crabbed over the half step to the urinal device. The autocannon shells to his brain continued as the warning bells kept at their incessant bleating, eroding his will to live. Never had he experienced such pain. Not in his MechWarrior training, not in the sibko life before it and the Room and the Machine, not even the time a group of young trueborns caught him alone outside the crèche and let him know what they thought of mystics and the tainted blood he bore—five weeks in the infirmary, and nothing compared to the pain that made him wonder why he could not feel the blood coursing down his cheeks from burst eyes.

Where did this pain come from? But he knew.

Finishing bodily functions, Kisho used a quick-squirt sponge to wipe away the worst of the salt-encrusted sweat and ungummed his eyes—it felt like snails had crawled into the corners and died and dried during the night. As he opened the hatch and stepped into the corridor, he ignored the source of the headache. Ignored it about as well as he ignored the pain, as well as he ignored most things of late.

Not well. Not well at all.

*   *   *

"I have two DropShips on an intercept course to the *Santin*, Star Admiral," the technician casteman said. From her position at the sensor board on the bridge of the *Comitatus*-class JumpShip, the woman tapped through several screens, verifying information. "Ten thousand kilometers and closing at G plus two."

"Relative position?" the captain responded, voice no more hurried than for a discussion of a new wheat hybrid by two merchant castemen.

"Twenty-two degrees, downspin. Aft."

"Another JumpShip?"

"*Aff*, Star Admiral."

From his position, ensconced in a corner of the bridge—only there due to his mystic status—Kisho nursed a small water bulb, trying to rehydrate his tongue. *Must be a dead* surat *in there.* While he fought against the slowly abating pain, helped by the Star admiral finally terminating the proximity-warning alarms, Kisho took in the surroundings.

Several dozen meters across, the circular bridge contained numerous banks of computers in several rows, centered around a large holographic display. Unlike many JumpShips, the *Comitatus* did not have a forward viewport. Off to the right (*was that starboard?*) of the holoprojection, the Star admiral sat in his mag-chair, a grandfather with peppered hair and just-wrinkling hands, proudly taking in his whelps—almost a dozen personnel, all frantically working to bring the admiral relevant data. Though Galaxy Commander Ket Lossey stood on the bridge—almost at the Star admiral's elbow, but just outside the discomforting field of the mag-chair—in this situation Star Admiral Bavros, despite Lossey's ultimate command of the entire force, held the reigns of decision-making.

The worst situation for any MechWarrior . . . to be

attacked while in transit between worlds, where their fate rested in the hands of someone else. Kisho nodded in sympathy at the distaste on Lossey's face.

"The rest of the fleet is due?"

"Seventy-four minutes, by my mark, Star Admiral."

Enough time for the *Comitatus*, as the most heavily armed of any JumpShip in known space, to clear away any obstacles this side of a WarShip. With the pain lessening to manageable levels, Kisho's sardonic smile flared momentarily. *And if we run into a WarShip, then it is all over anyway.*

Star Admiral Bavros decisively stabbed open an intercom. "Star Commodore Leroux, I want both Stars deployed immediately. Those ships are not to close within a thousand kilometers."

"*Aff,* Star Admiral."

The man shifted position slightly—whether by design or not, the chair slowly bobbled in the magnetic field that allowed the admiral to spin it in any direction when needed—opening up another commline. "Star Commodore Jit," he said, voice still casual enough for a night in a local bar.

"Star Admiral?"

"We have company."

"I noticed that." The sarcasm in the DropShip captain's voice surprised Kisho, especially considering the frown creasing the Galaxy commander's face. But Bavros only smiled.

Long-time friendship, that one.

"Fighters are scrambling. Your *Sacred Rite* will act as last defense. Can you manage?"

Several smiles washed features, as even Kisho appreciated the humor. The *Sacred Rite,* a *Noruff*-class DropShip, could put the fear of the Great Father into even some smaller WarShips. Between the *Comitatus,* the *Sacred Rite,* and its complement of twenty of the finest aerospace pilots in Clan Nova Cat, they were eminently prepared to blaze a trail into any system. And that didn't include the other aerospace fighters attached to individual Clusters on board the incoming *Odyssey-* and *Invader*-class JumpShips.

Laughter boomed back. "*Quiaff*?

"*Aff*," came the smiling response.

"Star Admiral," Galaxy Commander Ket Lossey said, harsh voice filling the sudden vacuum.

As the admiral signed off, his fingers gently coaxed the chair around and the two warriors squared off. "Galaxy Commander?"

"You cannot destroy these forces out of hand."

"I cannot?"

Ket's minuscule nod almost verged on disrespect. "I would request you not destroy this force out of hand. It is paramount we find out who they are. We are only a jump from the first of our designated targets. Have they discerned our arrival and are they preempting it? Has our arrival been given away?"

Kisho nodded. *Glad to see I am not the only one leery, like her or not, of Warlord Tormark and her ultimate motives.*

The admiral nodded. "Of course, Commander. They shall not all perish." He spun the chair back to the holoprojection. "Technician Tiral."

"Star Admiral?" a diminutive man responded, peeking over a computer console, as though he were a crèche child attempting to be a man before his Trial of Position.

"Tap into battlerom feeds and ship beacons. Feed the data into the tank. I want a holoprojection of what's unfolding."

"*Aff*." A flurry of keystrokes bespoke instant response, despite the admiral's surface lackadaisical attitude.

He runs a tight ship.

Several minutes drifted by in relative silence as the star admiral settled into the mag-chair, setting it to angle back as though he were reclining in the most decadent of Spheroid loungers, while setting it spinning slowly. Kisho was confident his half-slit eyes missed nothing.

After a shorter time than he believed possible, the holoprojection burst to life. A rainbow of hues cast the bridge into harsh contrast, the shadows highlighting sharp edges until everything but the holoprojection looked like a two-dimensional image; the depths washed away like running ink from rain. Like a *stravag* Spheroid voyeur peaking into a forbidden rite, Kisho actually leaned forward to try to grasp the nuances unfolding before him. As a swarm of aerospace fighters met a like swarm, trying to shield the incoming DropShips, the information fell into a confused sensory overload of flashing lights and gyrating images, and suddenly the pain began to mount once more.

Kisho immediately closed his eyes and leaned back to try to avert the return. *Anything but that.* As he did, the memories, as though conjured by the aerospace battle unfolding in the deep cold of space, surfaced and the nightmare surged.

He'd had nightmares. All mystics did. What else could you expect as a result of their . . . training? But this. To be so frightened and yet not remember a single thing. No, this was different somehow. Something new. Fingers clenched in frustration and nostrils flared, pulling in stale air, while his ears stoppered against everything around him. Nightmares always stalked whenever he began to unwind and let down his inner defenses, as when he talked with Hisa. But not like this.

He breathed deeply three times, then let it out in a single long exhalation and slipped into a trance. To forget about a nightmare! To forget about the fear— no, not fear! *unease*—of the crumbling walls between him and Hisa. Of the sharing of his darkest secrets, even if he only scratched the surface. He pushed all thoughts aside and floated in a void of nothing.

"Mystic." The word rudely intruded, a reedy light in luxurious darkness. Kisho ignored it.

"Mystic." It came again, more determined, though still respectful. In a haze of contentment, Kisho waited, unwilling to answer. Yet training could not be ignored, years of indoctrination. He slowly cracked lids, to find a technician casteman solicitously standing before him.

"Mystic."

"*Aff.*" The word seemed strange, as though it were the first spoken in ages.

"The admiral requests you leave the bridge."

The words jarred with his contentment, to the point that he slowly leaned forward from his slouched position, opened eyes wide, and glanced around the bridge. Consternation prickled flesh at the almost empty bridge; neither the Galaxy commander nor the Star admiral were present and the bridge appeared to be on a low-duty shift. The battle?

He looked again at the technician and hated what came next, but there was no helping it. "What happened?" He chewed his tongue for a moment to abate the anger. Asking a lower casteman!

"You were in a trance, Mystic. The battle is over, the ships returned."

"What?" He chewed on that, surprised. Not often did he lose control of a trance. Almost never. What had he been thinking about? Hisa? The *stravag* nightmares. He slowly realized the man still stood before him.

"Who was it?"

"What?"

"The ships we fought, *surat*. Who was it?" The man winced as though struck full in the face. Weakling.

"Mercenaries."

"Mercenaries?!" He slipped a hand towards his back, massaging a cramped muscle. Was The Republic now hiring mercenaries? Had they fallen so far? Become so desperate?"

"*Aff*, Mystic. Mercenaries hired by Lambrecht."

Confusion stripped away a measure of arrogance. "Lambrecht?"

"*Aff*, Mystic. They've declared independence and hired mercenaries to try and blockade against any Republic counterattack. Once they realized who we were, they hailed us. Begged us to let them be."

He cocked an eyebrow.

"We allowed one DropShip to limp away."

"Watch those contractions," Kisho said absentmindedly, standing and moving away without giving the man another thought. *It is as I feared. How I saw it on my first trip to this rotted husk of a failed empire. It is shattering.*

Breaking apart under the strain.

Kisho reached the hatch and began to make his way back to his quarters, knowing he must review Tivia's codices one more time. But he could not help a final thought.

Shattering. As am I.

Interlude II

Ways of Seeing Park, Barcella
Nova Cat Reservation, Irece
Irece Prefecture, Draconis Combine
18 March 3129

Ghostly lights wove a skein of second skin across Kanaye's features—a multijeweled mask of light to hide behind. One more layer. One more mask. Would it be the beginning of the last? His shoulders bowed under the burden.

"Subject Seven, eliminated." A disembodied voice echoed in the darkness.

Kanaye ignored the comment as he finished his role in the previous disqualification. Regardless of his own actions, he almost shuddered at their detachment.

"Outside the appropriate parameters," another responded with equal discourtesy.

"*Hai.* Failures are almost beyond projections."

"Four remain?"

"*Hai.*"

"Then the projections still remain viable."

The two individuals seemed to soak in the darkness, as though more accustomed to shadows than light. He tried ignoring their conversation as more numbers scrolled across multiple monitors.

Subject One seemed a statue of ice: cool, total control, moving forward with absolute precision. His numbers were way off the chart. Twice, now, he'd almost failed, one leaving him wounded, and yet not an emotion moved his features. Kanaye shook his head, though, well aware the eyes would be hot enough to melt 'Mech armor. *That one projects cool, but the depths . . . ah, the depths.* Despite misgivings on Kanaye's part, Subject One seemed to surpass all expectation. A reedy desire blossomed. *Perhaps.*

Subject Two, in chamber three, progressed well. Polar opposite to Subject One, he savagely clawed forward, even bypassing some sections through stunning mental agility. His emotions hung on his features, disdaining to hide the usual Clan arrogance, tempered by a mystic's training. Zealot.

Subject Three, in perfect mimicry of her usual decorum, ghosted through every angle, passed every obstacle. Without the savagery of Subject Two, but also lacking the apparent detachment of One, Subject Three possessed a self-assurance at her age that most adults lacked. She appeared a perfect blend of the other two. The one that should have sparked Kanaye's interest. And yet, no matter how many visions he sought, no matter how many times his mind cast within for answers, she fell below the radar. Needed, of course. Useful, absolutely, if she passed. But the one? She *should* be. But he could not convince himself.

Subject Four? Kanaye barely glanced at his numbers, knowing with absolute certainty he was on the verge of failing.

Kanaye glanced away from the monitors momentarily, sinking down and within to find that vision, while allowing his eyes to reacclimatize to the darkened room outside the kaleidoscope of holographic images on which all their hopes hung.

A scant fifteen meters on a side, it seemed more the home to a crazed computer fiend than to the five individuals trying to find a place amidst the blizzard of computers, monitors, and endless tangles of wires, like the stripped muscles of some mammoth beast. A 'Mech howl leapt to mind, screaming at the depravity of a shorn-off limb, left to molder in darkness, disgrace. *As we molder?* He pushed that aside, knowing the answer. All for a single purpose. All to monitor and track the ongoing Trials begun by ten individuals. Only four were left.

A Trial of Mysticism.

"Subject Four progresses well?" Despite attempts otherwise, the voices of the two interlopers (technically not, but Kanaye would forever consider them such) focused him back to immediacy.

"*Hai.* Well within operating parameters. He might succeed."

"The others?"

"The modeling shows two. Subject Three."

"Subject One is too detached."

"Two, too savage. Undesired."

"*Hai.* Both. Undesired. Numerous cross-referenced modeling demonstrates a ninety percent probability of failure."

Glad for the darkness, Kanaye stared with fury and mocking in equal measure at the hunched forms clustered closer to the monitors than the technician castemen assigned to monitor each candidate's progress—aged

Spheroid crones, needy, desperate. And they were desperate. Desperate for contribution. Desperate to maintain a hold on a program no longer theirs, a program from which they would only get the cast-offs from now on.

He smiled, a cruel, satisfied smirk hidden among secret shadows and comforting darkness. *You made the deal and now you must abide by it. A quarter century is more than enough affront to these sacred chambers.*

Of a sudden, a part of Kanaye's mind centered and then spiraled down as his face slackened slightly, focusing him in an instance of recognition. *The time is now.* He glanced back to the monitors, ignoring the endless regurgitation of raw data fed through a mesh suit worn by each candidate and augmented through an endless series of relays and additional sensors buried throughout each chamber, and found an actual holodisplay. As though immersed in the image, as though having an out-of-body experience, as though he were a specter irrevocably tied to the supplicant— everything but Subject Four sloughed away.

The thirteen-year-old boy—sharp eyebrows, high forehead, and gray-eyed (genemother heritage breeding true, despite the new mix of genefather; as always), muscles still not fully developed, the hint of the child still apparent in the preman—wove through an intricate landscape of mathematically generated terrain: cubes, trapezoids, decahedrons, rhomboids . . . a bizarre, endless topography climbing away not simply in two dimensions, but in three, as the chamber slowly rotated—a massive, existential Escher landscape to warp minds and rend souls. Quantum mathematicians would trade their lives for the prospect of once, just once, sitting within such boundaries and contemplating the endlessness of perceptual existence and the absolute exquisiteness of numbers . . . despite the knowledge they would lose their sanity.

Every dozen paces, as the boy moved up and down and around the wicked landscape, he would freeze, a kilometer stare (mirrored exactly by Kanaye at that moment) savagely slicing away all humanity from his features, as though he contemplated things none else might see. After a moment, his face animated with some small emotions, he began moving again.

"Two minutes." A small thread of Kanaye's concentration eased away from the boy's experience into another trough of contemplation.

Out of the corner of his eye Kanaye noticed the two interlopers huddled over the monitor displaying raw data and, despite resolve, he almost whirled to strike them. *Look at the boy. Look at him! Look what we have done to him.* But he would not. For all relationships come with crosses to be borne and this one was no different.

Perhaps more importantly (he wallowed momentarily in the spitefulness of it all), he assuaged his anger with the knowledge that he'd surpassed their modeling. His vision had shown him Subject Four would fail this test, despite the endless modeling that *they* so clutched to their chests like the vain to the smooth skin of youth. He ignored the bass rumbling of knowledge that he was to blame as much as any for what he put these possible mystics through.

Subject Four continued his stop, go, stop movements, young limbs easily transitioning through such chaotic maneuvering, but the strain began to tell in the fluttering of hands and quickened breathing Kanaye noted. The boy's face still moved through the nightmarish transformation of dehumanization at each stop as he strove to focus his vision and discern the exit.

Kanaye remembered his own trial, the Byzantine chamber pressing against his senses until he thought he might explode. Yet he'd traversed the room with so many more years hanging on his shoulders than this young man—a room Subjects One, Two, and Three had already passed.

It was so different for him. No pretraining. And only the single room, so long ago, the caste so young— he chuckled soundlessly, darkly: *still* so young. And no blood. No blood. He tried moving his tongue and found it sealed within a dry mouth.

No blood . . . a mantra forever running through him. A Moly. That was what the interlopers called him, mocking him with a silly Spheroid female's name. An anomaly. Outside their parameters and their graphs and their modeling. Come to visions without their training and their program . . . now *our* program. And yet, in the depths of so many nights, before the sun burned them into submission, he knew the name fit all too well.

And now purebloods tested, the program so much more advanced. Each supplicant must pass a randomly determined number of chambers, in an order provided by the interlopers' endless modeling. *Will I change that when they are gone?* Despite a rampant desire to wrench away all aspects of the training and remold it, some things were sound, despite their origins.

The spark of possibilities in Subject One drew desires and need. To put aside the endless years of burden and guilt. To remove his unclean hands from the office and pass it to another. Despite his Clan upbringing, despite the voluntary bereavement of any claim to a Bloodname . . . he would pass on immortality in the gene pool. He would pass on a dozen Exclusive Bloodnames, pass on inclusion in The Remembrance. To just pass the burden he was not worthy to hold in shepherding this mammoth project . . . no greater gift, no more desperately needed vision fulfilled.

"One minute," a voice intoned, misplaced confidence bloating the words.

Subject Four. He cast back, delving into memory for a name he himself bestowed. A name. What name? *Ah, Kin. Now I remember. Star. You will never be that star. Never bear your name as is your right upon passing this Trial and becoming a mystic in training . . . not just a subject in training.*

Abrupt thoughts of his own naming ceremony, alone on Zane Plateau, gifted with the honor of becoming the only mystic who might choose a name. And after long fasting and vision seeking, he set aside his first name and that of his Bloodname House forever. And there could only be one choice of a name, one choice to guide him.

Kanaye. Zealous.

Finally, as though an internal pressure pushed the boundary of pain beyond all ken, tics flickered on Subject Four's face as his internal timekeeping told him the truth before the interlopers could discern it. Failure loomed. The boy paused prematurely from the go, stop, go movements in the last fifteen minutes, the nothingness of facial expression showing a delving for answers.

Answers you will find and you will know you failed.

And yet, despite the knowledge of failure, in spite of what failure would bring, Subject Four moved on, using the training and knowledge given him to work towards his goal until the last possible second—never retreating, never admitting failure until failure grasped him in iron-banded grips.

Startled exclamations eased the majority of his concentration away from Subject Four's Trial and back fully into his own surroundings—coldness, in the control room. He shivered momentarily. Not the cold of temperature, but the sterility of their diligence. As though to underscore the idea, the stench of too many individuals packed into a small room palpable—their nervousness and the two groups' mutual distaste for one another bleeding into sweat—until noses practically curled with the stench.

Once more, he leapt to a new understanding.

That, that is the difference. That is why a Moly already surpasses your modeling. The supplicants will forever be assets to you and yours. And, though I cannot deny the need, though I must and will see this program continue, I will never forget what they are and what we do to them. The price they pay so that we might survive. That is why one of them must lead this program . . . so that those in power can never forget.

"Time has expired, Oathmaster," a Nova Cat technician finally spoke, for the first time in long minutes.

The two interlopers shook as though coming out of a dream, as though just realizing for the first time that the Oathmaster of Clan Nova Cat, per the agreement signed with blood so many years ago, was now fully in charge of the Trial of Mysticisms, in charge of the entire training program, to these Trial chambers and beyond . . . their standing mattered no more. They'd be off-world within days, never to return.

"*Aff,*" Kanaye responded, sadness choking the word off before he could continue. He glanced at the monitor again, and noted Subject Four had assumed a lotus position, already into a level-one trance, face open and ready to accept anything. So young. Thirteen. Yet so ready for his responsibilities.

They think you failed, Subject Four. They think you failed, Kin, but not completely. The mind may have faltered, but the spirit is true. In that, you show we are on the right path. He contemplated the boy one more time, then slowly reached forward for the seventh time that day, placing his thumb onto an optical reader in the computer console. A quick scan authorized the initiation of the program and then paused, waiting for verbal authorization as well.

"With great power comes greater need for absolute control," he intoned solemnly. "In the Trial of Mysticism, there can *only* be success."

"Seyla," the two technician castemen sealed the small ceremony.

With both authorizations confirmed, a microburst of orders spewed from the computer to the suit worn by Subject Four, initiating a coded sequence that burned out the small microbattery pack as it drew all its energy in a single massive jolt of volts, directed right at the young man's brain and heart, shutting them off like a thrown switch. He slowly slumped forward, as though simply falling asleep, a child going too long past bedtime, falling asleep where he played.

Once more Kanaye raged, and yet an assurance that, despite his unworthiness for this honor, he was indeed on the right path, banked the heat down; he continued watching the boy for a moment longer as the interlopers immediately dove into the piles of hard copy printouts of endless sensor data, trying to discern why their modeling failed, when they should have looked to the other three.

All three stood in the central hub of the entire subterranean training facility, glancing at one another in equal parts stunned joy (they all passed . . . all three!) and no little amount of wariness (a by-product of training, regardless of how closely the training attempted to bind sibkin).

Aff, *the right path.* For the last decade, when any supplicants were able to pass the Trial of Mysticism—all too often, those who did not flush out of training previously, failed here; their bodies disposed of with surgical precision, rendering them for possible genetic material—only one stood in the central hub, filthy, ragged, and triumphant.

And now three. Three! *My visions outpaced their modeling.* He glanced momentarily in their direction with scorn, before returning to the monitor. *We are on the right path. One of you will replace me. A pure-blood mystic to lead.* He smiled, despite the years still left to finish their training and then to lead them into the universe, where they might find the experience to match their training and live up to their potential.

A vision made flesh of a future without him. He straightened his shoulders, as though readjusting a heavy burden now made lighter, and moved to the door, ready and anxious to induct them into the new roles and finally call them by their names.

Kisho. Tanaka. Hisa.

9

Captain Josef Yoland stared blankly at the table as he gulped down a sandwich. Meat a hair on the rancid side, but no time to be picky. *Cook's doing all he can. Like all of us.*

Shit. No time to be picky, but his stomach told him *no way.* He threw the sandwich down on the edge of the rickety table, wiping greasy fingers onto even dirtier fatigues.

"Captain. Ben coming in."

Josef glanced up to the head poking through the ajar door, and nodded acceptance. "Send him in. And I mean the second his ass leaves the seat."

"You got it, Cap."

He shook his head as the smooth-as-baby's-butt face

disappeared. *Kid's not even sixteen, or my mother was a saint.* He chuckled. *Oh, what a saint, eh, mother? Hope you finally fell in a hole.* He thought better of that. *No, I want to be there when you fall in so I can kick some dirt in, so stick around. I'm sure there's one more bastard you can screw and take his money to get you through the day.*

Josef shook like a dog coming out of the rain, trying to dislodge his mother's memory. Ever since he'd left Deneb Kaitos all those years ago, he'd managed to keep her memory pushed down and out of the way.

Pretty soon they won't even be in puberty yet and we'll be grabbing 'em and slapping them into tanks, or even trying to stick 'em into 'Mechs. Got to power the machine, right, Bannson? Got to bring in the cold, hard cash and who cares about the rest of us.

He reached a hand into his jacket—he had to find a clean shirt to wear under this itchy bugger—and scratched thoroughly as he glanced back to the old-style paper map. Two stuck daggers and a hard-edged basalt rock (as if there were any other type of rock on this godforsaken volcanic hell-ground) kept the map in place against the errant winds that could bring a fresh breeze as easily as vomit-inducing sulfur fumes and ash that made him want to tear his eyes out of his head.

He'd stared at it for thirty straight minutes and nothing had changed. No magic shift in the flags of where he'd deployed his forces—damn small numbers. No new flag marking a grounded DropShip with desperately needed reinforcements. Absolutely, positively, nothing.

Josef ran a hand back through ruddy hair, trying to count his blessings and could only think of one. "The snakes would've at least killed me and I'd be off this rock," he said out loud as he grabbed the only folding chair not breaking down like the rest of his equipment and plopped down. He yanked out a dagger and began to strip dirt out from under a fingernail. *No, snakes would've killed me, but not sure I want to go down that path just yet.*

As though they were a hurricane, the snakes stormed across the border, driving and annihilating everything before them. In wave after wave of red 'Mechs and ships and personnel, they gobbled up a dozen worlds quick as you like and then grabbed more. As obvious as a whore at Sunday meeting, Josef knew they were coming for him. Not because he was worth a good goddamn, or that Athenry was worth the effort to pee sitting down (though try telling that to Bannson, the bastard!), but because Athenry sat as the final line of defense in the snakes' advance to the world of Dieron. And Dieron was just about everything to the snakes. Might as well talk about their capital, Black Luthien, as mention Dieron. Fortress Dieron. Capital of the defunct Dieron Military District. Never fell in centuries of fighting. And then the Jihad, and the high-and-mighty snakes got their heads handed to them as much as the rest of us and they had to give it up to Stone for his Republic—god, how that must have smacked their samurai chops—and now it's time to come get what's theirs. Time to take back the ol' fortress, and they were jonesing for it something fierce.

And then, from one month to the next . . . nothing. Suddenly their swords are sheathed and they're walking around their new worlds as if six months before they weren't hacking off heads and screaming in their wack tongue. No, almost an entire year passed without any new major advances. Something stopped them. Stopped them cold and he had no clue. After all this stinking time, no clue. Talk about being in the dark. Damn Bannson!

But it didn't matter.'Cause they were as two-faced as you could get and they carried their stupid swords around in their cockpits with them! And when they got over whatever it was that slowed them down, beady black eyes and a topknot would be staring from a raised blade. Staring at him and wanting his blood all over the ground.

"What?!" he growled, jerking his arm back as he found the sandwich in his hand again, the mildly rancid meat coating his tongue like he'd just licked the underside of a fry vat. On the verge of throwing it to the ground this time, he slowed, stopped, and finally heaved a huge sigh. *Hand knows better than my stomach what it needs. Nothing else for another two days at least.* Bracing, he stuffed in the remains, swallowing without chewing so he started coughing to the point where small chunks of bread were flying onto the map, landing, and squishing. He reached for a bottle of tepid, foul water just as Ben pushed open the door.

Light blue eyes creased into laughter, catching Josef sputtering food and trying to trickle down vile water to keep from choking to death.

"Cap. Damn. You know your gun will do the job a lot quicker than choking down crap like that."

A great retort refused to come as Josef continued to cough until his chest hurt. A hand pounded on his back until he finally got it under control. Tears filled his eyes and shallow, shuddering breaths finally tapered off.

"Thanks."

"Don't mention it. Again, gun next time, Cap. Gun."

"Go to hell."

"Aren't we there?"

"Damn straight. What you got?" He sloshed the last of the bottle's water (more like piss) into his mouth, swished it around, and spit it on the ground, then took a seat again.

"Nothing."

"What?!" he raged.

Ben slowly took off his helmet, scratching at sweat-soaked hair as thin and straight as angel pasta, then shrugged as though that said it all. "I met the merchant and he's got nothing. Said the JumpShip passed through without even relaying any messages. Took everybody by surprise, not just us. Even the few cast-off Republic troops, it seems, were expecting some type of message on that ship. Passed through like we were ghosts." They both averted their eyes, the words a little too close for comfort.

"What the hell is Bannson thinking? Just leaving us here to die! And why the hell did we take this rock so far coreward of any world he controls?!" The dagger he'd been using on his nails flew to thunk satisfactorily into a wooden box on the far side of the prefab hut.

"Don't know. Either way. Perhaps his new bride is keeping him too occupied."

Josef gave his best scout the evil eye. "That's just a rumor, dammit."

The other man shrugged it away. "Hey, if the rumor's made it all the way up here . . . just saying."

And he knew it for truth. Deal with the devil, Bannson, and you'll get caught. Nobody plays with Daoshen Liao without getting burned. Nobody. Even a backwoods soldier like him knew that. And getting hitched to that family . . . might just be worse than this hellhole. He shivered and shared an equally disquieted look with Ben.

"Then what the hell do we do?"

"Don't know, Cap. But we got men who need to know this is all for something."

Josef sighed heavily, then cursed as rotten eggs crawled up and burst in his nostrils. Damn sulfur. *One of these days a magma geyser's just going to open up and take me away.* He finally stood and took a last look at the map, just to be sure. "Yeah, I know. And it will be worth it."

Maybe not to that bastard Bannson who's forgotten us, but it'll be worth it in the end. I'll make it worth it.

Santin, Comitatus-*class* JumpShip, Zenith Jump Point
Kervil, Prefecture II
The Republic of the Sphere
10 September 3136

Hisa packed in silence, the heated words still ringing the air, though spoken almost five minutes ago. With exquisite care, as though bundling up her most precious possessions in place of the standard Clan apparel any warrior received, she continued methodically.

"So we will part like this?" Kisho finally spoke, anger and hurt warring for equal dominance as he floated in the corner of her small berth, as though he were a cadet sent to the corner to discover what he had done wrong.

With the arrival in the Kervil system, each of the saOathmasters and the forces assigned to them were splitting off to their designated worlds. Tanaka was on his way to Styx, Hisa to Saffel, and Kisho to Athenry.

"Like what?" she responded without turning, her voice never shifting off its serene tone, as ever.

Fists pumped once, sending him into a bulkhead before he could grab a handhold and stop his movement—not enough to cause real hurt, but enough to possibly bruise. *As my ego is bruised?* "You know what."

"Of course I do."

"Uh?"

"Do not ask irrelevant questions if you do not want irrelevant answers."

Anger spiked a notch. "So we are irrelevant."

"Of course not," she responded immediately to his hot words, finishing up the small bag of personal wear and moving to restore the berth to cleanliness.

"Then this conversation is irrelevant."

"Of course not."

"Then *something* is irrelevant."

"It is?"

"Do not use those techniques on me," he spoke between teeth, hands clenching and unclenching. "We trained together. Remember. I know all the tricks."

Finished stowing the cot, she turned to do a final wipe on the small sink/urinal area. There were labor castemen for such jobs, but Hisa always said she preferred to do the work herself. "Brings a calm you can seldom find anywhere else," she liked to say. Kisho, after a particularly bad nightmare, actually tried it and found nothing but the desire to punch a bulkhead.

"What do you want me to say?" she responded, her back still towards him.

"Something that does not throw my words back at me."

"But they are your words."

"*Aff.* I spoke them."

"Then?"

"You disagree. I understand. But I thought you might . . ." He trailed off as he slowly rubbed the bridge of his nose and momentarily closed his eyes against the sight of her back, careful to not send himself into another bulkhead with a hasty limb movement.

"You thought what?"

"That you might have an answer," he responded, frustrated, opening his eyes.

"There are many answers."

"Stop it."

"I am only saying what you know is true."

"Of course I do."

"What does that say, then?"

"It says you are pushing me with the same callousness as Tanaka."

Hisa's back moved every so slightly. It might have been a need to clean an extra spot he could not see, but Kisho, despite anger, felt shame at the barbed reply. She had never been, nor ever would be, like Tanaka. That's why he had opened up to her. Why he had begun to feel she might be the person he *could* open up to—well, not completely, but as complete as anything . . . That she might bear some of his burden for him, just for a little while.

That she might understand.

And now this. But he would not apologize. Absolutely not. Especially when she would not even look at it. "Am I no longer good enough for you? If your faith in our path, if your faith in what we do is so strong, if you are so *stravag*-bent on giving me a helping hand, then why not help me with this?" He despised the self-loathing evident in the words.

Without a response she snagged her bag, opened up the hatch, and slipped through as though fleeing, leaving him floating and openmouthed. *This is it? She leaves like this? She leaves* me *like this?* Arrogance and fury overcame a desire to turn his back on what she obviously held out in falsehood and he struck legs out behind, pushing off the bulkhead and arrowing through the hatch, expertly grabbing a handhold, and with a well-placed foot on the opposite side of the corridor, shooting after her.

"Hisa. How dare you walk away without even answering my question?!"

"But I have answered it," she said softly as he caught up to her at the turbo lift.

Anger, still firmly entrenched, sank talons deeper at her refusal to look at him. *You* surat. *You are worse than Tanaka. False friendship. False understanding. And now you throw it in my face.* He raged until he almost saw red, and he ached inside with the possibility that the easing of his burden, that the slow easing of the nightmares, would all be surging back, redoubling their efforts to annihilate him.

The door to the lift opened and, once more, Kisho contemplated letting her go. But for the first time in his life he'd allowed a door to open, and his fury at her betrayal could not be vanquished without a final showdown, without him stripping her with words, so she might hurt as well. Kisho slipped through just as the lift closed, reorienting feet to the left as that became the floor and the lift moved to the right, now "up."

He opened his mouth, intent on unleashing a torrent of vitriol to strip her flesh as a nova cat would its prey, and she finally turned towards him.

No shields.

No protection.

Nothing but the depths of her soul, of her mind, of her heart laid bare.

Her entire being awash in her eyes, waiting for his judgment.

He thought their previous encounters were powerful. He thought she had lowered all her interior walls at previous couplings. But nothing could prepare him for the sheer dazzlement as she bared herself to the full powers of his reading ability. He wanted to shut his eyes, desperate to stave off the flood of such horrifying intimacy, and simply could find no will. The very humbleness with which she handed herself to him stole all thought but that he was a *surat* of the basest sort for his disparagement of her actions.

"Kisho, I have tried. I have tried to help you, but you will not accept it," she began softly, the very gentleness of her delivery more devastating than any bombastic recital of dogma. "You think visions and faith come from without. As though it is a giant river you are trying to find, so that you may lie down on its soft banks and dip your hands into the blessed waters when you will.

"But it does not work that way. Faith is not something from without. It is not a river I can grab buckets of and hand around, hand them to you. By the *Founder,* if it was only so easy," she whispered, eyes entreating with a power to pull his soul out from his body. "But it is more precious than that. It is not out for all to see. Faith is within you. Faith has always been within you. It cannot be shared. Only my actions, based on my faith, can help to nurture another's. I cannot give it to you. You have to see what I have to offer. I have tried to offer all these weeks . . . all these months and, yes, even years, though you probably would not remember. I have offered my testimony of what I know."

Her voice strengthened. "You have to see it and you have ask why you do not have it. Why I bear the same nightmares and the same hurts and burden as you, and yet find a tranquility you lack? And then you look for it. You *want* to look for it. And if you truly want to find it, you will. It is that simple."

She closed her eyes and he almost collapsed to the floor, as though released from being pinned to the bulkhead by the power of her honest desire to help him. When she opened her eyes, all of her safeguards were in place; once more the demure, over-tall, slightly ugly little mystic. Or so he had concluded so often. But the power he had seen! The utter conviction! For the first time since the final days of the Room, his eyes itched with a need to shed tears.

"Look inside you, Kisho," she breathed softly as the lift came to a gradual stop, allowing them enough time to grab one of the hand railings to arrest their forward movement before the door opened. Then she was gone.

But I have, Hisa. And I find only blackness.

**Jesica's Revenge, Merchant-*class* JumpShip, Nadir
  Jump Point**
Athenry, Prefecture II
The Republic of the Sphere
15 September 3136

The shuttlecraft finished maneuvering, attitude jets
bleeding off all but a fraction of the remaining velocity.
With a hollow boom that shook teeth and rattled bones,
the craft expertly nestled into an unusually configured
docking point—exclusively built for shuttlecraft—on the
tramp freighter *Jesica's Revenge*, a *Merchant*-class
JumpShip.

As the ship held a self-contained small craft bay,
Kisho initially could not understand such lavish expense. Comprehension came as he concentrated on
thinking like a Spheroid. *No honor. Only tricks at
every turn. How can I take what is yours for nothing?*
If the *Revenge* kept the shuttle and most of its person-

nel outside the confines of the JumpShip, it became difficult for such a craft to take over the ship—a very effective brig, as they could lock down the docking collar.

Of course, the shuttle might try thrusting free. He chuckled as he undulated out of the seat and somersaulted with passable grace over towards the hatch, where there was already a knock. *Then again, in that case, we would all likely die,* quiaff? The humor hung hollow.

Before he reached the hatch, a Nova Cat technician casteman tapped back on the door, answering loudly. After a moment, a return tap and the hatch began to spin open. No electronic intercoms? Then again, that required added expense. And could break down, adding more expense. An expense a tramp freighter likely could not, or would not, afford. Especially as a handy wrench and a good shout did the job. He already liked this captain and her tight ship. No waste. Only the business at hand.

The hatch swung open and two burly men stood on the other side, their well-used coveralls spidered in a dangling harness that included everything from wrenches and hull patches to what appeared to be a holy book of some kind and a thermos. Men used to working straight twelve-hour shifts carrying everything they might need. Again, they rose a notch in Kisho's book, despite their Spheroid natures. *Competent is competent, regardless of your station.*

The man on the right, holding a wrench, rubbed a stubbled jaw, smeared with some lubricant. "Welcome to *Revenge*. You Kisho?" He spoke in short, clipped tones as he directed the words to the technician.

"Neg," the Nova Cat said, waving a hand in his direction.

If not for the Spheroid presence, he might have instructed the lower casteman on proper decorum towards superiors (especially to a mystic!), but knew this was neither the time nor the place.

He drew in a deep breath to focus on calm, and almost gagged at the strong stench leaking from the ship into the shuttlecraft. *Do they kill and gut animals right on the ship?* He swallowed and focused. "I am Kisho," he said, stepping lightly forward in his mag-slips and bowing low, before meeting their eyes again.

They both appeared to be sizing him up, with half-hidden smiles despite their best efforts. For this first of what he knew might be many meetings with merchant ship captains, he had donned not the ceremonial leathers of his Clan (they were not worthy of such honors), nor the simple suit of a MechWarrior, but the subtle and powerful accoutrements of a mystic.

Though sheathed head to toe in leather, it was not the glossy black of ceremonials. Instead, soft, doe-skin-style pants, with stitched glyphs across their surface, covered legs from waist to soft-soled black ankle boots. On his left, thin twin belts woven through the fabric of the pant leg fastened to a small, ivory, obe-lisklike stav, fifteen centimeters long. At the top of the stav, several lines and diagrams signified rank and caste, analogous to the glossy black polymer staves worn by other warriors. Below that, for each event deemed worthy by the Oathmaster, a small bas-relief—minuscule, requiring an artisan of exceptional skills—etched the ivory, wedding the mystic to his spirit stav. The upper garment—swathing torso and arms to the wrists—made of alternating gray and black stripes of doe-skin leather, a mimic of the nova cat's poisonous and barbed mane. On each upper arm, a gray cat eye—a Nova Cat mystic was all-seeing, all-knowing.

Kisho knew their derision, yet wore his caste as a

shield better than any diamond-filament armor. He might not have believed in all the mystic caste conveyed to outsiders, but he *did* believe in his caste and its value . . . especially when it came to *surats* like these.

"I am expected by Captain Veronica," he finally said, breaking off their rude stares.

"Ah, that's true. Right, mate. This way to the bridge." The right one leaned over and whispered something as he turned to leave, eliciting a barking laugh from his companion.

Allowing a Nova Cat to get away with such insubordination was one thing. Allowing this *surat* to get away with it was something altogether different. Kisho stepped forward with his left foot, planted his left hand on the edge of the hatch, then swung a hard-edged roundhouse kick into the laughing face. Completely unprepared, the man didn't even blink before his head snapped back into the bulkhead and he went unconscious, like lights cut out during a thunderstorm.

The momentum carried Kisho up off the floor and he used his left hand as a pivot point, spinning with the momentum, tucking legs into a ball as he hopped over his arm, rotating both laterally and vertically, and back down and around to the ground, where his magslips readhered. All before the other merchantman could do more than turn around and yell.

"What the hell is this?!" The man shouted, yanking a pistol out from a concealed holster. "You trying to take our ship?!" His other hand reached towards a comm device at his neck.

"Of course not," Kisho responded, as though nothing untoward had just happened. "If we wanted your ship, it would be ours. Your companion needed to be taught respect."

The other man stared as though Kisho had sprouted

horns and a tail, then slowly raised the pistol. "The hell you say! Stupid, arrogant Clanners. You can't just come on our ship and lay a smack down." The man's voice continued to rise, face slowly flushing a deep crimson verging on purple. "You can't just do that!"

"And you cannot disrespect a mystic of Clan Nova Cat," Kisho responded with a calm arrogance that slicked the room with power. The impasse stretched until Kisho finally broke the silence. "If you are going to shoot me, get it over with. We have a world to take and you are holding up the operation. Beware, though; if you kill me, any scavengers will have trouble finding anything bigger than your wrench on this wreck."

The calm delivery seemed to get through to the man, and his mouth slowly opened wide before he gulped and reluctantly put the weapon away. He reached up to his comm device. "Jak, send a medic down to the shuttle collar. Make sure Spinner is okay." The man nodded once more, then turned away, unhitched his feet, and sailed down the corridor.

Kisho almost laughed harshly at the sullen but beaten look on the man's face. *As it should be.*

At less than half the length of the *Comitatus,* the coasting journey to the captain's ready room took little time. The placement of the shuttle docking collar was purposeful, allowing little to no access to the rest of the ship. Perhaps this section could even be sealed off from the rest of the ship.

He entered a small room, to find the man (he had not even introduced himself properly!) talking rapidly to a woman he assumed to be Veronica. Dull-eyed, short, and frumpy, without the deference paid by the crewman to the captain's bars on the too-large jacket she wore, he might have dismissed her. As Kisho entered and stopped, the woman held up a hand to silence the other, then spoke bluntly.

"You hit my man?"

"*Aff.*"

No other response. He noted a tightening of her eyes and quickened breathing. Violence. On the edge of violence so easily? Then he understood how she maintained control on this ship, despite her obvious lack of charisma.

She abruptly smiled, waved away the other man (ignoring his expletive), and slipped smoothly into a chair, locking the restraining bar. She waved a hand towards him. "Spinner's needed an attitude adjustment since I brought him on at Bethel," she said, motioning him to take a seat.

Kisho nodded, pleased at her subterfuge—pleasant words in direct contrast with her body language made the game more interesting. For a moment he almost smiled at the situation. *Am I becoming a Sea Fox? Enjoying the art of the deal as much as a battlefield?* His thoughts spun to the disc he carried, before settling back to the matter at hand. Despite their strange ways, there was much to respect in the Foxes.

"Why you here?" she finally spoke.

He reached—slowly so as to not provoke her; she carried a weapon or three on her person, he felt certain—into a small pocket in the front of his mystic uniform and pulled out a small bag. With a magnet mounted on one side, the clear polymer shrink-wrap held a small data cube. He casually placed it on the table between them, the magnet latching to the table with a clear snap. He nudged the bag and shrugged.

Her dull eyes flickered to the bag, then pinned his face until he pulled his hand back. She then reached forward, pulled the bag free with a scrape, and slowly squished it as she looked to see what type of cube it might be.

Kisho's eyes roved over the small room, but found

it utterly empty except for the table and chairs, which were bolted with a strength that would defy an Elemental's attempts to free them. No one could use something from this room to stage a boarding action. He tasted the air with a quick tongue flick. At least they had closed the hatch, walling off most of the stink. Would they be worth this effort? Perhaps too far down for any type of honor? He kept the sigh silent. *Too late now.*

"So, what am I to do with this? You just giving it to me? If so, I got a trash compactor and an air lock date next week," she finally responded, setting the bag spinning between them.

"Of course, I would not expect someone of your station to work without proper remuneration." He watched, amused, as she vacillated on how to respond, but could find nothing to get upset about—the deadpan delivery robbed it of context. "I would bid for an open transmission of the data on that cube to every system you enter from now until one year has transpired. Additionally, when you encounter any other merchant ships, you transmit the data and request they do the same."

She cocked an eyebrow and tilted her head, as though suddenly trying to figure the angle. For the Nova Cats to request a direct audience, there must be something else, right? She might as well talk out loud. "Don't know," she responded. "A whole year is a long time. Might forget after the first two systems. As for other captains . . . don't like them much and they sure as hell don't like me."

Obviously. Once more, his right hand dipped into a pocket and pulled out a data disc, without a sealing bag, and set it spinning slowly towards her. "I think you might find the information on that disc . . . interesting. Perhaps enough to cover my bid for work."

She shrugged, but the tightening around her lips spoke of intense curiosity. Hunger. Hook set and reeling in. All too easy.

"Perhaps I might. Perhaps not."

Kisho nodded in return, playing the game to the hilt. "Perhaps not."

After just a long enough pause, she reached and grabbed the disc, then motioned to the man standing by the closed hatch. With a sullen look still printed firmly on his face, the man reached towards the back of his harness, unhitched a small data reader, and handed it to the captain. She slotted the disc and began reviewing. Avarice lighted dull eyes as they opened until they appeared on the verge of popping from their sockets. She finally looked at him.

"This can't be the real deal."

Kisho nodded gravely, teeth pinching cheek in a pinprick of pain to keep from smiling. "I can assure you, it is, as you say, the real deal."

She glanced again at the screen, then back at him. "How can I verify it?"

He shrugged. "That is up to you, Captain. Obviously that is only a fraction of Clan Sea Fox's network in this region, but just enough of a slice to allow . . . the right merchant to make significant headway in several markets." For a moment he hated the idea of turning over the hard-fought Trial of Possession *isorla* to this *surat,* then shrugged it away. *We do what we must.* He hated how much he sounded like the Oathmaster at that moment. Placing a hand on the table, the cool metal a nice contrast to the stuffy room, pulled him back to the present. "If it proves false, then you can jettison the data cube at your earliest convenience."

Tongue darted several times to wet lips, as she forgot to maintain a distance from her desire. "What about the other captains? You don't expect me to share this, do you?" The perpetual violence in her eyes flowed back, occluding avarice.

Permanently flawed. In the Clan, I would call for a Trial of Annihilation against you . . . perhaps against all your genetic offspring. But I am no longer in just my Clan . . . and must make accommodations to accomplish my goals. Quiaff, old man? The bitterness quickly tempered any elation over playing the captain to a mystic tune.

"I care not, Captain," he abruptly said, gruff and direct. "You toss them whatever bones will slave them to our desire." His tone deepened, hardened, eyes piercing hers, mirroring back all the violence she could muster. "And Captain, remember this. We will know if you do not keep your side of the bargain. We will know and we will come for you."

Anger flashed across her face and darkness sparked in her eyes, but it eventually lost to overflowing greed. As he knew it would.

Kisho unfastened the locking mechanism and stood, finished with his part in the Oathmaster's plan, and began to leave. *I have laid the groundwork. A net cast to the void as you wished, old man.*

Now let us see if it will bring up anything from the depths.

Nearstar, Outpost-*class* DropShip
Nadir Jump Point (Initiating Intra-system Burn)

Not even twelve hours from his meeting with the merchant and now he faced a different situation, if one of equal distaste.

Kisho moved stiffly into the conference space on board the *Nearstar*, an *Outpost*-class DropShip. With thrust pounding out behind the vessel, propelling them on the start of their journey to Athenry after so long, a standard gravity pulled at his body with strange yet incessant fingers.

Star Colonel Tivia, already in the room, glanced up and nodded in his direction, before turning her attention back to the other occupant. Kisho moved to the bolted-down table and eased into the hard-backed seat.

Tai-i Jing Smith was full of whipcord muscles, and Kisho felt sure the Dragon's Fury (wait, now the Combine?) officer would look Kisho eye to eye if they stood together. The short-cropped dark hair and smooth features gave him an ordinary look, like someone to dismiss. Yet a commanding aura nestled easily on his shoulders, despite his casual attitude. A good commander, despite appearances?

"Look, I'm just telling you how I see it, Star Colonel," Smith said, tapping the table as though to draw attention to the terrain of Athenry displayed in three-dimensional detail on the holoprojection. "This should be a total cakewalk. We're in, we're done, we're on to a world where I actually might want to vacation."

Irritation and amusement surfaced in equal measure as the commander continued to ignore Kisho. He poured his senses into the man, noting all the small biological tics and signs, which always told the truth no matter the words spoken, and came up even more amused. Something large lay under the surface, but he couldn't draw it out just yet. Emotions the man held under an absolute iron will, the only reason Kisho might not pull the truth from him immediately.

"As you say, *Tai-i*. However, is there a reason to not follow my plan? We are coming to this war fresh, relying on your intelligence," Tivia responded, while pausing momentarily—her desire to not offend an of-

ficer they must deal with was as plain to Kisho as the
holographic display before them. "And despite you
calling the Raiders 'rabble,' they have managed to survive for over two years, against repeated probes by
Fury forces. Not to mention the original Republic
forces they pushed off the world. This does not sound
like a force that should be taken lightly."

Smith waved his hand, as though to dismiss these
concerns. Tivia masked her response, but anger
bristled.

"*Tai-i* Jing Smith," Kisho interrupted; he might hate
the assignment, but he might as well get on with it.

Smith turned a ready smile and a nodded head towards him, but his cool eyes bespoke something else
altogether. The look in his eyes, combined with the
other minutiae already taken, dropped Kisho immediately into a light trance—his features fell away into
inhumanity as he wove paths and hunted clues for a
pattern. After several moments he came up, anger and
disappointment and no small sense of inevitability
sloshing within him until they seemed to permeate
every pore.

"Damn, that was freaky. What the hell, you have a
seizure?" Smith cursed, amazement opening up
greater fissures in his facade, simply confirming what
Kisho knew to be the truth.

"He is a mystic," Tivia snapped, anger and astonish-
ment painting her voice in equal measure. "Have respect." She turned towards Kisho. "A vision," Tivia
said, doubt and hope warring on her face in equal
measure.

Kisho looked in her direction, restraining a sudden
contempt. *A vision. Right. And will I deny it? Or will
I use this chance to resecure my facade once more? To
start a new phase of the game with a better layout of*

stones? Thoughts of the strained good-bye with Hisa jounced, before he ruthlessly pushed them aside. *Of course I will use it to bind Tivia closer to me. Right, old man?*

He turned his gaze away from Tivia—knowing full well that no denial would turn to affirmation in her mind—and took in *Tai-i* Smith. *You have lived your entire life in The Republic and yet you also harbor the same sentiments held by so many still within the Combine. Despite the decades, despite all we have done to cement our loyalty, you still cannot trust us; you still consider us inferior.*

After Hisa, after the distasteful meeting with the merchant, this was too much. He uncharacteristically poured that frustration into venom as he spoke. "The Nova Cats have not fought alongside another nation in long years, for reasons I am sure you are well aware of, despite your birthplace. As such, it is by my hand that we choose this path. We will honor the oaths made to Katana Tormark, but we will do so in a manner of our choosing. You may ground as you will, but the orbital insertion goes forward as planned."

Smith leaned back as though trying to distance himself from a large heat source, while throwing up his hands, a surprised look seizing his features. "Wow, vision man, calm down. Just throwing out options, here. Orbital insertions are dangerous business. Just don't want you all splattered across a thousand klicks while my troops are left to clean up the pieces."

"You will show respect," Tivia once more cut in, before Kisho could raise his hand to cut her off.

Kisho leaned forward, the cool metal of the table a balm against the heat washing through him— frustration at his losing control, of this situation; of everything, it seemed. His iron control over the game slipping away as though greased fingers to ferroglass. *You may have your mask back in place, but you cannot hide your contempt from me.*

"I believe," Kisho continued, reining in his volume, but retaining the edge of mutual contempt, "that is our decision to make. And though you may find it difficult, we do not. We proceed as planned."

Unable to bear the situation any longer, he abruptly stood and left the room without a backwards glance. He would likely pay the price later with Tivia—even though, regardless of how much Tivia would deny it, he had just taken on all the burden of blame for any rough spots between the Star colonel and *Tai-i* Smith, allowing them, hopefully, to work together more smoothly. But he would also convey his . . . *vision.* They would need to be careful around the Dragon's Fury, especially *Tai-i* Smith, else they might find a PPC at their backs at the worst possible moment.

As he stormed down the corridor, no destination in mind, his shoulders hitched, as though he felt a phantom PPC already pressed to the nape of his neck, energy capacitors already charging.

12

Kisho walked across the 'Mech bay of the *Outpost*-class DropShip as the ship's mammoth fusion engines bled off transit inertia, the resulting pressure almost mounting above a standard gravity. Coming to the berth, he stepped forward and laid a hand on the foot of the *Wendigo* as he glanced up, the metal almost alive to the touch.

The fifty-ton 'Mech, with all its rounded edges and smooth, sloping shoulders, bespoke power and feline grace—a fitting epitome of a Nova Cat 'Mech. Even the forward-thrusting cockpit and the unique design of the ferroglass reminded one of a stylized nova cat head. Off the hips of the *Wendigo,* small twin stanchions of rank and power thrust down, to mirror the spirit stav bound to the left leg of his formal mystic attire. The combination of back-canted legs and a clean star of five weapon ports placed in arms and head beckoned Kisho to lay aside his worries and problems and take up the latent power in the walking titan of metal; to solve his anger and frustration with the stomp of metal-shod feet.

It has been too long, old friend.

"Mystic, I beg your pardon, but time is short and yours is the last 'Mech to be cocooned. Insertion in one hour, *quiaff*?"

He turned towards the technician casteman, irritated at the interruption, then stepped back with a nod, said, *"Aff,"* and continued moving well away, until he backed up against the bulkhead. *Only doing his job. And doing it well.*

The man, along with almost a dozen subtechs, swarmed around the machine. He'd not noticed as he approached the cubicle, but the technicians had already laid the groundwork for what was coming. A huge myomer hoist at the back of the 'Mech berth—clawed hand latched onto the 'Mech across six points to relieve undue pressure—slowly began to lift the 'Mech into the air. Shutdown and rigid, it looked like nothing so much as a Spheroid child lifting a metal toy soldier. *Ah, but this one is ten meters tall.* He chuckled. *Am I the child, then?*

As the 'Mech reached the minimum height required, the technicians exploded into action. Myomer operation (and even hydraulic) machinery whined and hummed in the almost vacant bay as several different exoskeletons and larger pieces of equipment were put to use. Ozone—from the sheer volume of electricity used to power the various myomer hoists—stung the back of the tongue and wrinkled the nose.

First, an endosteel framework was rapidly built

around the 'Mech—the image of the toy escalated, a child placing connector rods around the metal soldier. Pressure points were heavily padded where they met the BattleMech, with dozens of studs extending out in every direction, especially along the base, where the feet were tightly ensconced in a latticework.

Once the framework was finished, monstrous slabs of geodesic ceramic were elevated into position from other myomer hoists (for the larger pieces) and a few hydraulic arms (for the smaller sections), operated at several different levels of the gantry works on three sides of the 'Mech. Predetermined indentations in the ablative ceramic sheets took the framework studs like finger grips on a well-designed rifle butt. Heat-resistant metallic foam, prelaid in the edge of each section, grew white-hot under several thousand watts of electricity, molding together with almost no change in form as the sections quickly cooled. Kisho covered his nose against the chemical stench, but still sneezed several times before the ship's scrubbers could dump the toxic mix.

Another set of technicians sheathed in heavy exoskeletons manhandled a giant cradle into place, locking it into the recessed track that ran all across the deck of the huge 'Mech bay. The whine of exoskeletons changed pitch as they backed off, then powered down, as the myomer hoist lowered the half-shelled 'Mech into the cradle. The construction and sheer number of studs on the inside of the ceramic cocoon distributed the weight of the entire 'Mech without distressing any plates, or rupturing seals.

Kisho began walking to the gantry as the crane disengaged and hoisted out of the way, while its smaller cousins hoisted the final plates into position. He began to climb, while the rest of the plates were sealed—remembering, this time, to hold his breath—and reached the top just as a gantry swung into position, allowing him to move to the very top of the ceramic egg and the hole preserved there for his own insertion.

"All set, Mystic," a technician said. Kisho couldn't tell any of them apart and didn't try. He waved absentmindedly as he scaled the short ladder down into the interior of the orbital insertion pod. Darkness took him, as though he moved into a giant's crypt. *A giant I intend to awaken.*

With long familiarity, despite the waning illumination from the opening just above, he found the hatch in the back of the 'Mech's head, spun it open, and slid through. If it were dark before, now almost pitch blackness greeted him with its soft, velvety hands and its promise of an eternity of nothing.

Again, from long practice, he stripped out of his suit down to a small T-shirt and shorts, pulled out the cooling vest, and stowed the jumpsuit in the back of the command couch. Having dressed, he sealed the hatch, then slipped around the side of the command chair and dropped into the seat.

A memory of mystic training from crèche days enveloped him. Totally blind and deaf, with only tactile senses to lead him through the cavern system to safety. Slick bone stabbed into his thigh, and the putrid stench of failure assaulted him until vomit flecked every stitch of clothing and he blacked out.

He came back to the present, momentarily rubbing the scar on his leg where the puncture wound had gotten so infected he almost died . . . yet survived. *Like you will this?* Not the coming battle, of course. But everything else. *Of course, you will.* His usual arrogance almost reasserted his confidence in his ability to play the game. Almost.

Reaching over, he threw a switch and the beast beneath his feet awakened, fusion reactor powering up systems and forcing a rapid series of blinks as the too-bright lights sparked a constellation across numerous consoles, monitors, and secondary screens. He reached forward and toggled several switches, initiating a full systems inquiry. He knew the technicians would not have released the machine without their own pre-system check, but at times a warrior must make such checks as well.

"Voice authorization required," the battle computer spoke.

"Kisho," he responded. Of a sudden he wondered if a warrior who gained a Bloodname actually changed the voice pattern recognition code, so he could speak his full name. Though Kisho banked many coals of anger within himself, unlike some in the mystic caste, he never questioned their inability to claim a Bloodname. Simply a consequence of who they were. A consequence of the blood that every new mystic sibko carried from the same genemother. First Mystic. Yet a melancholy set in. *Did they know? Did they have a vision of what they would create in the mystic caste? Of the suffering we outcaste warriors would endure for the greater glory of the Clan?*

"Voice authorization confirmed," the electronic voice interrupted his reverie. He slowly shook his head, knowing there could be no answers.

"Authorization code required," the modulated voice responded.

"No blind paths." He gritted his teeth. It was not about a lack of faith. It was about finding the faith and accepting the path yourself. Not simply because someone else showed it to you. Rumblings of Hisa reared and he pushed them aside. Not now.

"Authorization confirmed. Command transferred." With that, power cycled up to full parameters, and the remaining darkened monitors and systems sparked with inner life. He reached with his left hand to expand the systems check, taking in the weapon systems now unlocked for his use. The particle projector cannon and twin medium pulse lasers in the *Wendigo*'s right arm registered a cool green of capacitors charged and focus mirrors aligned, while the LB 10-X autocannon in the left arm showed a full complement of ammo. The small laser in the head, almost an afterthought, shone its small glow of readiness.

Even the small laser is accepting, regardless of how little it will do . . . The sigh slipped out then, full and heavy. *Not now. Not now!*

While the 'Mech cycled through additional systems, he pulled out medical pads, attached them to his thighs and arms, plugged in electronic cords, then reached for the neurohelmet shelved above and behind him. Sliding the helmet on, he cinched it tight, then tied the medical monitors into the helmet. Finally, he withdrew a cable from the command couch and snapped it into a mate at the bottom of the vest, as liquid squirmed across bare skin, with only thin ballistic cloth to keep possible shrapnel from his flesh. *Then again, if shrapnel is flying around the inside of the cockpit, I will have much bigger worries by that point.*

"Lancer Alpha Trinary, this is Star Commodore Sollic," a voice bounced around the inside of the 'Mech cockpit, from the now-activated commline. "Insertion in two minutes."

The first tremors hit.

At seven thousand tons and one hundred twenty meters in length and height, the *Outpost*-class DropShip could rightly be called huge by most human scales. Especially for a ship meant to ground on a planet, as well as traverse solar systems. Though not truly gargantuan in size, like the assault *Nekohono'o* at sixteen thousand tons, or the mind-numbing civilian *Mammoth*, at fifty-two thousand tons, the *Outpost* nevertheless represented a wonder of technology; a virtual small city in transit.

It trembled like a child shaking a toy ship as the vessel slewed into the soup of the planet's upper atmosphere. All relative. To Athenry's atmosphere, the *Outpost* was a gnat. One it would swat from the sky without a thought if they were not careful. He chuckled darkly as he checked final systems.

Suddenly he swung back slightly with the entire 'Mech, and the giant egg enshrouding the *Wendigo* moved, then settled into the cradle as it began to track across the deck plating. Without needing to patch into the ship's video feed, he knew four other identical cocoons housing the rest of his Star mates were moving from their positions as well, heading towards the launching doors. Twenty-five miniature pods for the attached battle armor were also moving into position. The fighters would already be airborne, providing insertion cover should the defenders decide to match the assault, while the ten vehicles would wait on the *Outpost* until the 'Mechs and battle armor secured their landing zone and the *Outpost* grounded.

"Stravag," he growled. At the last moment, he abruptly realized he'd not fastened the five-point restraining harness and began doing so at speed, as a roar brushed in through two levels of armor and a buffeting rocked the fifty-ton 'Mech in its giant cocoon slightly. *Allowing too many worries to distract you,* savashri. Then, without so much as a warning or a by your leave, he fell up, the harness keeping him in place, as gravity went topsy-turvy and the cocoon rotated madly as it fell away from the DropShip, until

prepositioned attitude jets fired, aligning the ceramic shell for optimum insertion into the lower, thicker atmosphere.

As the shell dug into the atmosphere, and the friction turned the ceramic shielding into a blazing torch that etched a white streak across dirty, gray skies, Kisho felt as if the cockpit were warming. It was not, of course. Kisho knew the insulated cocoon let so little heat through that the *Wendigo*'s hull would only be tolerably hot to the touch. Enough heat to warm the cockpit simply could not pass all the way through the shielding, the near vacuum between the cocoon and the 'Mech, and the *Wendigo*'s own insulation as well. But when you looked like a falling star, the body assumed heat and acted appropriately, regardless of such knowledge.

Eyes closed, a trance walling off all emotions—sealing off this instant when a warrior found everything beyond his control and a single aerospace fighter could end his life before he might even grasp a joystick for return fire—Kisho rode out the atmospheric insertion. Replaying the plan in his mind, he could see the *Outpost* and the other DropShips of the flotilla, their cargo delivered like angry storks dropping bombs in place of children; their drive plumes flaring to brilliance as they poured on thrust, moving back towards orbit, their trajectories racing away across the horizon, where they would stay until the landing zone was cleared of enemies.

Finally, sensors in the cocoon detected sufficient atmospheric pressure—the doglike electronic brain determining the life of the pod had expired—and explosive bolts shattered the geodesic armor plates and latticework, which were then torn away by the savage, roiling winds. Now, a metal man fell at several hundred kilometers an hour, heading towards a very unforgiving ground below.

"Star, report," Kisho spoke into the commline before the expertly engineered waste metal sheared completely away. A chorus of voices chimed in. Eyes glued to radar, he catalogued positions and tapped through short- and long-range settings to pinpoint his own Star, while verifying the locations of the other Stars in the assaulting force.

"Flight Alpha. Report."

"Mystic. The sky is clear. There are no targets. I repeat, no targets." As though in answer, a brace of aerospace fighters tore through near space, their contrails leaving a wide wake through the churning moisture of a heavy rainstorm.

"Nothing?" *You come that close to me again . . .*

"Nothing?"

The adrenaline pumping through his system began to subside as disappointment set in. As the altimeter cycled down and he began the slow burn of jump jets to bleed off velocity in preparation for touchdown, he could not help but wonder.

All this way. We came all this way. Where is the enemy?

13

"**Y**ou are sure?" Ramadeep Bhatia's fingers itched for the *tsuka* of his katana. He wanted to feel the perfect balance and edge latent in the hilt and know decisive action would soon flow. Itched for something.

"*Hai*, director," the *Musukosan No Ryu* agent said.

Ramadeep grunted. A *shinai* thrust from a kendo master through a face guard would not have caused as much consternation. Not pain. No. Consternation. And amazement she had flowed so easily past his guard. *Why did I not think of this?*

The small, wiry agent continued kneeling on the *tatami* mat in the director's secret chamber reserved for such receptions, slightly to his left but in arm's reach, as Ramadeep's fingers twitched and he flogged the failure. The bioluminescent glass beads hung from the low ceiling generated an eerie, sickly blue light, which blanched faces and washed away subtle facial nuances. Yet, in this room, the traditional Combine facade was left at the door. Considering the trouble and expense Ramadeep went through to build this buried chamber—bioluminescent lights (powered by sugar and fertilizer) so no unusual energy drains off of the palace reactors could be traced; no electronic devices, so unusual readings by scanners could not trace to the source; no wires of any kind penetrating walls for taps; and so on—one spoke plainly or never spoke again: one of the first things any Sons of the Dragon learned when inducted into the director's innermost circle.

He reached to the small bamboo tray at his right knee, where a neat stack of rice paper met his fingers, and he smiled, once more flogging himself for his vanity. In this room, of all rooms, he could not avoid the truth that in some things he was more like the Peacock than he wished.

Ramadeep's left hand reached with precision to the small teacup at his left and he sipped cold sake while his coal black eyes scanned lists, names, and time stamps. A new thought emerged.

"Warlord Saito?"

The man glanced up, intelligence gleaming in the odd light. "He was made aware, but by then Katana had already jumped out of the Pesht District."

"And if he'd found out when she was still within the Irece Prefecture?"

"You know Warlord Saito better than I."

"Taigo."

"*Hai*, director." The man said, bowing deeply, then straightening to a full kneeling position before answering him directly. "He would not respond. Or would 'lose' the information. She came alone, so he can ignore the affront. Especially as he will bury the information as deeply as he can. And when it comes to Saito, there is no one with deeper closets and more piles of skeletons."

He nodded, according his best pupil the acknowledgement. To this day, he remained surprised Saito ever managed to gain the warlord's seat, much less retain it. Never did find out what he held over Vincent. "And the Peacock?" Ramadeep watched for any telltales and only found a slight flicker in the left eye before the man responded.

"He will ignore it. It is warlord business."

Very good, Taigo. You still have trouble accepting my conclusions concerning the strength of the Dragon and yet you hide it well. You are coming along. "Hai," he finally responded. "Saito has no reason to trumpet the weakness, and with the Benjamin Warlord seat *still* vacant, the geisha could troupe through all three military districts like a Canopian pleasure circus and it would only cause a small stir." *And when, oh mighty Peacock, will you replace the Benjamin Warlord? With wars looming on all sides, you cannot wait much longer. Can you? And why are you waiting?*

"And Warlord Tormark?" Taigo's lips hardly moved as he spoke.

A cool smiled curled lips. *You may follow my lead, but you do not do so blindly. You respect the geisha and dislike my diminutive name. But of course, it would be impolite to explain such to me directly . . . even here, in our room of open secrets.* He bowed fractionally, letting Taigo know his point was taken, if not accepted.

He replaced the teacup carefully, the tingling in his fingertips still demanding answers. Or action. "Her bold move to contract Nova Cat forces was brilliant." He gave that up grudgingly. "However, there are many types of battlefield victories and not all victories lead to success. Taigo, you may respect her for her battlefield accomplishments. She is, without doubt, an unsurpassed warrior, worthy of the blood of Minobu Tetsuhara that flows in her veins and his sword, which she carries. And she is quickly demonstrating her acumen for courts." Though he would love to see her in the Black Room, attempting to deal with the other warlords. The cool smile grew perceptibly. Warlord New Samarkand in particular would enjoy breaking her.

"If she is all you say, then why is she wrong for the Combine? Sakamoto was a fool and Saito craven, and the Peacock lacks the strength of his forefathers. Only Matsuhara appears to hold the strength you seek. You say we need more strength for the Dragon? Why not Katana?"

Ramadeep slowly lowered the rice papers, placing them back on the small bamboo tray, as eyes raked his brightest pupil. Though intelligent, dedicated, and fanatical, not even Taigo could stand up to such scrutiny for long. He slowly wilted. Though his posture remained ramrod-straight, Ramadeep could almost feel the man's *ki* wither and waste away, a rock-hard sheet of ice sloughing under the brutal assault of summer's high sun.

"There is much you don't understand. There is no true strength in the Peacock. He will never have the strength, regardless of the steel of his warlords. Even if all warlords were of the caliber of such men as Takashi Kurita himself, the Peacock would still be the Peacock. And the false strength he draws from the dedication of the likes of Katana can only weaken us in the long run. Can only crack a hard facade, which will cave if pushed." Silence washed through the room as he watched Taigo stare inward, contemplating.

Ramadeep once more cradled the earthenware teacup, savoring the gritty texture that almost made his fingers feel wet. Memories of a youth spent in the fields where such pottery sprouted from endless grandfather hands filled the moments before Taigo finally spoke.

"An empty dragon's egg."

Ramadeep closed his eyes for a moment, a quick prayer flashing silently, given for such agents. He would need all his Sons of the Dragons if they were to weather the storm already starting to break across the Combine. He opened his eyes and began to speak. "A false strength all the Pillars of the Dragon will fall prey to. Steel. Jade. Even Ivory and Teak. All will be seduced by the supposed strength of the Pillar of Gold, the Peacock. And when our enemies come for us, like an empty egg shell we shall shatter, and the scavengers will feast on our flesh." He slowly clenched a fist and raised it before him, making sure to focus Taigo's attention. "Katana," he began, naming her for once in Taigo's presence, in the hopes of hammering in his point, "is the most dangerous of all our enemies. For she will make the Peacock believe he is something he will never be. Worthy of the Dragon's throne."

He slowly lowered his arm until it rested on his knee. "She must be stopped, and with Warlord Tormark there is only one way to do so."

Taigo slowly nodded, hopefully, finally convinced. *We shall see if you are, Taigo.* Time to step up the plans already in motion.

14

Kaona Island
Wandessa Chain, Athenry
Prefecture II, The Republic of the Sphere
3 October 3136

Rotten eggs sat in the back of Kisho's throat, while liquid oozed from every pore, making his hair limp and soaking even the ballistic cloth of his cooling vest—an image of a fruit squeezed for all its juices flashed through his mind. *I hope whoever drinks me chokes.* He smiled wryly and raised the water bottle to squirt his face, thought better of it, and took three long swallows as he strode through the field of volcanic rocks in the small clearing of what appeared to be endless jungle. *No use wetting my face. Feels like I am standing in a shower.*

"Kisho?" A voice spoke behind him. "Wait up."

He stiffened, on the verge of ignoring the call, then slowed and looked over his shoulder, the best he would offer while continuing towards the command tent.

Tai-i Jing Smith, looking at him eye to eye as Kisho had guessed, strode towards him. "Mystic," Kisho corrected.

The other man held up his hands and slid on his usual sarcastic smile, but increased his pace to catch up. "Yeah. Sorry about that. Mystic. Forgot."

No, you did not. You forget nothing. Despite the man's facade, after Kisho cracked it, it might as well have been a window for the *tai-i*'s ability to hide anything.

"Man, is it hot here or what?"

Kisho turned away from the absurd statement— might as well call the sun yellow-white. They walked almost in lockstep, their equal strides maneuvering past rocks too inconvenient to step over. The command tent for the on-planet forces loomed near.

"So, had a chance to cool off yet?" Smith tried again, just as a towering shadow cut off the sun and blessedly lowered the temperature by a few degrees. In the distance sat the grounded *Nearstar,* intermittent smoke columns still rising from foliage smoldering after the ship had burned itself a clear area to land.

"If not, I took a quick jaunt at the crack o' dawn, about three klicks to the ocean. Warm as piss at this latitude, but felt good, even if I'm still scrubbing salt out of my crotch. Check it out."

With an effort, Kisho kept harsh words at bay. He knew the man referred to the meeting on the *Nearstar* and not any physical temperature. "Do you have a specific question you want to ask?"

Underlining Smith's friendly tone, animosity lurked. *Why would the man not speak plainly? Afraid to offend? Afraid your superiors will send you to the back-*

*waters of some Periphery world if you botch up this
liaison?*

"Hey, just trying to make friendly conversation,"
Smith said, losing most of his bantering tone.

"And if I do not wish to have a friendly conversation? Then what?"

"Dammit. What the hell do you want?"

"Honesty."

"You want honesty?!" the man spat, coming to an
abrupt stop.

For a moment Kisho contemplated continuing, then
thought better of it. The uncalled-for animosity
seemed to seethe below the surface of the man's eyes.
Time to see if the wound could be lanced, staving off
problems down the road. He stopped and turned,
while keeping just far enough away. The other man's
prowess as a kick boxer would not be brought to bay
without needing to close, giving Kisho time to react.
Not that it should come to violence, but you were
always prepared. . . .

"Did I not ask for it?" Kisho said, words flat and
hard as a strip of sand turned to glass by PPC fire.
"Is it that I am a *Clanner* and you cannot abide us?
Do you hold the sentiments to heart that led to our
secret war with the Dragon during the Second Ghost
Bear–Combine war?" Kisho continued, interrupting
Smith before he could respond, his harsh words exploding between them. A good defense is a better
offense. Throw the man off his guard and see what
happens. "Have you encountered our lost brethren
and been found wanting? Or is it that you cannot
accomplish the aims of your mistress and so she must
contract for outside help that eats at you? Or is it
something about me personally? Is the idea of a
mystic—a 'vision man'—offensive to you?"

The other man blinked rapidly and opened and closed his mouth several times, as though he were a fish out of water. At some other time the look would have been amusing, but Kisho barely paused in his verbal pounding.

"What?" Kisho continued, cocking his head as though speaking to a small child. "I thought you wanted to talk? Apparently that is not the case." He turned and resumed walking towards the command tent. Though the other man did not follow immediately, burning anger washed across Kisho's neck like noonday sun. *This is not finished. Not finished by a long shot. But to heal a wound, you have to cauterize it.*

He reached the command tent and entered to find a bevy of personnel moving about assigned tasks— Dragon's Fury personnel, as well as Clan Nova Cat warriors and technician castemen. Even two labor castemen moved large computer consoles and finalized the setup of the holographic generator. A power cord bundle snaked out under a tent flap to the fusion generator, kept at some distance as the radiation shielding on the recharger was not as adequate as that of vehicular-scale engines.

"Ah, Mystic," Tivia Rosse said, waving him towards the edge of the holomap.

Setting aside his encounter with Smith, he strode up beside his nominal superior, coming to a loose-limbed rest. He admitted for a moment that he wished the air-conditioning of the tent was active, but it had yet to be set up.

"What think you?" she said without preamble, indicating the map.

The holographic map detailed the Wandessa Chain islands, one of four such landmasses on Athenry. Their current island, tagged as Kaona, was by far the largest in the chain, though another dozen could easily hide a small force of BattleMechs in the heavy foliage. The humidity and heat, combined with the density of foliage, guaranteed infrared scanning was almost worthless and magscans only worked when you got close enough that weapons were likely already flying.

On the main island, several blue lights burned, indicating the on-planet forces of the Fury and Nova Cats. With the lack of evidence of any defenders, despite ample proof they were still on-planet, the initial plan was aborted and a third of the Nova Cat forces assigned to Athenry were kept in orbit. All the easier to deploy them when the main defenders' location was determined. A half dozen red dots indicated last known locations of the Raiders—information taken from locals, thereby suspect.

Kisho's stomach had begun its familiar churn when an individual joined them at the table. *Tai-i* Smith stood across the holomap, anger etched on his face in dark lines limed with sweat. "*Tai-i*," Kisho said respectfully, and went back to studying the holographic display. *Perhaps I should not have been so direct with our Fury liaison commander?* He shrugged. *That path is already chosen. And I have something far more critical to deal with right now.*

As the relative silence stretched—the hubbub of the tent swirled around, as personnel finished prepping the room for an extended campaign—Kisho casually reached up to wipe away the sweat that began to coat his forehead and trickle down along the sides of his face.

The fear began to take on a life of its own—a primal beast, clawing its way out of its cage, teeth tearing and claws rending. The fear that seemed to constantly plague him of late, now that Hisa no longer lent her aid. The fear from the moment he understood he was heading to war and that he would be assigned as a mystic to offer counsel. No, not counsel. That he could do. No, to offer portents. And visions. To provide Tivia with mystical guidance, when appropriate. After all, they could not sit forever on this world, *quiaff*?!

In an effort to stall, he reached forward and toggled several switches. The holographic display flickered several times, then spun the main projection down thirty percent in size and moved it slightly off center, while a new projection blossomed, showing near space in The Republic. As he stood on this stinking rock island, Nova Cats were also assaulting Styx and Saffel, along with small liaison Fury forces. Meanwhile, Fury forces under Warlord Tormark's direct command were attempting to solidify holds on the worlds taken during Sakamoto's fourth wave of assaults, including Deneb Algedi, Nashira, Telos IV, and Kervil.

No more than three months. The words rang as though spoken from Katana's lips. And with minimal casualties. Because just beyond, less than a jump away, across the imaginary border into Prefecture X, the ultimate prize hung like a ripened fruit, waiting for the right warlord to grasp it and bite into its sweet flesh of victory: Dieron.

And to do that, and to keep to the schedule Katana outlined, they could not waste time. The four chains on-world contained literally thousands of islands. If the defenders were looking to make the assaulting force's life a true hell, all they needed was to go to ground. A single 'Mech to an island, or move it out and plant it under a coral reef, and they would never be found, unless they wanted to. *Never*.

But Tivia held a secret weapon. Her pocket mystic, to pull out and rub like a lamp, awaiting the magic genie who would pop out and grant her wish. *Quiaff*?!

A tremor moved down Kisho's leg and he gripped the edge of the table to hide it.

"Well, *Mystic*," Jing spoke with no attempt to hide his doubts. "Throw your dart and let's get this going."

"You will not—"

Kisho leaned back from the table, raising a hand to cut Tivia off as he glanced in her direction. Though she tried to hide it, he could discern her thoughts as though the words blazed in the air between him, her eyes flickering away from his. Though she felt true anger at Jing for disrespecting a Nova Cat mystic, her own doubts caused her shame. Doubts over Kisho and his strange behavior of late, his storming out of the command space, only one of many such erratic behaviors that seemed to plague him of late.

The knowledge brought pain, despite the clear truth that cut like a glass shiv. *She does not doubt mystics. She doubts* me. For all the long years of playing the game, he had always managed to convince. For the first time, he witnessed the power of doubt towards him . . . it brought *real* pain.

He turned back to the table, ignoring Smith for now. *We will have our confrontation, you and I, but not now.* He stared at the table. *How do you do it, Hisa?* For a moment he tensed, afraid he'd asked the question out loud. *How can you believe we can simply stare at a table and a vision will come? How?*

He swallowed in a throat parched to sandpaper, despite the one hundred percent humidity soaking everything to the bone. The words from their encounter on the lift surfaced, like a neodolphin cresting the water in a breach that sent it soaring into a sparkling, red-tinged sky. Spray. A halo.

Testimony.

He closed his eyes, her words focusing actions, slowly opening his mind as he began ransacking. *Where would I be if I were a Raider? Where would I hide?* All the reports he had pored over stacked up before his inner eye and he allowed them to fall down. Not sorting them, but instead tossing them to the winds of thought and waiting until their flutterings ended. Then he would open inner eyes to find their surprising design laid before him.

Three quick breaths and everything fell away as he dropped into a first-stage trance, his humanity dropping unconsciously from his face, and then into a second and third stage, quicker than any previous time in his life. His inner universe seemed to expand like a living breath, as though his own lungs ballooned reality into existence. Everything took on a distorted image, as he continued breathing, hot and humid breath loud as a universe awakening, yet as silent as the moon slipping through a starry landscape.

Suddenly, he opened his eyes, fear gone and finger pointing determinedly towards a single bright blue spot. Without hesitation or doubt, he spoke. "That is where we will find Raiders."

Lightning forked into the fleeing hoverbike pack. Bodies hit directly were vaporized, leaving afterimages on retinas, while the concussion of the energy bolt's passage skewed the light, one-man machines to the sides, or outright flipped riders headlong into tangled, moss-covered trees, leaving smears of bright red against dark greens and wet browns.

Kisho relaxed his index finger from the primary target interlock trigger on the right joystick. Spoke loud enough for his throat mike to activate. "They are fleeing."

"Of course they are fleeing," Smith responded, the sarcasm easily transmitted even through the electronically reproduced voice. "You expect them to stick around for a welcoming committee of 'Mechs and battle armor? With an aerospace strafe thrown in for giggles?"

Kisho ignored the words, wondering why Tivia did not respond to such words. Using foot pedals, he maneuvered the 'Mech around the smoldering remains of a *Hatchetman,* caught between the furious fusillades of power projected by Tivia's *Shadow Cat,* Jing's *Thunderbolt,* and the *Wendigo.* Even as the 'Mech stepped past, the impact of fifty tons of walking metal on the hardened ground caused the armored carcass to cave in, the internal structure of most of the center torso of the hapless *Hatchetman* completely vaporized, a rotted corpse unnaturally dug up from the comfort of the grave, collapsing under the harsh light of day and the truth of its death.

A sympathetic explosion snapped Kisho's attention towards his secondary monitor, but sensors registered no additional enemies. The small encampment only held a single 'Mech, a half Star of vehicles, several squads of infantry, and the elusive hoverbikes. He knew most of the battle armor, after a quick defense, had melted away into the underbrush after the *Hatchetman* and the four vehicles were annihilated in short order. Beyond that, a few burning buildings were all that marked the spot for this cache of Raiders.

But to where? He pulled the *Wendigo* to a halt as fear began to worm its way back from its trapped cage deep within him. Has to be another camp . . . not the primary camp.

"Well, seems like you sure did find the Raiders' camp."

The words burned like laser shots from a pulse rifle, stitching a bruised soul, tearing away the last vestige of the cage. His pulse quickened and breathing became claustrophobic in the tight confines of the cockpit as realization dawned. *I made it up. There was no vision. I just pointed and pretended I found a vision. Found anything . . . and I found nothing.*

He began to tremble, as not even Tivia responded to such a provocation.

How did Hisa . . .

15

Spirit Cat Encampment
Addicks, Prefecture III
The Republic of the Sphere
10 October 3136

Kev Rosse, one time senator of The Republic of the Sphere from Prefecture III, now leader, commanding officer, and cult of personality for all those, civilian and military alike, who wore the name Spirit Cat, held the data cube in a curled hand with rigid fingers, as though to ward off the poisonous strike of a hissing serpent.

The secrets you hold.

An echo of his vision spiraled through the room and the tent flaps seemed to waver into the image of wet stone walls.

"The vision?" the old warrior said almost immediately upon entering.

"Do you think?"

"I asked you."

"Stop that." The easy banter drove the fluttering wings of doom away, though he could sense the vultures settling into treetops just out of sight, waiting for their chance. His breath sounded hollow for a moment, as though the sound bounced within a small, underground room. "So quickly?"

"That your vision has actualized?"

"No," Kev said impatiently, waving a hand and staring at twinkling eyes and bearded face. "It came right to us. You heard the captain's tale."

"Do we believe it?"

"Do we dare not?"

"Does it matter?" the Visionmaster said, shrugging as though casting aside an unneeded weight.

Something I cannot do, Davik. Especially not now. "Perhaps it does not. But she acquired the cube from this Kisho in the Athenry system and then jumps to Nirasaki, then Helen, and then Addicks? A merchant ship passing through two systems without stopping except to charge solar sails?"

"She had business on Addicks."

"Of all the ships, in all the void this Kisho might contact, and he connects immediately with the one with business in our system?"

"Convenient."

Kev searched for levity, or seriousness, and only found shadowed eyes. *Aff. Convenient.*

"Play it again," Davik said, coming around to the side of the table.

Kev nodded, opening a small drawer to retrieve a player, slotted the cube into the device, and turned it on, placing it so both could view the message. An ancient head coalesced out of scintillating lights, craggy face and deep-set eyes a map of knowledge that even put Davik to shame. Eyes flickered to the Visionmaster to find blanched features and glued eyes.

You feel the power too. Across half a thousand light-years and through a holorecording and you can feel his power. It can only be the Nova Cat Oathmaster. Chagrin and anger mixed in equal measure. At the power of this man and, though Kev had never set foot within the Combine, much less on a Nova Cat Reservation, that he felt the pull—at himself.

"Welcome," the ancient began, voice warm and knowing. "During the dark days following the collapse of the second Star League, Khan Santin West beheld a vision. A searing portent some say blinded him. A summons that, unless the Nova Cats joined the fighting against the zealots, all would be lost. And so we answered the call before any other, sending our warriors to stave off the collapse of humanity." The singsong cadence of the delivery and the power of personality projected, even through the holodisplay, almost conjured images, until a kaleidoscope of history swung before their eyes.

"And during that quest, our warriors found a Spheroid worthy of respect. More, a warrior to follow. Devlin Stone proved his loyalty and integrity and honor on countless battlefields and on countless occasions, facing down despots and the corrupt of the Inner Sphere in his quest to rebuild from the shattered remains of the Jihad. To build his golden halls. The Republic. And so those warriors stayed; to find a dream of a Star League we survived Abjurment to obtain and watched collapse around our ears and flow like mercury through helpless fingers."

The Oathmaster paused and Kev let out a pent-up breath, fascinated by his own reactions. A history any Spirit Cat knew like a Spheroid quoted nursery rhymes. And yet, the power of its delivery! He clenched and unclenched fists, as though to crush the data cube, remove its existence . . . yet knowing he would not.

"And generations passed in progress. Yet the snake head of the past, ever devouring its own tail in history, is swiveling into our present. The golden dream dies and the darkness takes our kin. Those who chose a different path now find it blocked. Can they return to the fork in the road? Can such a great distance be retraversed?"

The eyes never wavered in their grandfatherly delivery. *You are good, Oathmaster. So very good. Makes my Visionmaster look like a charlatan.* Shame sparked and he once more gazed at Davik from the corner of his eye, only to find a similar expression. He knows and is not angry, but awed. He sees a goal he wishes to reach.

Kev resettled into the chair, back creaking from the long strain of sitting, and refocused on the holodisplay. *And what are* my *goals?*

"*Aff.* Of course they can. Never once was Abjurment considered. Never once were those who chose this path in danger of being cast out. Instead, like prodigal sons returning from a far land, we would slaughter the fatted calf and welcome our brothers home. A new festival should be dedicated and lines added to The Remembrance, so that, for centuries to come, the reunion of our two peoples will be sung in chronicle and rituals of battles. My saOathmasters are even now within The Republic, answering the call of duty. Yet they are there to receive any who would answer this call. Who would hear their blood sing and respond . . . *Seyla.*"

The holoimage went dark and the two men stared

into space, afterimages ghosting above the table, before their eyes finally adjusted to the dim light.

"Such power," Davik breathed, awe coloring his words.

"*Aff.* But should we answer the call?"

Eyes met to find no answers as they stared at one another. Davik finally dropped down into a sitting position, as though no longer able to stand. "I cannot tell you. But we can, at the least, meet with this saOathmaster. This mystic."

The strange way Davik wrapped lips around the odd words reminded Kev of how far the Spirit Cats and their brothers in the Nova Cats had moved apart, despite so many similarities. He chuckled darkly, realizing the visionmaster was a title and office unique to the Spirit Cats, albeit a pattern of the oathmaster. And these mystics? A new caste? Will wonders never cease?

He bowed his head into calloused hands, scratching his scalp against the heavy pollen in the air, the tickling sending shivers down his back. *You say one of us can move back to the fork in the road, Oathmaster. But who will do the moving?* And the mover will then have to move again; forward down a road long ago trod to try and catch up. *Who will move?*

He knew the answer, as surely as he knew he would answer this message. Would travel to meet this Kisho. "As usual, Davik, you are right. We must meet with this man. This mystic," he responded, tasting the strange word as well.

The look of relief on the visionmaster's face almost brought pain. *Are you so quickly cowed? Have you so quickly forgotten all we have done?* His sight wavered as the doom of his vision pressed once more. His right hand plucked out the data cube and began to squeeze, until it cut into his palm before collapsing and twisting beyond recognition.

I will meet you, Kisho. But I will not come as a lamb to the slaughter. You have a vision of the future? Well, so do I. And it may not include you, or the Nova Cats.

16

Kisho hefted another pile of moist dirt out of the trench, onto the growing mound. A myriad of wiggling alien fauna squirmed like dead, white fingers twitching in the sunlight, before burrowing back to the safety of the dirt and its protective darkness. He rested the shovel against the ground, leaned, and partially wiped away a flood of sweat from his face. Hoisting up the bottle dangling from a belt harness, he took a warm swallow, then got back to work.

"Mystic, that is deep enough."

He glanced up to find a labor castemen standing next to his rather large pile of dirt, a distinctly uncomfortable expression twisting his features. Straightening from the last thrown shovelful, he stretched his neck and felt vertebrae snap and crackle as he arched his back. With a swift jump, he leapt out of the trench he'd help dig. "This will do?"

"*Aff*, Mystic. More than do." The man bowed more deeply than strictly necessary. "I thank you for your efforts. You did not need to aid us."

"*Aff*, I did not. But the stink was getting worse and with most personnel drafted into repairs . . ." He shrugged. "Someone had to help dig this new latrine."

The man bowed even lower, a pained look etching deep lines as Kisho verbalized what he'd been doing. No matter. The stink was getting bad. *And sanitation is needed on this* stravag *ball of rocks and rotting vegetation, or we will all die before we even find the* stravag *Raiders*.

Without a backwards glance, he left the shovel standing in the mound and began walking towards the small shower stalls set at the far edge of the clearing. As he moved through the camp he made several detours around working groups of individuals, and soon anger began to replace the calm he found in simple, manual labor. Several vehicles (those that could even traverse such rough terrain), two 'Mechs, and even several suits of battle armor, were currently under repair. The damage to only one of which came from enemy fire. The rest were the result of the pitfalls of the rocky terrain. The 'Mech had almost completely snapped off its foot assembly when it punched down into an empty lava tube; they were lucky not to have lost the entire machine.

And now, almost everyone was drafted into repairs, while three different probing raids—one included a suborbital hop of the *Nearstar* to another island—were under way, each trying to locate any sign of the Raiders. After their first brief taste of battle—the pain of failure still lanced, white-hot as ever—not even the back of a Raider's helmet had been spotted.

He reached the stalls, mind wandering far afield, and began prepping for a shower. A quick twist set the pneumatic pump funneling water from the make-shift rain cistern, through a short series of tubes, to a nozzle head. Stripping out of the filthy single suit, he laid the garment on a wire rack where he'd spray it down shortly, then stepped into the stall, latching the chest-high door shut.

The water, while even warmer than his drinking bottle, still washed away sweat and grime, bringing a momentary reprieve. Quickly sinking his head into the water stream (only thirty seconds of water allowed per individual every three days; warriors every other day) he didn't initially hear the sound. Not until the tremble tingled his feet and worked up the backs of his legs did he jerk his head out, looking around.

What? The next explosion rocked the camp, close enough to be heard distinctly across the breadth of the Nova Cat base, sending people milling about like a kicked anthill.

Without hesitation, Kisho rammed through the stall door without bothering to open it—tearing the small lock completely off its hinges—already at a dead run. *They are attacking? Attacking us?!*

Stark naked, Kisho ran on bare feet, unfeeling of the rocks tearing at flesh and leaving a trail of smeared crimson footprints. *The* Wendigo *is the only operational 'Mech here. They will target it.* "They'll target it!" he yelled, devolving into the vulgarity of contractions in his anger and shock. *They are attacking us?* Despite the rage, a grudging respect grew. Such audacity. *This leader is no standard Raider. No, no standard Raider at all.*

Halfway to his 'Mech, the high whine of servomotors and a steady thumping, like the world's largest kettledrum, of a 'Mech closing caused Kisho to glance over his shoulder. A towering giant hove into view from a slight dip to the southeast of the clearing. Its flat head swiveled above the shortened trees, before using its left hand and sheer mass to bash through the remaining vegetation, exploding into the clearing. Like a startled flock of birds reacting to an enraged labor casteman farmer, personnel stuttered in different directions, before streaming away from the metal titan.

A quick stream of small arms fire splashed ineffectually across diamond-filament-impregnated armor, sparking fierce pride. Not all are crèche kids, running at the first snap of a twig in the woods!

With a deliberateness that spoke of arrogance, the pilot ignored the sniping and raised its right arm, where the underslung weapon aperture glowed a brilliant blue-white, before energy speared directly into the torso of the *Wendigo*. The laser-straight blast of invisible protons that followed was marked by eye-searing lightning as atmospheric molecules visually expressed their outrage at the subatomic abuse. The passage of the beam overhead stood all of Kisho's hair on end, singeing it and roasting skin across his body with a first-degree burn. The blast of the impact threw Kisho off his feet, rocks gouging painfully into naked flesh upon returning akimbo to the ground, while a whole other light show exploded in front of his eyes.

Shaking away the spinning, multicolored spots from the bounce his head took, Kisho scrambled to his feet, but swayed a moment as bile surged in the back of his throat. He swallowed stomach acids back with an iron will as he started to shamble again towards his 'Mech.

An explosion echoed dangerously close and he slewed

to a stop, hunkering down before he realized the sound came from behind. Glancing over his shoulder, he saw a Demon medium tank circling the *Panther,* a small dog to an enraged big cat. Coherent beams of ruby brilliance slashed from the dual medium lasers in the turret, runneling armor in liquefied streaks across the 'Mechs' legs. Instantly, a metal rain sprouted from the torso of the *Panther* as a phalanx of missiles washed towards the Demon, explosions obscuring it behind a wall of thrown dust and debris.

Must get to the Wendigo. He launched back into a run, feeling the bruises but stretching into it. Out of the corners of his eyes, an army wearing alienlike hardened carapaces surged from the trees, flickering beams of crimson burning and killing indiscriminately, before an answering call of like-suited battle armor joined the fray, the crisscrossing beams of energy searing afterimages that Kisho tried to blink away.

Among the Nova Cat defenders scrambling with half-fixed equipment, an Elemental missing one arm of the battle suit ran—did the lacking arm create an imbalance too severe to use its jump pack?—directly into the teeth of the fighting. Though it lacked the right arm laser, its missile pack's twin salvos still found their mark, and the warrior leapt right onto a Ranger vehicle just sliding into the clearing. Using the myomer-driven claw, the Elemental began tearing into armor like a maddened animal. It could not last, and a shot found the gaping hole in the warrior's protection, vaporizing the man's arm and stabbing into the chest cavity to kill him instantly.

Pushing forward again, Kisho bowed his head to honor such sacrifice. *You will be remembered for such honor.* Almost to his 'Mech, he could see wide swaths of destruction already wrecked on the base, with tents, half-fixed vehicles, and piles of supplies burning. For a disconcerting moment, his eyes picked out the region where he'd just finished the latrine and found it a churned mess of obvious tank tracks.

It burned far more than it should and he redoubled his speed to the *Wendigo*. On the verge of gaining the ladder, the universe turned inside out, as silence became noise, black became white, and gravity upended. The titanic explosion of another PPC strike into his *Wendigo* detonated around him, tossing Kisho aside like a used toy from a child's hand.

The last image, which spiraled down to occupy his mind in the darkness: the *Wendigo* slowly tilting, falling.

"Damn if the kitties don't fall down as good as anybody else," Josef said aloud to no one in particular.

The Raider captain feathered jump jets as he pinpointed the next location on the topographical display and brought the *Panther* down smoothly in a clearing just large enough to accommodate the 'Mech. He immediately stomped down on pedals, launching the machine into another ballistic arc towards the next small clearing, uncaring of the smoldering fires and their towers of smoke left behind, marking his line of retreat. "You can see me, but you won't get to me before I'm out of here. And by the time your egg makes it back from its useless trip to Phula, we'll be long gone."

He laughed out loud, bringing the machine down once more, overcompensating slightly and slamming the left arm through a tree's upper branches. The impact didn't damage armor, and before the flurry of leaves and snapping branches even settled, he was into the air once more.

He clenched his jaw twice to cycle to the right frequency, then spoke. "Remind me to give you a big, sloppy wet one for this idea," he said, eyes glancing towards the heat indicator, watching it slowly climb under such extreme use of the 'Mech's jump jets.

"Will do, boss," Lieutenant Collins responded.

A quick look to the radar display showed the much slower, but still mobile, platoon of battle armor flowing away from the savaged Nova Cat base by all three planned routes. The effort to try to cut the holes for a quick escape without giving away their plans had been considerable, but now, for once on this god-cursed planet, things looked a little better.

His smile grew perceptibly less at how quickly the Nova Cats responded. *We caught them with their pants down*—the smile turned crooked at the memory of the running warrior; had that been *his* Mech?—*and yet they still managed to rally enough to force me to pull back or risk taking too much damage.* He had had run-ins with Steel Wolves and even some Spirit Cats, but this was something different.

All the Clanner stories he'd ever heard surged and suddenly he wondered once more if this world held a rocky patch of ground with his name written all over it. No answers. Not today.

The smell of his sweat filled him as he breathed deeply after hammering down into the ground a little too hard, then raged at such carelessness, for letting his mind wander. *Six feet will come lightning-quick if you don't pay attention. And regardless of what tomorrow brings, we skinned a few cats today.*

That would have to be enough.

$$=== \mathbf{17} ===$$

Kaona Island
Wandessa Chain, Athenry
Prefecture II, The Republic of the Sphere
16 October 3136

The flames beckoned like a lover to forgetful pleasures and then sleep. Hunching forward, Kisho ab-
sorbed the warmth of the fire as though suddenly cold,
regardless of the heat of the night. On Kaona Island,
at least, even the nights brought little relief from the
heat. But enough. He ignored the discomfort of the heat
washing against reddened skin, the pain of a heavily
bruised shoulder, the knot on his forehead, slashed
feet.

Made it all a focus for the ceremony.

Without looking down, his left hand probed across
the small leather mat on the ground, fingers slowly

caressing several objects, while eyes burrowed into sparkling reds, transcendent yellows, and vivid oranges. Claw from a sphinx raptor; a broken spirit stav; small chunk of carbon-nanotube-reinforced graphite from a 'Mech gyro; a child's right index finger. With eyes washed of surroundings by the intense light, each vineer seemed to open a window within the cavorting blaze, to a time and place where each object held significance. Nova Cat warriors traditionally saved vineers only from battles but, for a mystic, these mementos could be any object that aided in finding a new path. In finding a new vision.

In finding self.

The tension strummed within until his right arm shook slightly, a branch in a stiff wind. A wind increasing and a branch on the verge of not bowing, but breaking. *I do not believe in my mystic blood. I do not believe in what they would have me do. And yet, when all else fails, I fall back on a warrior's path to visions.* The irony of it brought a bubble of laughter, which hissed between thin lips, more like the hysterical sniping noise of a hyena. A wounded one at that.

And shall I feed my most precious objects to the fire and gain my vision? The snap of the fire, almost a full kilometer from the damaged base only now returning to some normalcy, sparked in sarcastic silence, unwilling to answer, while the night hugged its secrets like a jealous lowercaste lover.

The finger bone? The sphinx raptor claw? What shall it be, old man? I am mystic enough to know you are at a fire right now, even if in stravag *daylight. Seeking visions to aid your saOathmasters. To send us strength. Do you keep the fire vigilance as long as you can remain awake, passing out and resuming your vigil upon awakening? Yes, that would be you. Are you proud of*

*me, old man? Are you proud of how your pupil has
failed you? Failed us all. . . .*

The noise in his throat churned through several in-
carnations, until it broke free in an animal growl of
pain.

He grasped the piece of gyroscope, wrapping fingers around the jagged chunk as though it were a
balm to a tortured soul, and began to squeeze. The
sharp edge spiked pain through the palm, up through
raw nerves to an already overstressed brain. On the
verge of breaking skin, a rustle of undergrowth at
the edge of his makeshift clearing loosened muscles
in surprise and he looked up with a flash of annoyance. Who would seek a mystic in the middle of a
ritual?

The flames divided and flowed around the intruder
who entered the clearing from the other side, and sat
without asking permission.

Tivia Rosse, her features catching fire as though an
artist worked to create a flaming warrior of death, sat
in stony silence. Her features, despite the flames, were
etched in the deepest ice caverns of Tarazed. Any
other time, Kisho would have thrown the person—
superior or not—physically from the clearing, righ-
teous indignation his for the taking in her blasphe-
mous disregard of mystic privacy and contemplation
in ritual. But Kisho could hardly look Tivia in the
face, much less raise the ire to confront her. Instead
he glanced back to the vineers at his feet, hoping silence would convey a cold disdain for the commander.
Several minutes passed, eroding confidence further,
shedding it like a snake, the tender, new skin underneath unable to withstand the rigors of her stoic
assault.

She will not leave. The thought wafted on warm
currents from the ever growing pile of coals, stinging

eyes and hitching breath as though he took in a lungful of smoke. Another handful of minutes and another
truth slowly dripped into consciousness. Not only
would she not leave—she would not speak. And with
his turmoil, Kisho would fail in the silence game.
Would fail to ignore her. *How has the game come to
this? How have I lost all my ability to function without
anyone knowing the truth?*

With a sigh he barely managed to conceal, he carefully laid the chunk of metal down with his left and
scooped up the finger bone in his right hand. The
memory of its owner surged. Usually so sarcastic and
painful, arousing nightmares from the Room—
nightmares he would gladly now accept compared to
this new, unknown fear that tore him down—it actually seemed to bring a modicum of strength and calm.
The cool bone was almost a spirit stav, the hard
ridges and small indentions where ligaments once
rested, its own bas-relief carvings of a life cut short
by his own hand, before it could serve Clan Nova
Cat. The condemnation did not seem so forceful this
night. Perhaps *surkai* will finally be done, forgiveness found?

He looked up. "You come here?" He tried for
angry, but managed only stern, and that only if one
were generous.

"Aff." Her lips hardly moved.

"Others have stayed away."

"Others are not the commander of this mission."

He bowed his head, trying once more to avoid her
piercing eyes.

"You are a mystic."

Did he manage not to jerk at her harsh statement?

"You were assigned by the Oathmaster to guide this
mission. To provide me with insight that will lead us
to victory." If possible, with each word her voice

thinned more, as though transforming into the tungsten-tipped sword of a *Shiro*. "And yet, you have not given me what I need." Haft swinging and blade vibrating with the speed of the descent. "You have given me . . . nothing at all." The tip a blur, cleaving for his skull.

He almost slouched, but realized conceding, even physically, would tear away the last of his shields, the defenses he'd begun to shed so many months ago. He rallied, drawing upon strength, gripping the finger bone until it threatened to break. "Visions come when they will, Tivia." He watched through high lashes. Her expression did not change over the lack of title.

"You were confident of your first vision. The vision that netted us nothing."

He shifted his gaze to the fire, as though dismissing her. Shrugged. *Leave!* "We found Raiders." Even to his ears it sounded weak.

"And when will we find more? When they strike at us, while we stand naked, our troops scattered and worthless?" He winced at her blatant reference to his current condition. Somehow she managed to convey more power than if she were looming over him, spittle flying and voice echoing into the night.

The wind picked up, funneling the fire's smoke straight into her face. He watched her in his peripheral vision. She remained motionless, unblinking, with tears pouring down her cheeks. Finally her relentless composure cracked as she bent slightly out of the way.

As though released from paralysis, he took in a harsh breath of carbon, fresh-cut wood, and endless moisture and wet foliage. "If I were not interrupted, perhaps a vision would come now."

She matched his stare, and another level between them fell away. Unlike so many Nova Cats, who struggled to hide from mystics and their truth-telling abilities, Tivia never resorted to such tactics. She wore bluntness on her sleeve, as though to defy anyone, mystic or otherwise, to not take her at face value. From the moment she met him, she doubted and yet she did not care. Results were all that mattered to her, not the form. Just function. But now, he failed. Failed her numerous times, and for that there might never be forgiveness, no matter *surkai* and the gross penance.

She abruptly uncoiled to her feet like a leaping cat and Kisho actually stiffened, as though preparing for an assault across the fire.

"Perhaps," she whispered, her word more felt than heard. With that, she simply turned away, silently disappearing into the tangled forest, as though she were a nova cat indeed. Kisho realized she'd let him hear her coming the first time.

He unclenched white-tipped fingers, the pain flashing momentarily in his joints, to find the outline of the finger imprinted heavily on his flesh. His blanched skin flooded crimson, the raised edges of the bone still visible. The impression would fade shortly.

But his encounter would not.

Of a sudden, the finger bone seemed to sear like a hot coal and he dropped it to the leather mat. His stupidity as a crèche youth rose as though conjured from the bleeding, glow-effusing sight, towering into the form of the young girl he had killed. He shook, a nova cat slouching out of water, and the image slowly receded, though the echo of Tivia's words would not, nor the pain they invoked.

Calm lost, the thick, overgrown forest swiftly

twisted from an oasis against problems to a grotesque monster, tentacles and writhing feelers and teeth. Waiting to take him.

But there is nothing to take. Nothing to hide from. Nothing . . .

18

Kaona Island
Wandessa Chain, Athenry
Prefecture II, The Republic of the Sphere
17 October 3136

The *Wendigo* wobbled, as the machine pounded along, sand flying as though explosions rocked the beach. Kisho cursed, knowing the medic had been correct despite his protestations, as the pain along his shoulder and back caused him to wince, hitching his left leg in a minor tremor. The 'Mech, already finding it difficult to traverse the soft sand, wobbled further, and the whine of the gyro trying to compensate for the shifting balance crescendoed. The slight direction change imparted by the altered angle of the foot pedal ramped the broken-glass-edged sound until it hurt his teeth.

Watching the retreating Raider hovercraft through the blast of sand left by its passage as it effortlessly skimmed across the sand—distance increasing—he added to the burgeoning headache by gritting teeth. No choice. With a distaste that choked, he reached to the throttle and slid it smoothly back by ten percent, waiting for the balance of the machine to adjust, then slid it back again, then again until it dropped well past half the *Wendigo*'s maximum speed.

"Alpha Base, losing target," he spit into the throat mic. "Terrain untenable. Will follow best able."

"Confirmed, Alpha Star."

He clenched his jaw to open another commline. "Parak."

"*Aff*, Mystic?"

"Slow down," he spoke, hating the words as they slipped out.

"*Aff*," the other man said, apparently content to follow orders, despite aborting the headlong flight after the escaping Fox armored car. After all, Parak's Pegasus hover scout could swat aside the Fox without breaking a sweat, but if it ran into any larger units it would be in trouble. And unlike the Clan mentality for so long, that a victory was a victory regardless of the outcome, regardless of how many Clansmen died and how much equipment was lost, the Nova Cats currently fighting for Warlord Tormark had to keep the ultimate objective in mind. Then again, of all the Clans, perhaps the Nova Cats had come the furthest, adapted the most to the Inner Sphere style of fighting, where a battle, regardless of how honorable and glorious, was only one set against the larger war. And no matter how many battles were won, it meant nothing if they lost the war.

How long it took us to figure that out . . . and so many Clansmen still cannot accept it, no matter the decades that passed. Instead they reach for other explanations. The Elstars. The neo-Crusader philosophy, ru-

mored to have started with the Hell's Horses and now growing with parts of the Jade Falcon Touman, of total war. The entire Sea Fox Clan? Mystics?

He opened his mouth until it cracked, ratcheting the jawbone back and forth to unseat the tension riding as thickly as beetles on dung in his neck muscles, while his mind chewed on that line of reasoning before letting it go. Bad enough to be so handicapped in a fight, but then to have the weight of failure bowing him down . . . *What I would not give for Kopek's* Cat *or Liso's* Hawk *right now.*

"Commander, the Fox has left the beach, heading up a river that cuts through the jungle. Looks like we got a small canyon about a klick or so upriver."

"Hold for the rest of the command." *Not that I have much of a command.* He gritted his teeth again, further tightening already tight-as-strung-wire muscles.

To be stuck with such a small command, knowing what was coming. . . . He ran his tongue along his teeth, pinching it in frustration. That they must split up through the entire region to search for any clue of the Raiders made sense, as they were pushed for speed. But despite Clansman arrogance about their superior skills in a one-on-one duel, it never came to that. Two 'Mechs were down for repairs in the last week alone due to ambushes.

And yet they had no choice. They had to keep to the timetable. Had to hope that the combined-arms Star of a 'Mech, two vehicles, and three Points of battle armor would be enough to hold out against a concerted attack long enough to allow reinforcements to be dropped in via *Nearstar,* constantly kept one step from liftoff for just such an event. Had to hope the Nova Cats' skills were sufficient to pull out a miracle, or be a worthy sacrifice to the glory of the Clan if they . . . were unsuccessful. Except they could not afford to lose so much equipment . . . and regardless, to date the plan failed. Miserably.

Kisho glanced at the radar monitor, picking out the other Pegasus as it protected the armored personnel carrier, which slogged through the sand like a bloated hypogat out of water. Kisho pulled up to a quick stop to avoid hitting Parak's ride, accidentally kicking sand onto the flanks of the Pegasus. He punched up the magnification through the forward viewscreen, and the perspective dizzyingly swooped forward into a natural swath through the thick forest-style jungle. Though the foliage on this side of the island usually fell well below the height of a 'Mech, near the freshwater river the strange trees ballooned in height and girth, until the setting sun threw long shadows, like arms of oblivion stretching across the gap. He tried not to shiver at the image it presented, and talks with Yori on his first trip to The Republic surfaced. Bakemono. Demons. Monsters.

Have you become afraid of shadows as well, surat? The derision almost coated the inside of the cockpit in the thickness of his scorn. Yet it did not keep the shiver from raising the hairs on his arms.

"It is a trap, Mystic," Parak spoke after almost thirty seconds. The doddering APC finally pulled up, sand cascading like a child's tantrum, flying in every direction. The whine of the Pegasus vibrated even into the confines of the cockpit, the wash of high-pressure air adding to the general visual maelstrom.

"Of course it is a trap," he replied. Why not state the obvious a few more times?

"But we will move forward, *quiaff*?"

Kisho toggled through radar, magscan, and infrared and could find nothing. If only his aerospace fighters were not flying a defensive position over the Nova Cat main encampment to stop another raid. He clenched and unclenched fists and arched his back, trying to ease the throbbing. No good. *"Aff."*

Silence greeted the statement. Not much else to say. "They will hit us from within the canyon."

"Aff, Mystic. That is where I would lay such a trap."

Kisho's eyebrows slowly rose, as the silence stretched out like myomer pulled taut against heavy current.

"If I were ever to lay such a trap," Parak finally added, his voice a mix of annoyance and scandal for such a statement.

Despite everything, laughter bubbled—not enough to activate the throat mic, but enough to lessen the tension in his body. *"Aff,* Parak, so would I. So would I."

"Then let us be about springing it," Bordi spoke, the other Pegasus revving its primary lift fan like a Spheroid teen gassing a hoversled in challenge.

"Aff." Without another word, Kisho revved the *Wendigo,* drawing more energy off the fusion reactor, sending the machine forward at a good clip.

The sun dropped away, a verdant curtain cutting off its bright stage light, throwing shadows into every crooked tree branch and darkness under every bush. The sounds of heavy military machines sat heavy against the susurrations of nature, all but annihilating the soft wash of shallow water across a bed of centuries-smoothed stones, and the sigh of a light breeze through the lush vegetation. Almost Eden.

But sights were deceiving. The entire area reeked of rotten eggs. An active vent on the slope of the secondary cone of the island was located not five kilometers from their current location, and spewed sulfur and who knew what else into the region. The twisted vegetation would kill as quickly as any PPC. The flora had adapted to the poisons constantly infecting the ground water like a disease eating the body of the island, spoiling its blood with pollutants and heavy-chemical effluvia.

"Star Commander Fost, prepare to deploy your Elementals on my mark."

"*Aff,* Mystic. Preparations under way."

They moved forward, fanning out as much as the limited terrain allowed, the twin Pegasus flanking ahead right and left, with the APC behind the central hub of Kisho's *Wendigo.* "Alpha Base."

"Confirm, Alpha Star."

"Alpha Star, proceeding to"—he checked the coordinates—"thirty-four by twenty-seven, to grid Beta-tango four."

"Copy, Alpha Star. Do you want *Nearstar* prepped?"

Tension spiked again. Prepped did not mean prepped, it meant launched. Against Warlord Pesht's forces four decades ago, the Nova Cats learned harsh lessons of broadcasting clear intent, even on encrypted channels. But if he told them to prep and they found nothing . . . Tivia's eyes haunted him almost more waking than asleep. One day she would call him out, and if he did not find something to show for it . . .

"*Neg,*" he finally said. It might be a death sentence, but better to die on the field of battle than to find your honor stripped and your disgrace paraded through the entire Clan. A mystic who is no mystic. An unbeliever.

A heretic.

"Copy, Alpha Star. Advise, *quiaff*?"

"*Aff,* Alpha Base," he managed to respond, breath hitching and shoulders and back twinging under new spikes of pain running steel fingers through sickened muscles. A heretic. Might as well call me a freebirth and a Spheroid and get it over with.

While his mind played this way and that, like a

Lyran trying to decide what new shiny thing to buy, eyes roved over the terrain. The river—more like a large creek—meandered, the dense forest carefully following its route. Though the canyon walls loomed less than a kilometer in the distance, the river cut hard to the left and, less than a hundred meters up ahead, swung back to the right, as though a drunken god had tried for a straight line and failed miserably.

They had made their way past three such bends when, of a sudden, Kisho knew he could not stop, but also could not go forward. Pain, always a constant weight on his stomach, spiked hard, but in a new way. Not in worry, or remembrance, or shame, but in something else. Despite his frantic state of mind, he smoothly kept at the controls, knowing he must not slow down, but not why. Something within. Something. A feeling swept from toe to forehead, face instantly dehumanizing, raising goose bumps, pinpricks springing along shoulders and scalp, bringing a sense of understanding: knowledge.

He knew.

Mind already in a heightened state, he immediately threw a hitch into the *Wendigo* and slowed it considerably, coming to a stop a handful of meters before the next bend. Though he hated acknowledging weakness, the alternative would be worse. Far worse. "Need to stop for a moment. Shoulder"—he swallowed, gritting teeth, not just for show!—"spasm. It will pass."

"*Aff,* Mystic," came three sets of perfectly neutral responses.

Eyes beat across sensors like hands battering themselves bloody. Nothing. Absolutely nothing. Not on magscan, or infrared—could not trust it anyway in this infernal heat and thick foliage—not on any sensor. Not a *stravag* thing. Yet the knowledge burned like a new star in the firmament, bright and incessant.

He also knew he could not use their encrypted channels. It made so much sense now. The pieces came to him as though his subconscious had chewed on them continually, choosing this moment to present them in ordered fashion. How they managed to always avoid them. Always stay one step ahead. No idea how they managed it, but they must have deciphered their encryption and, despite the Nova Cats' attempts at subterfuge, still divined their every battle plan. Once more, the knowledge burned within him, the sun at high noon, scouring away any vestiges of foggy doubt. Under such pressure, there could be none.

He knew his Star mates. They would follow. They were good warriors and they would follow their mystic. With smooth actions, he powered down primary targeting acquisition systems to avoid detection, while powering up weapons. "It is passed," he said curtly, sliding the throttle forward, while sidling towards the edge of the coming bend, as though trying to avoid some particularly slippery section of river.

From one step to the next, the knowledge once more sank into his gut, blossoming in an explosion of light and understanding: now. Legs automatically stomped down onto jump jets and he feathered venting pressure slightly to realign and send the 'Mech sailing over the foliage bridging the river. If not for the aerial view, he would have missed the shapes lying in the water—submerged pop-up turrets of some type, perhaps jury-rigged, in a deeper part of the river. Even without the targeting reticule, he swung the PPC into line, *feeling* the shot, unleashing a fusillade of azure fire as the 'Mech peaked the jump and began to descend towards the river. Steam exploded like a winter avalanche defying gravity across a swath twenty meters long as the particle cannon sizzled water in a torrent of energy.

A rain of missile fire leapt downrange towards the bend in the river, as though nervous fingers, surprised by the assault, had triggered preset coordinates without assessing the situation or revising for new circumstances. Following contrails, Kisho throttled jump jets to full power near touchdown, while easing into a shotgun blast from his LB 10-X. Trees exploded in an avalanche of flechettes, scythed down as though by a series of spinning, giant machetes. A sympathetic explosion rocked the jungle, argent fire throwing harsh light onto a series of portable rocket launchers and screaming men milling about. *Not enough to down me, but enough to peel off some serious armor and perhaps take out a vehicle or two.*

Plasma screaming from magnetic baffles, the *Wendigo* slammed into the rocky edge of the river as two untouched makeshift turrets boiled up out of the water, lances of ruby slicing towards his position. Yet both shots missed, their remote pilots finding it too difficult to track the turrets so far off preprogrammed firing arcs. With casual ease, whips of cerulean energy popped the small black canisters like ugly zits, and black, burning metal vanished into hissing water and charnellike rapids of oozing, smoking oil.

You may still wage better strategic wars at times, but you will find, as ever, a Clansman is without equal in immediate tactics. The grin of satisfaction for biting back at the striking Raiders, albeit against only a handful of desperate infantry, brought a relief so powerful his vision seemed to waver momentarily.

The three vehicles gunned around the bend, weapons already tracking and missile launchers spewing towards targets he could not see. He smiled sheepishly and reactivated the primary targeting systems, and several threat icons blossomed onto the screen, while the target reticule appeared, ready and begging for a dark gold tone of hard lock.

He watched as the Elementals disgorged from the APC like a bird regurgitating food for its young. But this food struck with a vengeance. Though it could not compare to taking down a 'Mech, the chance to finally *do* something more than made up for any lack in the battle, and he knew his Star deserved a taste as well. The battle armor swam into the trees, army ants eager for the slaughter.

He moved the *Wendigo* slightly, facing the canyon and checking sensors once more, then slowly shook his head. They will be gone by now, knowing we sprung the first part of their trap. But perhaps this is a sign of things to come. A turning point?

A sign. With an abruptness to steal away breath, the realization of his line of thinking clenched iron-banded fingers across his chest, and the maelstrom of events leading to the discovering of the trap cascaded back into consciousness. *How did I know? How?* His stomach clamped again, while hands gripped joysticks until tendons popped. *I did not hunt for it. I did not fall into a trance to find it. It came to me.*

It . . . just . . . came. . . .

He changed his mind and throttled the machine up, slamming into the nearest woods, hunting for a few elusive infantry desperately scampering away from the metal god bringing their doom. He shied away from his own memory of a similar event.

Better than to face his own reality at the moment. Laughter seemed to follow him. Laughter from a voice that never laughed.

Interlude III

The Founder:
We will do what we must.
Three centuries ago this day,
Operation Klondike ended,
Golden Century, imminent flowering;
justification and fulfillment.
We follow hallowed footsteps.
We will do what we must.
—The Remembrance (Clan Nova Cat),
   Passage 467, Verse 29, Lines 21-28

Ways of Seeing Park, Barcella
Nova Cat Reservation, Irece
Irece Prefecture, Draconis Combine
26 May 3122

He huddled, today's hurts and black marks starting to go away. The Machine was done with him and he didn't want to think about tomorrow.

Three cried in his arms, while Two sat with a small space between them, but they could still touch each other. If they needed to. But Two was looking away. Two always looked away now.

The cold floor made his right leg hurt extra bad—not *his* fault, Eight should *not* have gotten in the way of the Machine and they *both* got it—and he needed

to pee in the corner hole. But it could wait. He had
to make Three stop crying. They didn't like that.

"Three, it's okay. Your bad feelings will go away."

The deep grooves in the skin across the top of her
head showed like extra bad black marks. Like the Machine beat her extra bad today, but she was only in
Dark, right? And it didn't matter if it did or didn't.
They told them no. Told them no over and over and
over again. Told them it was only in their heads.
Sheesh, never mind the black marks on their heads!
Right there on their heads! He tried yelling that one
time and spent an extra period in Dark.

"Three, please. Come on," he said, young voice
barely above a whisper, as he looked around. The rest
of the kids in the darkened room were trying to sleep,
or stared at walls like they wished they could just walk
through, or were scrunched up into as small a ball as
they could make themselves. And he didn't want to
pay attention to those, 'cause if they stayed that way
too long, they came and you never came back.

He saw Seven waving real hard to be quiet. He also
saw Nine, Fourteen, and Twenty-two were inching
their butts along the floor to get away. He hated them
for that. He might do the same, if it wasn't Three. But
still hated them. Hated them bad.

"Two, you don't have bad feelings at night. Right?
Right?" He had to talk softly, 'cause he didn't want
them to know. And you couldn't really talk loud,
'cause you could only take little itty breaths, 'cause
you just never seemed to get enough air if you
breathed hard at night.

He looked at Two, but Two wouldn't look him right
in the eyes and he knew that, too. Scared eyes. But
never scared out loud. No, not Two. But they drew
his number first. And it had been forever since they

told all of them that *today* were all a cycle older and
they had a special present for everybody. But they
couldn't do it together. So they called numbers and
five kids went away and five came back. But they
didn't all come back sometimes. But no one would
talk about what the present was. But the black marks
were sometimes worse. And more kids would curl up
into the little bitty balls you did when you were just
a baby. And they'd lie there and you couldn't get
them out. Even when you told them to stop it. Tried
to even take an extra deep breath and yell real, real
loud, 'cause they didn't want to not come back. Did
they? And so, even though they told them it was going
to be a great present, some of the kids started to kick
and scream real loud when they came to get them.
And they read their numbers out loud. And it never
worked, 'cause they were all giants. And you could
scratch and kick and bite and they wouldn't say
anything.

And later, Two told him the present was an entire
whole extra period in Dark. A whole extra period!
And so Two only shook his head, but wouldn't say
anything now.

And that only made his heart jump and he had to
lick his lips some—they were chapped something bad,
and the salty taste made him thirsty, but no water
bulbs till light—'cause most of the kids had gotten
their presents, but he hadn't yet. And Three got her
turn four lights ago and then they brought her back
and she wouldn't sleep and when she did, it was bad.
Real, real bad. She kept making funny sounds and she
moved and he tried to hold her, like they always did
to keep warm on the cold floor, and she pushed him
away. Honest. Pushed him away! And now she talked
about bad, bad dreams. And he wasn't sure what to

do. But he just knew it was almost light time and they'd come and they'd call numbers and he knew One would be read aloud. Just knew it. Just knew it.

Then he was mad, 'cause he was crying, though Three was still scrunched up on the floor and Two looked at him and didn't say a thing, just looked away. And that made him start crying more. 'Cause Two always made fun of him and that time he caught him crying, 'cause the Machine cut him when he didn't do what he was supposed to in the drill and he missed blocking the sword and Two laughed and laughed and laughed and then he had to beat up some other·kids, 'cause he couldn't beat up Two, but you just couldn't laugh at him like that and let him get away with it, or you'd be Forty-four, or Thirty-two and they'd have to come in to stop the fighting and clean up the blood and that was the only time they ever talked, and all the kids involved got extra Dark, but one time he wanted them to talk to him and yelling didn't do anything, so he decided he would make them talk and so he picked Sixty-three, 'cause she was small and little and he just started to beat her up and five or six others started hitting her also and pretty soon there was just lots of blood on the ground and then they came and he felt bad, but he made them do what he wanted and that felt good, but he spent extra, extra time in Dark and that always scared him and made him mad and feel funny, like his thoughts weren't his thoughts anymore and he floated and his mind went away and did funny things and when it came back to him it didn't really feel like his mind and today would be the day and he cried and Two didn't laugh and that scared him more.

And then Three was there and they cried and they hugged and it felt good and it didn't make the bad feelings go away, all away, but some away, and he stopped crying.

"The bad feelings will go away," he said in his most small voice. But they didn't say anything back and they wouldn't look at him and he knew he was still scared.

All the kids cried out when the lights came on. The light hurt bad and everybody's eyes got itchy and watery and One thought he would just die, 'cause his heart was beating just so fast and he knew they were coming for him. And he looked around and saw kids crawling over each other to move away from the door as it opened. And Two wouldn't look at him and he kept looking at the black door and it was a monster's mouth and it would eat him and Three grabbed his hair and gave it a yank and he yelled and looked at her.

"The bad feelings will go away," she said. Her lips were moving funny and she looked like she was going to cry again. So he wasn't sure he should believe it. But he started trying to help her and then he cried and then she helped him. So maybe he could.

"One, seventy-three, twenty-seven, forty-nine, sixteen," the Voice said, but nobody came in. They never ever came in. Only when he made the blood happen. And yeah. He made the blood happen. And they had to come in. He made them do what they hated. Just like they made him do what he hated. Yeah.

So he stood up big and tall and walked right at that big door.

He'd show them.

Chamber processed. Primary sequence initiated; five subjects prepped.
Initiate initial submersion.

Subjects inserted into deprivation chamber.

Sequencing. Systems verified.

Initiate full null-sensory feedback.

Null-sensory submersion initiation phase executed.

Verification of null-sensory automation.

Null-sensory verified. Systems report nominal. Within parameters. Subjects are in the void.

Drop for forty-eight hours.

Sir.

What?

We've lost a lot of 'em, through several sibkos. Lots of shells to dispose of. Are we sure the modeling is correct?

Hai. *All the modeling converges consistently. If they can't take total sensory deprivation for that time period by five, they'll fail when we ratchet it up to the next level. After all, the big room should prep 'em for dislocation, as does the physical training mechic—those that survive it, that is.*

But we're churning through subjects. And they're just kids.

The price to pay. If the Cats want their Oathmasters and the Abbess her Budojin *Neophytes, can't have a human upbringing if we don't want them to think like a human. And you're new, so don't worry. Once past the room and the full depravition phase, they get coddled like kittens; they get beds and toilet. Besides, no sense in wasted resources past five if they can't take it.*

═══ 19 ═══

Kaona Island
Wandessa Chain, Athenry
Prefecture II, The Republic of the Sphere
21 October 3136

Kisho paced outside the command tent, a cat restless and on the prowl. The heat of the day waned, the sun sinking towards an endless cobalt ocean ready to quench its light and bring blessed darkness. Though he refused to look in that direction, the newly grounded DropShip's pings and twangs of cooling metal reached his ears even at this distance.

He spun around to continue the track in the hard-packed dirt, confident that at any moment he would be summoned. He'd been saying that for over an hour.

Tanaka. Of all the people to deal with at this moment, it had to be Tanaka? Burnt ozone from the *Spiritaker*'s fusion fire stung the air and tweaked nostrils. His nose scrunched, not from the heavily laden air, but thoughts, rebounding like an out-of-control warrior in zero-gravity for the first time, slamming into bulkheads, crunching bones and spewing floating droplets of blood, spinning off into a new trajectory and another incoming bulkhead, unable to latch onto a ringlet or other handgrip to bring a halt to the chaos and pain.

Tanaka. Tivia. Their failure on this world—*his* failure. Tanaka's obvious victory on Saffel. How was Hisa doing on Styx? He ground to a halt, the slight dust kicked up settling unseen across boots. Hisa. Shame flared and caressed skin pink. *I have not thought of her in so long. Too long. How? So much . . . so much to think about.*

And the fight? A vision?

He shied away from that last thought, launching again into a purposeful stride, using physical movement to bank away mental activity. But it didn't work.

"Mystic," a voice broke across chaotic thoughts like a wave to a blazing beach campfire. Kisho stopped, turned to find Tivia holding open the tent flap. Her eyes were angry, restive. More like liquid hydrogen, not water. He kept a shiver at bay, inclined his head lightly, and moved towards the door flap.

He almost expected her to drop the tent flap and force him to move it aside. No. Never such pettiness from Tivia. Too respectful of mystics, even in her fury and confusion.

He ducked in and shivered despite willful attempts otherwise. The squat form of Tanaka seemed to fill the entire space. *What I feared from the beginning! So many long months past. I am breaking down. They will expose me. I know it.*

Hisa! The name conjured strength to fortify suddenly weakening knees and allow him to push onwards into the tent and stand slightly to one side, while Tivia worked around her makeshift desk, but did not sit down.

"Tivia has spoken of your actions," Tanaka said in his usual clipped, deep voice.

Which could mean anything, he tried to console himself, but found it useless. *Sure, she praised me for my visions and expert handling of each situation to hand us victory,* aff? He remained impassive, staring at neither individual, hoping his self-scorn did not translate. After all, another truth-reader stood across the way. A truth-reader, as far as Kisho believed, who would as soon skin him alive as allow him to walk out of the tent.

"What have you to say?" Tanaka asked after only the briefest pause.

Expecting a lengthy silence in a test of wills to see who would speak first, Kisho involuntarily glanced at Tanaka and made eye contact. *Surat! He traps you so easily!* Now unwilling to look away, he responded methodically. "I am sure the Star colonel's report speaks for itself, *quiaff*?"

"Oh, *aff.* An endless series of fights. Which have accomplished little, but drain us. And no closer to victory. *Aff,* it does indeed. *Mystic.*" The silence this time did stretch, after the obvious accent Tanaka tossed onto his title.

A slow anger burned at disparagement from such an arrogant *surat.* Uncowed, eyes met eyes, like discharging PPCs. The Spartan room, with its handful of chairs, small holotable, and makeshift desk spun out of focus as the world tunneled down to Tanaka's challenging eyes. *Who are you to question my faith?* he raged, ignoring his own questions that plagued him even in dreams. The nightmares that refused to leave, old and now new, no matter how much meditation before slumber.

Heretic. The word almost hung in the air between them, as though fallen from Tanaka's lips. *And what if I am?* Kisho breathed deeply, the swell of chest against cooling vest a remembrance of all he gave to the Clan. *All I give. Every day. Everything I have. I hold nothing back, regardless of what faith or lack of it I may espouse. Nothing.*

Fury replaced anger in a wash of emotions threatening to choke off breath. A half-hundred words battled for egress, to assault the *surat.* An iron will sealed his lips. *I will not respond to the likes of you. If I am to be taken to task, it will not . . . be . . . by . . . you.*

Soundless laughter once more seemed to come from dry lips at a horrible distance. Kisho almost glanced aside, then pushed the impression away.

"Mystics," Tivia finally cut in, voice aggravated. "This accomplishes nothing. What we need to accomplish is the winning of this war. Of fulfilling the contract bid and won by Warlord Tormark, so that we may return to our worlds. With the additional forces brought by Mystic Tanaka, we should be making plans."

The words might as well have fallen among bull mastiffs, for all their effect, though Kisho did note how quickly Tivia seemed to want to step away from his lack of visions. Yet something moved across Tanaka's features. Only another trained for reading subtle muscle movements might have noticed the ever-so-slight shifting of eyebrows and eyes that moved from stern to slightly less so. Into . . . what? Confusion? Hesitancy?

Relief began to surge, yet Kisho wrangled it ruthlessly, hurling it back down. You could never be too careful around another mystic, especially one like Tanaka. One who could play you like a finely tuned guitar, regardless of your own defenses.

"Mystics." Her voice rose a notch, unused to being ignored. Once more, neither even blinked.

Who will cave first? Kisho moved an eye muscle a trifle in question. Another moment and an answering slip from Tanaka's mask. But an answer to his question, or one in return? Truth-readers they might be, but when two played the game, they might as well be norms and just as deaf, dumb, and blind to the larger world.

"Star Colonel," a voice interrupted, coming from outside the tent.

An annoyed sound erupted from Tivia. "I was not to be bothered."

"*Aff,* Star Colonel. But we have an incoming DropShip, two hours from insertion and already broadcasting in the clear."

That turned all three heads towards the flap as Tivia responded. "Enter."

A tall, lanky warrior stepped gingerly inside, but halted with the flap still open. Kisho detected the man's uncomfortableness over the tension in the room, like an oil slick on water.

"Who is it? Why are we not moving to defend?" Tivia demanded.

Confusion swept the man's face. "Star Colonel, it is a broadcast from Galaxy Commander Kev Rosse of the Spirit Cats. He comes in invitation to the mystic's call," he finished, nodding towards Kisho.

If the man had said the corpse of Warlord Minamoto was descending with legions of dead, he might not have dropped a bigger bombshell. Stunned momentarily, Kisho recovered, as an idea effervesced with strength. He slowly turned back towards Tivia, ignoring Tanaka, as though he were a freebirth.

"It would seem my visions have led us here, Star Colonel. After all, the mystics call was not simply to fight, but to bring the Spirit Cats home." It was not an outright lie. Yet pain seemed to dance through tightening stomach muscles over such a twisting of the truth. Completely unexpected that Kev Rosse would so quickly answer the call.

Tivia matched Kisho stare for stare, unrelenting. She slowly nodded, yet gave up nothing. "It would appear so."

With a salute to Tivia and a stiff nod to Tanaka—he would not be completely rude after Tivia's example— Kisho withdrew quickly before they might trap him. The air—despite ozone and lacings of less pleasant volcanic chemicals—tasted like freedom.

Yet a hand strayed to massage an unforgiving stomach and bad feelings still nipped at his mind, threatening a convergence of new and old nightmares alike.

20

Kaona Island
Wandessa Chain, Athenry
Prefecture II, The Republic of the Sphere
21 October 3136

Flames.

*How many fires have eaten wood and cast their ash
and light to the sky in my presence? How much warmth
have I siphoned from a heat source first used at the
dawn of time, while I ride the greatest military technological marvel ever created by mankind, making war
and seeking visions across the stars?*

The irony could not be avoided, making him slip a
smile on like an unused glove, while Kisho waited for
Kev Rosse to speak. But Kev hoarded words like a
nun her virginity; almost twenty minutes with two
brief eye contacts, and an endless stretch of staring
into spitting, hissing flames. Even so, the charisma of

the man could not be denied. *No wonder so many follow you.*

The other man's long mane fell like a river of blue-black equine hair, heightening the flame's effects on Kev's face. A glow permeated the strong lines, pushing features firmly into Kisho's mind and soul. *No, not equine. Feline. A nova cat.* The smile tugged; pushing, prodding itself more firmly into place.

And how would you respond to my smiles, Galaxy Commander? Offense? Ignore me? You have done a good job of that already. The smile teetered and Kisho took a firm grip on the indignity threatening to turn his good mood south. Not the time to show anger over his lost soul's lack of proper respect.

He shifted slightly on the small blanket, abruptly wondering if Tanaka might be trying to eavesdrop on this all-important meeting. His mood stretched even further towards a darker place, smile cast to the side like a shed skin—useless, itching, uncomfortable.

Of a sudden, Kisho stood on an endless blade, thrust out across a yawing crevasse falling away to the foundation of the universe. Naked, hair shaved, tough foot pads bearing the brunt of weight, pressing inexorably down. A line of sumptuous pleasure/pain wrought across both feet. A howling, as though built across a millennia of millennia, stretching from the first orgasmic burst of existence, to the insignificance of the infinitesimal blip of existence, rushing on towards a distant future so vast and incomprehensible that the mind quelled and he shivered against the awful enormity of it all. Body shifting, the pleasure/pain snapping over fully into pain as the balance changed and the spread of weight on the blade's edge pushed too hard. He heaved too far to one side; exquisite agony wrenched through feet, calves, groin, mid-section, chest, and head from one eyeblink to the next . . . body cloven in two, falling away into a darkness that did not enfold in warmth and forgetfulness, but devoured in icy remembrance for all the onrushing of eternities.

A soundless growl tore out of a parched throat into an uncaring night. Even sitting, he teetered forward, as though on the verge of collapsing straight into the fire. A firm hand shot down like the multiton grip of a 'Mech fist, steadying, drawing him back from the endless . . . nothing. He blinked rapidly to prevent the tears trying to course down his cheeks.

What is going on?

Hair swept across his face, shocking him into true wakefulness. "What?" he croaked. Looked, up and up and up into disturbed eyes looming over him, haloed with an endless nova cat mane. His brain finally reset itself, lurched and stuttered, then swam back into the currents of this world and Kev Rosse stood over him, left arm steadying.

Despite the horror that scrabbled just below the surface, threatening to send him gibbering once more into an endless pit of his own making, he turned aside, shame burning hot and searing. *What the* savashri *is wrong with me? I must have fallen asleep. The only way my* stravag *nightmare might have risen like this. Only way!*

And what made it worse, this was not the old nightmares: the Room, where so many of his sibko died, because they could not take the lack of adult human contact; the girl he killed for no reason other than to make the Acolytes talk to him; the Machine, the training device, which pushed their physical training, even at that young age, beyond all endurance, teaching them to focus their minds to a level that can only really be taught to someone so young; the Dark, the sensory deprivation chamber, which endlessly wove their minds out of their bodies, twisting and distorting their thoughts and their souls, until they could find the visions the mystic caste was decanted to provide.

No, this was the new nightmare, of something coming. Of something . . .

"Are you okay?" The deep concern masked other emotions, but Kisho could only focus on the obvious Clan response.

Weakness.

He will think me weak. The question of whether he *was* weak stewed and burned within, only to be violently thrust aside. *No. No!* Through the incalculable heat and pain he managed an *"Aff."*

Without another word, Kev moved around the fire and reseated, but spoke immediately. "A vision, *quiaff?"*

NO! *"Aff."*

"Powerful. Powerful. . . ." The voice trailed off for a moment, bringing Kisho's eyes like a moth to flame, to find Kev staring once more into the fire that drew *his* gaze, the blaze highlighting an expression Kisho could not discern.

"Why have you come?" Kisho responded, nervous of silence and what lay within each pregnant pause.

The other man jerked slightly, glanced up, then smiled and laughed, lightly. "You brought me here."

"Why have you come?" Falling back to training, Kisho breathed deeply—took several tries to enter a first-level trance!—and dropped into finding the truth behind Kev's words.

The other man pulled out a data cube, set it on the ground. Raised eyes back up, quirked an eyebrow high. Once more, the silence pressed against Kisho— a dark, fathomless bag cinching tight with each falling grain of sand. *What is going on? Am I losing myself so completely?* He fought back with words.

"I see you received the message."

"And I see you like to speak the obvious."

Anger sparked. Desperate for strength, for anything, Kisho spread cupped hands within and carefully fanned the ember to push back the darkness. "There are times for subterfuge. Times to hide your words so only those worthy might discern your intent."

"*Aff.*"

"And other times, when the worthy are already present, and the truth might be pulled from such obfuscation, to lie bright and gleaming, for joy and enlightenment."

"*Aff.* And is this one of those times?"

"You think not? Are you not the leader of those who follow you? Have you not named yourself the 'spirit cats'?" The spiritual coal growing, it warmed as he fell into this role he must play. *Always a role to play, eh, old man? Never one of my choosing, only those chosen for me.* Despite his own words spoken what seemed like years ago to Yori, he still seemed to fight against the inevitable, the spirit unwilling to bend to the mind's knowledge of inevitability. "Does that not show your desire for worthiness?"

"Worthy for what?"

"Ah. That is the question we all must ask."

"Ourselves?"

"*Aff.* Or others, when the time is right."

From one of the treelike plants, a blood-colored leaf—with a striated texture and so many points it appeared more needle- than leaflike—slowly tumbled into view, cavorting and dancing to an almost unfelt wind. Yet it soon caught within the whirling eddies of the fire and lofted into the air once more. The dance continued, lifting and falling at the vagaries of the fire's whim. Yet it could not continue. Would have only a single conclusion. Like the cherry blossoms.

The pattern continued for only so long before the leaf fell too far, gave in too much to the call of another's power and caught fire.

In a flash and pop of light and sap, the leaf disintegrated.

Their eyes focused on one another, expressions plain. A sign. A sign. *Am I that leaf? Do I let others dictate my actions, leading me to my doom?* The memory of the living nightmare swirled, threatening to quench the light within.

"Am I worthy?" Kev finally spoke. The words came across heartfelt, but something pinged Kisho's senses. Desperate to reach beyond his own battle, he focused on Kev's reactions, striving to match body to words.

"Worthy of what?"

"There is only one reason to come here, *quiaff*? Only one reason to ask such a question." Kev leaned forward slightly, mane and liquid shadows casting features into a wall of darkness Kisho could not penetrate.

The familiar whiff of smoke to nostrils long accustomed centered him, allowing Kisho to play the part, despite misgivings. "You are worthy if you have desire."

"A desire to return." It should have been a question, but instead came as though a statement. As though something he still mulled over?

"Aff," Kisho probed. "Spheroids fall back to old habits and war consumes us. You seek to find sanctuary for your people. What better sanctuary then that left decades ago as you wandered?"

Kev slowly raised his head, troubled eyes finding a mirror. *But are you troubled by returning? Or troubled by me? And if by me, then by a vision you believe in, or a mystic you cannot believe in?* Staring at Kev, running through the man's dossier again, Kisho quickly came to the only conclusion possible—a conclusion only partially supported by Kisho's observations. *Am I losing it, or is he that good at hiding himself?* No, this man believes in visions. Has had visions himself. Such a leader. To have accomplished all that he has done. To have so many follow him . . . and he believes.

Hisa's words tumbled up against this intelligent, admirable warrior, settling onto him like a life-size holovid display: a perfect fit.

"Time," Kev finally spoke.

Taken off guard, Kisho floundered, then latched on. "*Aff.* It will take vast time without working HPGs to contact your far-flung troops."

"Yet I can begin immediately."

The words fell with conviction into the fire, as though a benediction to their meeting. And yet something still seemed off. The words rang true, yet some shading marred their perfection.

"You will be in The Republic for some time?" Kev continued.

Kisho stiffened, then relaxed at the obviousness of the statement. *He can see as well as any what is going on here. And likely divined where we are going next. "Aff."*

Kev abruptly stood, shattering the meeting as cleanly as a booted foot through a stained-glass window. "Then I shall be about it." He inclined his head and swept away without another word.

Kisho sucked in hot, humid air, taken aback by the sudden departure. Eyes going unfocused, he ran through the meeting once more, and the few spoken words, and the implied meanings coating everything. *Despite talk of revealed truths, we keep so much veiled, quiaff, Galaxy Commander?* Aff.

He slowly stood, clenching and unclenching muscles, forcing a full-body stretch. Of a sudden, what both-

ered him dropped into focus as his eyes happened to
catch on the data cube on the other side of the flames,
the surface bubbling, the structure slowly collapsing
under searing heat.

*You will be off to tell your people. But what will
you tell them?*

═══ 21 ═══

Kaona Island
Wandessa Chain, Athenry
Prefecture II, The Republic of the Sphere
23 October 3136

Captain Josef Yoland caressed the Marx XX laser rifle's worn butt as though tracing the contours of a Capellan courtesan. He jawed for another moment on the wad of juicy bacco, then spit quietly to the side while lips stretched crookedly.

Not that I've ever had that *particular pleasure,* he groused. *Only ten-stone women for me.* But he let his imagination run in quick, exciting circles anyway, before letting go with a soft sigh. Snuggling further down into the newly turned loam, next to a particularly large tree of some type (his mother would drop a few stones into the poor box at the meetinghouse before he'd recognize one tree from the next), he pressed leathery skin firmly against the rubbed-smooth high-impact plastic and sighted in through the scope.

Like a god looking at mortals, the distant encampment leapt forward, the gnatlike figures scrambling around vehicles just over a kilometer away. A 'Mech, a dozen or so quick-fab buildings, and a DropShip zoomed into sharply defined focus. He beaded in on one person after another.

You're dead. You're dead. You're dead. Finger itched to make it so. The image of a haggard woman, trying to retain her beauty behind a putrid mask of smeared makeup and a miasma of cloying perfume, ghosted across each, crosshairs dead center between angry lines and loathing eyes.

His finger cricked until pressure verged on tripping the electric connection, then eased again as he remembered the plan. Eyes refocused momentarily to the small timer taped to the side of the rifle, digital readout counting down. He tongued the bacco directly, tears smarting at the acidic flavor, juices ballooning to almost overflow, then he spit and slid on the crooked smile once more. *Not gonna beat me this time, you old hag. Taunt me all you want, but I'll cap you when I'm good and ready and not before. I sure as hell ain't gonna spoil such a splendid trap.*

He sighted once more on numerous individuals—an obvious tech here, warrior there, and grunts for the dirty work all around—waiting for the arrogant one to show. *How many times I got to tell someone? Never get into a routine. I learned that when I was nine, 'cause a routine gets you beaten. Gets you killed. And here you are, so high and mighty warrior and you fall into a trap I would've avoided before I grew hair on my nuts.*

He shook his head at the injustice—ejected another lip of spit softly to the side—of the arrogant warrior basking in the military sophistication of his unit, while he lay in the dirt, launching a groundpounder's surgical strike 'cause they didn't have the spare parts to fix his *Panther*.

He grimaced at the injustice, his mom's words badgering him about the head like a vulture: *loser, loser, loser*.

Just then the warrior began walking down the DropShip ramp, as the clock ticked down past the ten-second mark. Josef lined up the shot. His instructors—more like thugs, but talent is talent—had tried vainly to teach him about blanking the mind, about breathing techniques and becoming one with the rifle and bullet. But it was all a steamy pile as far as he was concerned. He didn't need to know what he did, just like he didn't need to know how his 'Mech worked to be a walking avatar of death.

He sighted on the figure, while a wicked grin turned his features into a horrible, sick pantomime of a grin, while the image of his mother ghosted the warrior's features and he caressed the trigger like a long-lost lover. The electric connection made, the rifle purred like a cat stretching in a warm spot of sun and pulsed out a coherent beam, flashing the right eye to a brilliant white plasma, the head exploding in a soft thump as the brain's juices burst to steam. The body took another step before collapsing to the ground.

Take that, Mom! If I was a loser, my unit wouldn't have survived as long as it has.

He immediately pulled towards another figure and sighted, as the timer hit zero and a phalanx of missiles began cascading in from his far left, washing across the enemy camp.

An unfelt line of dark juices dribbled down lips and chin, the gun a constant hum of activity.

*   *   *

"And I'm telling you, it's *not* the entire MMSS. It's the DI's connection to the leg's MCU!"

Kisho watched, almost bemused, as the two technicians stood face-to-face, chests heaving and trying to throw around an authority only they felt. They should be wearing Falcon green.

"Do not throw your Spheroid vulgarity at me, *surat*," the larger, slightly pot-bellied man spoke evenly; no show of emotion compared to the outburst from the thick-limbed, taller female. Yet the stubble on the man's closely shorn head practically vibrated from the effort.

He will move to violence first if it comes to it.

"I am telling you," he continued, "I checked those connections. The DI subsystems ran through five complete diagnostic cycles with no indicators outside normal parameters. It *is* the MMSS."

Kisho glanced around the interior of the 'Mech repair bay of the *Nearstar,* the hustle and bustle of activity swirling around, as he tuned out the babble of the technicians momentarily. *Will it ever end?* Despite apparent visions. Despite the visit of Kev Rosse and the apparent "mission accomplished" of the task handed out by the old man, the raids continued. Another ambush and two more empty reprisals followed a slight victory by the Combine forces.

The raids continued. The doubts continued.

He reached up a hand and began to scratch at three days' growth on his chin. The dark looks from Tanaka did not dissuade him from working on a beard, though the man's very walk sang of walls and hiding. Kisho yanked the hand away as though bitten. *I am not hiding. I am cultivating an image. If Kev can create such a charismatic image with his wild mane, then why not a mystic?* He smiled darkly, knowing the words rang hollow.

He turned back to the squabbling technicians and took a step forward. They instantly ceased their arguments, turning with bows and the proper salute for respect. "I do not care what you think is wrong with my *Wendigo.* I *will* have it repaired by tomorrow. You understand, *quiaff*?" His voice never ventured beyond a soft tone, but it sliced into the two techs, causing them to flinch.

"*Aff,* Mystic," they intoned in unison, immediately bowing low once more and retreating back to the leg with its armor plating stripped back, like an insect pinned to an entomologist's desk, insides bared. For a moment, it almost made the *Wendigo* look embarrassed.

Kisho sighed heavily, turned away, and carefully made his way through the bulk of the repair bay, then into the bright sunlight, eyes squinting against the harsh light as he began to descend the ramp. The bustle of activity outside mirrored that within. *Is this all worth it?*

Worth it for me?

The questions plagued him night and day. They were a constant thrum of low-level static that seemed to eat at the bandwidth of his concentration. The final question seemed a subsonic perturbation running through every thought, a clarion call so constant it almost became invisible, until jarred by another thought.

Feet struck hard-packed dirt, and he leveled out and began walking towards the command tent. A sound snaked through the air, snapping his head to the right. He hesitated, on the verge of running back to the *Wendigo,* walking problems or not, just as the Balac VTOL burst over the foliage canopy, angling in for a steep descent, the dragon symbol large on its side. Wind whistled between teeth. *Not another assault. Not another . . .*

His thoughts trailed off as the Balac swept into the clearing, a cyclone of detritus whipping through the area. Fresh bullet holes and a carbonized slash from an energy weapon spoke of recent combat. Very recent.

Heedless of the spinning blades, Kisho raced towards the craft just as it touched down. From the corner of his eye he caught sight of Tivia emerging from her tent, beginning to move towards the Balac, albeit at a more sedate pace. A Combine soldier leapt out of the door, tangling with the wired headset before he wrenched it off and tossed it back through the door, then moved towards Tivia, but Kisho intercepted.

"What has occurred?"

The man looked Kisho up and down, then moved past without a word or a hitch in stride. Kisho balled fists against the impertinence, then clenched further as he followed the man towards Tivia. After a dozen paces the soldier met the Star colonel and immediately spoke.

"Star Colonel, our command has been attacked."

"What casualties?"

"Twenty-five, including seven warriors before we could rally. That includes *Tai-i* Jing Smith."

Kisho stiffened at the news. Once again, the audacity of this Bannson Raider upped Kisho's respect another notch. Yet, simultaneously, the blow of losing Smith sparked resentment. Not over the warrior's death—the reaper came when it would to a soldier. No, resentment because they'd not finished their own personal battle. One more failed task. He abruptly feared to peer behind him, for the trail of failed and broken tasks, of shattered promises, stretching like a cemetery line of crosses marching into the distance.

"Perhaps we were wrong to keep our command centers separated." Tivia's voice brought him back.

The Combine soldier nodded, as though unsure what to say.

"Do you need assistance?" she continued.

The soldier bobbed his head, as though on a string, nerves finally coming through. "Acting *Tai-i* Tolin requests additional forces to resecure the area."

Tivia glanced in Kisho's direction; though she made no real eye contact, facial tics and cant of shoulders screamed disappointment. *A failure for me and a failure for you,* quiaff, *Star Colonel?* He tried to find anger but only found a disappointment as deep and bottomless as the black hole at the center of the galaxy. Over his shoulder, the sound of another cross being raised echoed loudly.

"We need to stop this. Now. Mystic, please find Mystic Tanaka and inform him of this situation. We will need his advice."

Because mine no longer suffices? The idea and dismissal burned, but not as much as the truth of the matter. He nodded sharply, turned, and stalked towards the mystic's quarters.

As though in a haze, he walked without understanding. *I have lost my way. I have lost everything. Why am I here? I fail and every day that failure becomes more evident. Any day they will drag me from sleep and toss me to the wolves, declaring my fraud. My heresy.*

Of their own volition, his feet carried him to Tanaka's tent. "Mystic," he said curtly, through teeth unwilling to give ground, despite the growing certainty of an eventual loss. Silence greeted his call.

Anger grew. *No need to be rude,* Mystic. *You hate me, but there are forms to follow, even for us.* "Mystic," he finally repeated, voice rising. Another half minute. "Mystic." Just this side of a yell, as the anger boiled to a gout of steam and he yanked aside the tent flap and entered . . .

. . . to fall back outside to his knees, chest heaving, eyes wide, hands shaking, stomach heaving and mouth sucking at moisture to keep the vomit at bay, mind wiped clean of all thoughts but one: *how?*

The liters of blood and horribly dismembered body of Mystic Tanaka did not faze him. As with *Tai-i* Smith, death came to everyone, warriors most of all. But this struck a nerve, hit at something lying at the core of Kisho's lack of faith, yet never given voice, for the pain was too much. Nightmares rustled with black wings and hooked teeth.

If I am a mystic and am supposed to see the path forward, how did I not foresee Tanaka's death? How did Hisa not see it with all of her faith and come to ward this blow? How did the Oathmaster not foresee it?! A small voice spoke from a far corner of his rapidly darkening mind that the old man well might have seen it, but chose a path regardless. It was a voice easily lost to the cacophonic shrieking of a hundred different questions and exclamations that paralyzed him. Kisho's calloused, trembling fingers gripped his face painfully, blocking out sight as though hoping to block out the inner eye as well.

How?!

22

Kaona Island
Wandessa Chain, Athenry
Prefecture II, The Republic of the Sphere
23 October 3136

"**H**ow did this happen?" Tivia demanded, rigid figure looming over the entryway to Tanaka's tent.

"I do not know," Kisho mumbled, lips numb as the rest of his body.

"Of course you do not."

Though she spoke softly, so as not to carry to any of the others standing close, a Gauss pistol between the eyes would have been less painful. He flinched, though he responded before he could stop himself. "*Savashri.* I am a mystic, not a psychic."

Her cold eyes found his and they stared at one another, no answers evident in either depths, before they both turned to take in the scene of death.

Two people in nondescript jumpsuits carefully

moved about the room, numerous tags already placed. The constant strobe and whir of a holocamera knifed into Kisho's off-kilter equilibrium, threatening to over-balance him, cleaving him in twain on the sword of his nightmare. The other moved slowly, head canting to different angles as though seeing things only he could perceive: a smear of blood (head canted slightly to the left); an amputated leg below the knee, pants meticulously cut, but flesh mutilated (head canted over to the right); palms viciously lacerated, fingers un-touched, clean (head canted to the right until ear al-most touched shoulder)—all while talking into a handheld recording device in a voice too soft for any-one else to discern. Every few minutes both men would retreat to a large toolboxlike container—they called it a forensic kit?—and retrieve some item, which they put to use in a way only they might fully understand.

"Civilians," he muttered. *We allow civilians to touch a mystic?*

"These are not civilians," someone said.

Kisho turned slightly to find the helicopter pilot who originally brought word of the assault on the Kurita encampment. After the man became aware of the situ-ation and Tivia dispatched a force to secure the area, a brief discussion between the two sent the Balac loft-ing into the growing darkness, only to return less than twenty minutes later. Kisho barely managed to regain his feet at that point, as the pilot, Tivia, and two casu-ally dressed men immediately sequestered the tent and went to work.

"ISF."

Kisho immediately looked again and swore vehe-mently, causing Tivia to glance his way in annoyance before resuming her own vigil, while the pilot started and took a step back.

How could I miss the signs? Death hanging on their sleeves, despite the conservative look and low-key demeanor. Though all too easy to blame the shocking events of Tanaka's death on Kisho's ongoing struggles, the laughter of the dead mystic mocked from the grave. Despite all that had occurred, *he* would not have missed such obviousness.

Internal Security Force. Of course the Combine would have attached such individuals to the Dragon's Fury as a consequence of the coordinator's support. Not DEST—no, the elite commandos would be *too* much support. But a few nondescript individuals placed here and there, bringing their unique skills, when needed. After all, who thought to include any of our own Watch intelligence personnel?

The coppery tang of blood wallowed in the room like a beached and bloated whale on a too-bright summer's day, despite the rapidly cooling twilight. He swallowed, tongue too thick.

And even if they were here, would they be up to this type of investigation? Who would have thought it would be needed?

"The Raider. He will pay."

His internal dialogue continued, then stuttered to a halt as Kisho finally understood her statement. "No," he got out before thinking.

"No?" Her response came low, as cool, challenging eyes sought his. "And how, Mystic, do you know this?" The gauntlet slapped hard and ringing into his face, before falling to the ground.

How do I know? Some vision? Anything? No. Of course not. Nothing at all. But still . . . "He would not do this."

She cocked her head, as though examining an all too weakened animal, ready for the slaughter. "Did he not just assassinate a half dozen people with a laser rifle? Please, let me know of your vision, so that we can know how to proceed. I am sure these *civilians* would be very appreciative."

Even *she* noticed. He sought anger and resentment, but found only emptiness. And a chasm growing by the minute, at her all too blatant words. *Will it happen now? Does she blame me for the loss of Tanaka? Has the time come to burn the heretic at the stake?* He bit his lips until blood threatened, desperately casting about for something. Anything. "It is a large step from a surgical strike to this monstrosity. If he would dare this, why wait until now? Why not begin weeks ago? A terror campaign of mutilations might work against a lesser military. He has no experience with Nova Cats."

She started to speak, then paused as her eyes took on a faraway cast, before she responded. "Perhaps, Mystic. Perhaps. But if not this Raider, then who?" Another blatant challenge.

Hisa! My walls are crumbling. Something seemed to be changing within Tivia. Her turning aside of obvious questions concerning Kisho's abilities, or even his commitment to the mystic caste, seemed to be at an end. Like a caged animal, his mind beat against bars, trying to find an escape. *I am undone. I am found out. I am . . .*

A sudden thought blossomed like a ray of sunlight piercing an endless, looming cloud bank, as his face unconsciously slackened and then resumed normalcy. He knew what he must do. Knew there could be no other choice, despite the consequences. They did not need him here; his constant failures were evidence enough.

He unstuck his tongue and spoke. "I must go on a vision quest."

Tivia looked startled for a moment, then anger thinned lips and raised eyebrows. "Now. You wish to go on a vision quest now?" She took a step towards him, closing the distance, latent violence shimmering along skin.

A calm spread like a cooling balm to enflamed skin. Aff. *This is what I must do.* The righteousness of his caste, missing for so many weeks, seemed to settle onto his shoulders like a mantle, while he drew up straight from the accustomed slouch of long, long days. As though fitting back into a role long unused— he ignored the inner clamor of questions still battering, despite the newfound resolve—a mask of arrogance morphed his features into cool detachment.

"I do not ask, Star Colonel," he began, voice stronger and more crafted than before he began the journey to The Republic. "A mystic goes on a vision quest when called."

Despite misgivings as plain in the set of her shoulders and mouth as the blood-soaked ground behind her, long years of inculcation could not be ignored, especially in the face of Kisho's suddenly commanding presence. She slowly bowed in acquiescence.

He immediately turned away, booted feet slapping hard dirt, mind already casting towards his ultimate destination. Usually a vision quest meant long hours or days of contemplation to determine where to proceed, and might last weeks, if not months. But he already knew. Knew where he must go to find a vision. To find help.

To find . . .

23

Bannson's Raiders Bivouac
Athenry, Prefecture II
The Republic of the Sphere
1 November 3136

Damn you, Mother.

Captain Josef Yoland rearranged his jewels (wouldn't think about the crotch rot), while chewing savagely on the end of a well-worn pen—three hundredth time trying to quit bacco and it looked like this time he might actually succeed. 'Course, had nothing to do with him trying.

Oh, no.

Had everything to do with this stinking hellhole of a planet and eating weeds 'cause foodstuffs were almost completely gone and just trying to find potable water was becoming impossible and when you raided the enemy, you actually grabbed ammunition and spare parts and left the food, because you only had so much time in an objective raid and the enemy would kill you quicker than starvation if your autocannons ran dry or the giant rents in your armor weren't patched and you had to choose the lesser of two evils and when it came to bacco, it'd become so scarce it might as well have been caviar passed out by the high-and-mighty exarch himself. Last wads he'd scavenged, he ended up handing out to men in the makeshift hospital they'd set up. They deserved it more than him, after all.

He peered at the map spread before him, with pieces of dirty, worn, and torn paper dotting the landscape like forgotten memories, numbers of known attackers and defenders scribbled with the pen he just knew would run out of ink any second, trying to find the light of day, ignoring the now continual stomach rumblings and the bone-creaking strain of too many long weeks without adequate sleep.

Damn you, Mother.

"We're done, Cap," Ben said, his short summation a knife through the never-ending tangle of thoughts spiraling in a tight circle in Josef's head.

He glanced over at his right-hand man to find light blue eyes and that ever-ready-to-make-you-smile angel pasta the man called hair. But this time the usual mirth was lacking and the hair actually looked as if it'd gone thinner in the last few weeks. Josef ran a tired hand through his own hair, feeling the grime and grease caked in after a week without a shower (water given to the wounded who needed it). *Is it thinner as well?* Could almost feel it, as he leaned forward once more on the rickety table, slightly bemused—in a totally exhausted sort of way—that the table actually survived everything they'd gone through.

"Yeah," he finally coughed out, rancid bile piling up on the back of his tongue at the admission.

Silence took the room, broken by the sounds of camp around the makeshift tent, as they both studied the inevitability of it all. Regardless of their brilliant and unorthodox tactics, Kurita and the Nova Cats simply had the forces to win in an attrition fight, even with the decapitation they gave the damn snakes. And that's what it had become.

"Shit."

"You said it, Cap."

"How long?"

Shoulders slumped.

"That bad, eh?" Josef tried for a half smile and some levity, but Ben's blue eyes reflected only darkness. Captain Yoland slowly shook his head, returning to the map, but finding no solace. He began to pace in the small confines of the tent.

You cursed me, Mother. Damn you. Go ahead and fall into your hole. I'll find it later and water the weeds. A stale, hot breeze ruffled his too-long hair, scraping harshly across sandpapery dry skin. He stopped midstride, and revulsion rippled through him as realization dawned.

I don't smell it. The vile, sulfur stink of this place. He'd become accustomed to it. He'd actually gotten used to it.

He slammed his fist several times into his thigh in rage, turning to face Ben. "We've got to leave this place."

The other man leaned back from the table, scratching perpetually sweat-soaked hair while a small, almost wounded smile finally morphed lips out of a weeks-long grimace. "Um, Cap, you want to tell me how we going to do that? In case you hadn't noticed, we got no DropShip and Bannson doesn't take too kindly to deserters."

"Fuck Bannson," he said, fury making him shake.

Ben shrugged, as though it was no big deal to him, but he still scratched at his head—his telltale he was still worried. "Okay," he responded, pulling out the word like long taffy.

Josef continued pacing, fixing his eyes on Ben as though to hammer his points home with the laser precision with which he'd executed the Combine officer. "Bannson's deserted *us*. Left us here to rot and die while he's banging some Capellan whore. Good men who signed up for his dream of equality of the masses against the nobility. And now he's shacked up with one? Time to cut our losses."

"Okay," Ben once more drawled out, not sounding completely convinced, but still he moved on. "We still got to get off this rock. And when we do, what then?"

"What then? The universe is at war, my friend. And though we've taken a beating, we've got hardened troops here. Veterans all, baptized by fire in a way few commands are nowadays. Mercenaries are already in high demand and that demand's only going to increase. How does Yoland's Raiders sound?"

Light blue eyes rose a shade from their sheathing darkness, head slowly nodding as though possibly warming to Josef's idea, before a soft chuckle shook Ben at the name. "That still leaves the problem of getting off this rock."

"There're two DropShips right now on this rock."

"Okay."

"Ben, if you say that one more time, I'm going to stick my foot up your ass until you can taste the dirt on my boots."

They both shared a tired chuckle, but a laugh regardless, the second from Ben in one day! The sound was a precious commodity. "So, we just going to take one?" Ben finally responded.

"Yup."

Ben looked at Josef speculatively, then slowly nodded, as a true, mischievous smile peeked through endless thunder clouds.

"Okay."

24

Outskirts of Memphis
Epimethius, Styx
Prefecture II, The Republic of the Sphere
5 November 3136

"**W**hat have you done?" Hisa whispered.

Kisho breathed deeply, teeth clenched tight. The aches from the pounding gravities of the last twelve days felt like someone had taken a myomer-synching wrench to the length and breadth of his body. At one point he almost relented, allowing the DropShip crew to pull back on the terrible and constant thrust pushing relentlessly against their bodies with two standard gravities of weight. But something pushed, demanding he cut down on travel time as much as possible. And when a mystic requests, most Nova Cats take it as the most strident demand.

Yet all that paled into insignificance next to the horror in her voice. The horror that twitched muscles until he closed eyes against her unbridled reaction to his sudden appearance at her tent flap.

"Kisho, what have you done?"

He searched for words to describe the burning need to come, to speak, to find. But only a vast stretch of desert met an inner eye where once an oasis of firm decision and coherent thoughts flowered. Words died unspoken.

"How could you leave your command? How could you leave another mystic's body to be overseen by any but another mystic?"

"Tivia will oversee it." He wished the words back as soon as they fell into the room.

"But you were there. You are a mystic. It was *your* responsibility."

"A vision . . ." He began, opening eyes, only to trail off at the anguish effusing every magnificent line of her face.

"But you do not . . ." She trailed off as well.

"What?!" he demanded, stepping fully into the Spartan enclosure for the first time. The tent flap cut off the harsh yellow-white sunlight and the far-off sounds of sporadic gunfire as Republic guerillas tried once again to retake a portion of Memphis.

"Believe." Her soft voice a shocking contrast to the anger of his response. "You do not believe. You said so yourself."

The words stuck like shredding shivs from a needler—splitting, painful. He longed to touch her mouth, to smooth away the sorrow marring soft lips, but knew they mirrored his. "I need . . ."

"What?" Though spoken softly, she remained rigid, as though keeping taut against emotions raging within. "You need faith?" She slowly shook her head. "Do you not feel the déjà vu? This conversation repeating itself again and again? How many times can we speak of the same thing, Kisho?"

"Until I understand!" The tension of wracked emotions and physical exhaustion enveloped him, until he sank to the floor. To have come all this way, only to find . . . nothing. To find loathing from the one who should understand.

She swayed forward, as though to take a step, then snapped back into a stiff stance. "That is what is wrong, Kisho. That is where you fail every time. You try to understand. And there *is* no understanding. It either is, or it is not. As I have said before, you search and search for something, never realizing it is within and has always been there. You cannot find it. You cannot understand it. You simply accept, and believe. And it will grow."

"But what is it?!" he growled, pounding fists into already-tired leg muscles until tears tracked down his cheeks. Only with Hisa would he show such weakness.

"I cannot tell you. You have to find it for yourself."

"Savashri!" he yelled, the pain of the moment clouding out the emotions held dear for the one person who seemed to accept him, despite everything. "You *will* not tell me!"

Hisa mirrored his tears, her head slowly canting forward until salty drops hung on the end of her nose, splashing silently to the uncaring floor. "I have shown you, Kisho, but you will not listen. I do not know what else to do. You will not understand."

"And Tanaka did?!" Loathing coated words he could not stop himself from speaking.

She did not respond, or even look up, but simply turned away. The act seared, a universe-sized firebrand to burn him away. Of all the people to turn away from him. *Of . . . all . . . the . . . people!*

He bit his tongue until it bled to keep from spitting any more hateful words. Trembling with emotion, he staggered painfully and almost fell out of the door flap, heading towards a small one-man tent already assigned to him at the other edge of the encampment.

Visions! Savashri. *There are no visions,* surat. *There is not truth to find! There is only fumbling in the darkness, naivety and stupidity. I follow an urge to come and she turns away from me in disgust. Disgust! My fault for beginning to believe.*

The shouts of a technician as the man swerved a J-37 transport out of the way to avoid crushing Kisho went unheard as he stumbled on—glassy-eyed, slack-jawed, unhinged. Kisho finally found the designated area at the outskirts, crouched down, and bumbled into the tent, collapsing to the ground fully clothed. He welcomed the oblivion of sleep too long denied.

A fantastical field of white flowers (cherry blossoms?) spreads in all directions, stretching to a distance he should not be able to see. Yet each petal, each green stem leaps to sight as though he cradles every one in upturned palms. In the middle (yet there is no middle, or sides, and he is not in the middle, but above, or under) a massive throng of outlandish creatures cavort: proud, graceful, sanguine nova cats; ethereal chimeras with strong, feline features; dragons, yet not dragons, stunted, dull of eye and scale. Some lie, heads together in animal camaraderie, others lapping the morning dew from petals, chewing stems; carnivores turned herbivores. Yet something dark and foreboding stirs and strikes. Something of blackness and malevolency, eyes burning, stirs the creatures to anger and sudden savagery. The ethereal cats and pseudodragons ignore one another, falling famished on sweet nova cat meat. Crimson stains white fields in defilement, while whiskers flick unconcernedly, split eyes casually blinking, tips of pink tongues tasting air, while scales and ghostly claws rend flesh and devour it with the sounds of snapping bones and crunching cartilage. Feline lips spread in all too human smiles as they die, unaware . . . and the ghostly felines and stunted dragons begin to choke and die, leaving a perversion and corruption.

Horror ballooned until he could not breathe. He thrashed awake, bruised muscles screaming outrage. He rolled over and sat up shaking, chest heaving as though he'd run the entire night through. He shook his head, tried to work moisture into a sand-filled mouth.

This was a new dream. Something different. Unlike the old nightmares of youth, or the new nightmares of his own impending doom, this left an echo of others. Of events all around him. More importantly, as his breathing slowed and the adrenaline finally stopped pumping, allowing his pulse to return to normal, it stayed with him. Except for the single waking dream, the immediacy of all his nightmares passed quickly, leaving only a fragmented memory dropping away like a forgotten promise.

But this. This was different. A clarity sang within him. A clarity akin to the ambush on the river. A knowledge that seethed with assurance. With pure understanding. Not with an understanding of what it meant or what it might become. But with the knowledge that it *did* mean something. Something important.

Once more in a daze, as though following an endless, circular set of footsteps, he struggled to his feet in the predawn chill and made his way quickly towards Hisa's tent. He stopped abruptly, the hurtful words of last night piercing the growing elation. An elation that perhaps he might have found something.

She will forgive. She will! He staggered on, desperate to speak of his vision. To share it before it might evaporate and turn into a lifetime of rationalizations. He was so tired of it all. So desperate to have what every other mystic seemed to have.

Faith.

Without thought he crossed the threshold, slapping the tent flap aside. "Hisa!" He tripped over something on the floor, falling headlong towards the ground, hitting his head against something hard and angular. Stars burst bright and flashing, setting a bell ringing like a 'Mech fist to an armored chest, vibrating through him until he felt his teeth might shatter. Rolling into a sitting position, he felt something lumpy beneath him. A disquiet awoke.

"Hisa." The timorous voice sickened, but he could find no strength, as another *knowing* inundated his senses until the room seemed as ethereal as the felines from his dream. Eyes adjusting to the darkness, a slight shifting of light through the partially ajar flap showed a face he did not recognize, and the disquiet wormed into alarm and déjà vu slid across his skin like oily mucus.

"Hisa." Desperation sent hands scrabbling in the darkness, when a sudden stickiness slicked his hands, eliciting a scream of anguish. After an instant's hesitation, he continued, until his fingers found recognizable contours and lips already cooling, flaccid and never again to bless him with a smile.

Annihilating anguish overcame him and pushed him into an oblivion he welcomed with open arms.

25

The Café, Sapporo
Kushiro, Ozawa
Prefecture III, The Republic of the Sphere
15 November 3136

And the café bustled around him. Waiters weaving around each other, in and out of tables and patrons, in perfect, choreographed steps, as though in a ballet. They delivered food, picked up empty dinnerware, took orders, filled glasses—the dance always moving.

The patrons ate at a snail's pace. After all, this was the best café on-planet (according to some, on any number of planets), requiring weeks if not months to secure a reservation. Sometimes even nobility could not use their influence to sway The List. A list the maître d' would likely keep in a secret pocket in a shirt in which he slept. And he likely would sleep in a separate bed, so he wouldn't talk in his sleep and let The List slip to his wife. She'd tell someone, after all. He would know that.

And the food? Exquisite. Absolutely fantastic. To die for. Chefs rivaling any within two jumps of Ozawa. Chefs chained to stoves, performing culinary master-pieces night after night. Best of all, you could not slot the food (no, too mundane a word—cuisine, yes, that was the only word that came close) into a single cate-gory. It was not ethnic, nor world- or even House-based. Instead, the café presented a unique melding of every type of culinary treat you might find on a half hundred different worlds blended into a matchless dining experience.

And the ambience? Par excellence. The neo–art deco surroundings combined with a strange, almost primal mosaic of multicolored, glazed flagstones, all set off by basalt tables. The visual feast served eyes as starving for high culture as the stomach for cuisine. All taking place on a large patio ten stories above the crowded, obnoxious streets below, providing for an extraordinary outdoor dining experience under the stars.

And rain? Oh, never fear. Only the best for *this* café. A state-of-the-art ferroglass retractable cover, with a hydrophilic coating that reduced surface tension to smooth the raindrops into a tumultuous fall of liq-uid, creating a look as though eating underneath a waterfall, complete with sensory and auditory stimulus to accompany the experience.

And so people took their time eating, savoring each morsel as though it were their last. Knowing too many plain, boring dinners would fill the space until their next visit.

And it never hurt to have the patronage of some of the brightest stars on-planet, and one or two of the most powerful nobles (didn't seem to matter that it was *owned* by those same individuals). Thus it was not simply the fantastic food (it was), or the stunning ambiance and location (because none rivaled it), but the driving need to be *seen* at the café . . . *that* was what made it all work.

And work well.

Tuli smiled, the fork presenting the flash-grilled pink Angol fisherpike to his mouth like a sacred offering. The smile only grew wider as the juicy morsel exploded with a wild assortment of flavors, flashing sparks of hot and even cold along the tongue and quickly bringing a light sheen of delicious sweat to the brow.

But the food, the friendly bustle, the whole experience, was not what brought a satisfied smile to his face. Instead, the holoreader on the table, generating a discreet window for his solitary perusal, brought an almost real joy.

Though half a dozen such devices were scattered across basalt tables throughout the patio, allowing other solo diners to review work proposals, read the latest bestseller, do homework, or whatever else the mundane might fill their days with, he was well aware his work fell outside the norm.

Well outside.

He smiled wider, knowing the next forkful of delicate fish flesh would assuage any concern over a solo diner smiling widely. The beauty of such readers was that the projection required a person to not only be viewing it at a perfectly perpendicular ninety degrees to the reader, but the viewer had to be within a half meter. If either criteria was not met, then it simply appeared as a ghostly white outline, an ethereal frame for whatever the eye might see beyond.

And he was careful. Always careful.

And so, even if someone did happen to catch a

glimpse (those too-efficient waiters), all they'd get was an eyeful of a few paragraphs of a novel. Not a bad little bit of trashy romance mixed with Solaris VII intrigue. Never mind the writer had obviously never even set foot on Solaris, much less dodged gangs, police, and the underworld—not to mention that damn Toorima monstrosity that "escaped" into Kobe's sewer system a few decades back—in Solaris City's nightlife. And never mind the writer made the bad assumption so many of his kind made day in and day out. After all, assassins (at least the good ones) didn't hide out in slums, or live out of trashed flophouses, with drug addicts and whores for company. Could that be more obvious?! If one went looking for a rat and found one in a rat hole, bingo. Deader than a yak getting his hands on someone after they insulted his oyuban. But if the rat hid in plain sight? Better yet, if the rat hid amongst the gentry, with their preening and their foppish ways and their beliefs that anyone with the money and the looks and the panache to join *their* crowd couldn't possibly *be* anything but what he seemed to be? Well, then, one would be hard-pressed to find the rat, wouldn't they?

The smile tweaked a hair higher as he deciphered the code imprinted into the off-the-shelf e-novel, while secretly mocking everyone within eyeshot.

Geisha's gossamer wings.

The lead-crystal glass from New Rhodes III refracted the candlelight and discreetly placed lamps around the perimeter in an otherworldly mesh of unimagined colors as he raised the chardonnay to his lips. The horrifyingly expensive Harrow's Sun Winter Harvest 3130 dusted his tongue with a wonderful blend he failed to experience fully as he churned over the unusual nature of the activation phrase.

Not the Geisha, but her wings? For several long

minutes, not a facial tic or change of emotion marred Tuli's composure as he casually reread several pages, as though the experience of the dinner had actually drawn his attention away from the novel, something he knew had happened to four people that evening alone. The waiter came and went, the last of his meal was consumed, and the dessert menu discreetly placed, while he verified what the targets would be. Not the geisha. But those she sought to solicit for aid.

He clucked his tongue lightly, remonstrations against his presuppositions of what the boss wanted. Many man hours lost. Time equaled money in his line of work and wasting time was a graver sin than any he could think of.

He slowly stood to instantly find a waiter at his elbow, obsequious in his desire to make sure Tuli enjoyed his dinner (of course, yes, wonderful as usual, thank you, of course I will come again, my compliments, yada, yada), before leading the way out, as though he might have forgotten the way over the fabulous cuisine. No vulgarity of public payments here—if you were on The List, of course, you usually paid in advance with a carte blanche.

Stepping lightly into the elevator, his mind accompanied the descent in a dive down another vertical shaft, into a lifetime of training and technique, as he began preparations to visit several people who needed special attention. The elevator gave a microbounce as it settled, the doors whisking open, and he moved past a phalanx of security guards and cameras into the dank, musty night that enveloped him in dark arms that welcomed him home.

He consoled himself that his hours of preparation to aid the geisha out of this life could lie fallow for any amount of time before he picked them up again . . . if needed.

26

Fists of Truth, Broadsword-*class* DropShip
Orbital Insertion, Athenry
Prefecture II, The Republic of the Sphere
25 November 3136

"Where am I?" he managed to get out. Urgency echoed latent in words, budded behind every confused muscle spasm.

"You are on the *Fists of Truth,* Mystic," a voice said.

Fists of Truth? His brain felt trapped in a pool of cooling molasses—the congealing mess making it difficult, if not impossible, to think at all, much less in straight lines. The world shook.

DropShip. The world slowly filtered up through the morass, splitting open like a rotted fruit, splattering juices across his perceptions. He shivered as a kaleidoscope of memories and images rocked through him with more force than the vibrating DropShip making interface with the upper atmosphere. And through it all, urgency flowed like quicksilver.

"Mystic, do you need more medication?"

The words hesitantly seeped into off-kilter perceptions. A weighted *something* pushed against the sticky morass of consciousness, bursting memory bubbles in strobes of pyrotechnic brain activity. Calloused fingers gripped a brow furrowed with deep lines of hurt, confusion, and urgency until the sensations passed. He centered even more, coming up for a breath of fresh air as though he had lain drowning for long days, long weeks.

"No." He tried shaking his head to emphasize the point, but found it too much effort. "How long?" he croaked, then glanced up and saw a water bulb cinched to the bunk rail. He squirted the cool water—elixir to parched life—down a gullet that seemed to suck the moisture directly into cellular walls before it ever reached the stomach.

"Mystic?"

Perturbed, Kisho blinked rapidly, bringing the small berth into partial focus: white bed, rainy sea gray bulkheads, small medical computer bolted to the side of the bed, several wires and an IV running into different parts of his body. A diminutive medico with black, curly hair, swarthy face, bright, quizzical smile. His tongue scraped across salt-encrusted lips, tingling, and his throat worked convulsively, demanding more liquid. Despite the show of weakness, he shook the bulb and the medico immediately bent to a compartment underneath where he sat, cycled open a small compartment, extracted a new water bulb, and exchanged it for Kisho's. He downed another magnificent draught of fluid before continuing. "How long have I been out?"

"This time, you mean?"

For a moment the answer confused him, until a rapid series of bursting bubbles buried deep rose to the surface with flashes of the recent past: confusing bouts of desperate mania, interspersed with long periods of comatose inactivity. Demands for immediate transport back to Athenry. Demands carried out by Nova Cat personnel stunned over the death of a mystic and the apparent psychotic episode of another. And behind all of that, visions and memories of visions to send a man stark raving mad. An endless chiaroscuro of the mind, threatening to thrust up from its mundane flatness and flare to a three-dimensional reality that would tear free of its origins, becoming an all-consuming entity, first devouring its creator, then exploding in an orgy of rapid, grotesque growth to devour everything . . . everyone.

Trembling like a leaf in a brisk winter wind of need, waiting for the sudden snap and jerk dislodging him from the reality of the tree branch and sending him to a fluttering, aimless death, as the red leaf at his meeting with Kev Rosse, he spoke in an effort to secure his world. "What is the date?"

"The twenty-fifth."

Words trembled on lips, afraid for utterance, but knowing no choice. "Of November?"

"Of course, Mystic."

Kisho need not see the medico's face to hear the confusion. Despite the show of weakness, a sigh shuddered from lips almost numb with confusion, exasperation, but behind it, still a desperate exigency. *How has it come to this? Can I lose myself so completely?*

"What did I order?"

"Mystic? Just now?"

"No!" he said, blazing eyes raised to pin the medico to the bulkhead. The other man flinched back as though struck. "On Styx," Kisho spit out. "What did I order?"

"That you be transported back to Athenry as soon as possible."

"And?"

"And that if we made contact with any Spirit Cats, to treat them as hostiles."

The words triggered a sensory overload, sweeping him momentarily from the present to the past and back. Then he slowly leaned back into the angled bunk with a sigh.

I remember now.

Kisho leaned against the bulkhead after the short trek from the medical berth, cool metal a firm reality against uncompromising, betraying flesh. *I am not physically wounded and yet I move like a babe!* Words from the old man seemed to waft through a seething mental landscape: "Mental wounds can be more debilitating than any physical infirmity, while an alert, perceptive, and willful mind can overcome any bodily ailment."

Left palm against a metal stanchion, the rumbling of the ramp finishing deployment vibrated through his boot soles, tingling, while the boom of the locking mechanism echoed through the small 'Mech bay on the *Broadsword*-class DropShip. Kisho's hand traced the formal uniform of a mystic, stopping to feel the ivory stav of his rank and the small bas-relief of a young life—a life that felt as aged as a continental shelf. The minute images gave way to a mostly barren, smooth plane of off-white.

Potential. The word vibrated with power, yet pierced with pain. Will a bas-relief soon mark that surface showing the death of two mystics? The death of two mystics and once more the failure of the third? Another cross for the road behind.

Hisa!

Despair and loathing warred in equal measure, pulling relentlessly at self. Only a burning need for revenge kept him sane and rooted. Only an understanding of who killed Hisa and Tanaka. Of who likely tried to kill him, but Hisa proved more than the hired assassin bargained for. *You were always more than anyone bargained for, least of all me.*

The pain of loss brimmed until the desire to kill swam through his reddened vision. *The only person to understand me. Gone.*

A new sound intruded as the hot, sticky, despised air of Athenry reached through the widening bay door to welcome everyone with a moist slap and a sulfuric bouquet. *Not now. Grief will come. Not now.* With an effort, he straightened, drawing strength from that thought, and from the Mystic clothing not worn in so long.

He began walking down the ramp, and found Tivia already waiting. As expected. But he refused to cave under her shocked, questioning look. Eyes all too perceptive and piercing. Despite questions still brimming, the urgency of vengeance covered any doubts in a mountain of immediacy. Until blood washed his hands, any self-doubt would go unanswered.

He stopped at the end of the ramp, a step above Tivia, and met her stare for stare. The movement of other Nova Cats down and up the ramp made no impression as the two towering wills sought dominance. Finally, too many years of indoctrination forced Tivia to give, bowing and raising a hand to form the circular motion of respect. "Mystic. You have returned from your journey."

"*Aff.*And now I require leave and a small force to pursue my vision."

Eyebrows climbed until they seemed to disappear into her hairline, while doubts lay bare across her face and body posture. "You wish to take a force and depart Athenry? While we have yet to pacify this world? *Quineg.*"

"*Aff,* Star Colonel. *Aff.*" He poured every ounce of will learned across a brutal, inhuman upbringing; his voice was strident and looming with mystic authority. "I know who has slaughtered the mystics and he must pay."

She canted her head for a moment, as though unwilling to bend, before responding. "And who is it?"

"Kev Rosse."

Her mouth dropped open as though he had just spoken the name of the mystic caste genemother. "Why would he do that? He was just here. We have offered him sanctuary. He agreed."

"*Aff,* he agreed. He agreed that he would tell his people. But tell his people what?"

She pursed lips, but did not respond, as the rumble of a 'Mech returning from what appeared to be a patrol entered the camp. Kisho waited until the pilot locked down the machine before continuing.

"The Nova Cats in The Republic have lived apart from us for generations. And Kev Rosse has successfully forged a new identity in the Spirit Cats. A slice of all castes have followed his lead, his commands. The corruption by power is not wedded to Spheroids alone."

She nodded, and the minute changes in muscles as she spoke told a story as clear as a holovid sign at twenty paces. "But we have no wish to subjugate them. They are welcomed back with open arms."

Are they? Despite the old man's words, doubts still worried, like scavengers at long-dead meat, at Kisho's mission of bringing all Nova Cats within The Republic back into the fold. He shook his head, at his own questions as well as Tivia's, though tension eased at the first real victory over Tivia. "It does not matter, because they do not know that. And in their world, every hand has been raised against them. Why should this be different?"

She scratched her head, then pulled at her ear in a decidedly uncharacteristic move. "But kill mystics." Not a question, but a statement. A statement from a Clansman born and bred to revere mystics. Despite her personal doubts of Kisho, her devotion deserved only respect. If only all Nova Cats held her commitment to the mystics.

"But they have not. And despite their ignorance, they must know the deaths would sow havoc among our forces in The Republic. Enough chaos and they can take advantage of the situation, either to attack, or to escape the entire region."

She mulled the words over, before reluctantly nodding in agreement. "I hear and understand your reasoning, Mystic. Where will you go to find him? He will be five jumps and more distant by now."

I have no idea. "Where my visions take me." He waited for the gag response, but it failed to materialize. Perhaps it became easier with time. Finally. *Or perhaps I am returning to the control of the game I held for so long?*

He stepped down beside Tivia and walked towards the command tent to begin the preparations.

27

Light in Darkness, Scout-*class JumpShip*
Pirate Point, Addicks
Prefecture III, The Republic of the Sphere
28 December 3136

"**H**ow much longer must we wait?" Captain Bulic said.

Kisho actually glanced up, wondering what had changed. *You did not grit your teeth, Captain. What has happened?* But he could find no outward sign, despite the captain's expansive ability to project his thoughts like bright halogens for even a blind man to see.

Kisho slowly set hands against the holoprojection table, and carefully—no disengaging mag-slips—pushed fully upright, bringing to bear the authority of the office he'd been using like an overcharged stun staff to bully everyone the last few weeks. "Until I say otherwise. *Quiaff*, Captain?"

The words hung in the air, a visceral challenge, which the captain appeared on the verge of accepting, before acquiescing with a minute nod, a sickly smile. A twist and a muscle spasm sent the man shooting towards the far side of the small bridge of the *Scout*-class JumpShip, as though something urgent suddenly called for his personal attention.

Right.

Mask still firmly in place, Kisho glanced back at the holovid and began running numbers once more. Something to do to pass the time. The ever-expanding infrared signature of the arrived JumpShip had passed their position days ago, but still they must wait for an affirmation of inbound DropShips. Addicks was surprisingly busy, and four JumpShips had already passed through, only one unlimbering a DropShip, but it proved innocent. Perhaps this would be the one. Perhaps.

"How many times can you run these numbers, Mystic?" Kopek said.

Kisho met his subordinate's question with hard eyes, but relented. Unlike the captain, whose challenge rode every word like a strangling viper, Kopek's honesty shone clear, bright—a real desire for an answer, not an excuse to pressure him into movement. "Until they appear, or the numbers generate a better percentage and we move."

"But you know how dangerous this is, *quiaff*?" The words came out on an even keel, without an ounce of fear. Simply a statement, by an observant subordinate. Not an admission of the mortal danger of the situation.

"*Aff.*"

"If we are found—"

"We will not be," Kisho responded, cutting the man off. He tapped into the console, sharpening the focus on the map lasers already projected in three dimensions: centered on the world of Addicks, which rode the border between Prefectures III and IV, three jumps from Athenry, and well outside any space currently claimed by the Draconis Combine. All the worlds within a jump sprouted into existence, as though multicolored measles popping up on ethereal, black skin. Kisho snapped a wrist towards the diagram as it began to rotate, and tags rolled into position, with system names, known jump points, standard travel and recharge times, and more.

"Ankaa, Heah, Deneb Kaitos, Small World, Errai, Towne, Ozawa. And that is not all, only the closest. And Warlord Katana's O5P intelligence, filtered through our own information and cross-referenced against known ISF information"—he cocked an eyebrow, eliciting a tight smile from Kopek at the reliability of *that* information to be uncensored for their use—"shows most of these worlds attacked and owned by multiple factions over the last few years. Spirit Cats. Steel Wolves. Highlanders. Even the warlord's Dragon's Fury. With the full assault of the Dragon, the continuing incursions of the raptors and House Liao, and now rumors of unrest within the government structure of The Republic itself? Do I need to draw a Clan warrior a larger illustration? *Quineg.*"

"*Neg.* But it is still dangerous. The warlord might find . . . issue."

"*Aff.* But that is the price I must pay."

"The price we will all pay."

He accepted the words and the responsibility, and spoke as though answering an unasked question. "The worlds have been stripped of forces. There is nothing here."

Kopek nodded slightly, accepting Kisho's distancing. "Nothing but Spirit Cats."

"Exactly. Spirit Cats. The message Kev bears is not something to be broadcast, or entrusted to even the closest confidants. Especially as his message will be one of betrayal and violence against us." The remembered pain awoke, stabbing out with piercing claws and hot blades, as though only yesterday the blood of Hisa slicked palms with wasted essence. He breathed raggedly, wrenching control over a raging, endless fire within.

"But we have been here almost three weeks."

"He could have made several stops."

"And yet he could have come here directly, then moved on. From what you have shown me, there are strong indications he has several Stars as far away as Prefecture VII."

Eyes pinned and cut, before Kisho could leash them. He did not challenge, or usurp the right of vengeance. Simple questions. Questions of a superior subordinate. Of a sudden, a need to extend a hand, even to a little-known inferior sparked. "If we survive this," Kisho began, licking lips against uncertainty and the strangeness of such overt action. "If we survive all of this, upon our return, I will nominate you for the next Trial of Bloodright for your Bloodname House."

The other man jerked back, almost unsticking his own mag-slips, before lashing out a right hand to secure himself. "Mystic . . . I . . ." He abruptly stopped and bowed low, keeping it well past that required for even the lowliest labor castemen for the highest mystic, much less two warriors.

"It is the least I can do for your solid support, despite all the . . . strangeness of the last months."

The other man slowly straightened. "You are Mystic." He said it as though it said it all. Yet a question shone bright in the other man's still-stunned eyes and several long moments passed before he found the courage to voice it. "Mystics are not known for their nominations. In fact, they are almost never known to nominate, regardless of their prerogative."

Very perceptive. He struck a half grin, tried to keep the eternal pain—no, a dull ache after so many years—at bay. "It is not something we talk about."

"That you can nominate a warrior to wed his genes into the breeding program, to perhaps even have their blood mixed with the hallowed First Mystic, and yet you can never gain a Bloodname yourself?"

Now Kisho's mouth dropped open momentarily, before snapping shut, anger knotting shoulders into a hunch, furrows rippling forehead.

The other man immediately bowed deeply, shame radiating from every muscle. "Mystic. I have spoken too much. On matters not worthy of me. I ask *surkai*."

And you should have it! Yet he stayed his hand, despite the desire to punish the impertinence. Thinned lips dropped back to a mocking wave. *You honor him for his perception, then seek to punish him because he uses it?*

"*Neg.* Let it pass. You will have my nomination if it comes to that."

An alarm began in the room, spreading from a dropped rock in the sudden still pool of the bridge. All eyes searched towards the blinking light, found it. Dead silence, beyond the noise, gripped the bridge in hasty impatience as the technician pored over incoming information before turning towards Kisho and nodding, a smile growing on his lips. "We have verified the drive emissions. It is him."

One part of his brain noted the man turned to him before his captain, which would only infuriate. Yet he did not care. Dreams of blood sang in the air, and Kev Rosse would pay.

"Let them begin interface, so their sensors will be nullified, then begin our own run to Addicks."

* * *

Kaona Island
Wandessa Chain, Athenry
Prefecture II, The Republic of the Sphere

Josef chewed on his lip, watching through binoculars as Lieutenant Collins piloted the VTOL into the lightly defended Dragon's Fury encampment. The old, dented Karnov UR Transport swung its twin turbo-props from a forward position slowly into a vertical one as it slowed after clearing the trees and began to set down.

Shit. I hate this. Dammit. Should be me, not that kid. But it was a plan. The best plan they could come up with. Even Ben agreed, damn him. After all, the snakes made the mistake of using local vehicles to ferry in supplies from other islands. And it took some time, but they finally managed to bushwack one of the pilots. Then a series of remote-controlled, jury-rigged tube-launching rockets and the last of their high-grade explosives, setting off the illusion of a light firefight at the edges of the kitties base, to draw their attention and pull reinforcements from the snakes' camp. And they'd long cracked their secure channels, so using the right transmission codes to land without raising eyebrows wasn't a problem. *'Course, after this, even the dense kitties would know we broke their codes. Then again, after this, it shouldn't matter.*

He wanted bacco so bad he wanted to start chewing on his hand, or capping snakes or kitties. Or Mom. Yeah, that would do. At least for a half day.

I should've given you that kiss, lieutenant. He balled up fists in anger and turned away from the landing VTOL, burying face (of course he wasn't crying) as landing gear touched well-packed dirt . . .

. . . and a detonation seemed to rattle the whole

island as five tons of handmade explosives turned the VTOL's metal skin into shrapnel slicing down personnel like a giant harvester even before the expanding ball of gas shattered bones and the firestorm after it stripped flesh and detonated stored supplies of ammunition nearby, creating an endless cacophony of confusion and death.

Already up and running—he *would* lead this charge, after Collins' sacrifice!—the team of infantry, honed by a year and more of guerrilla fighting, stormed the DropShip's deployed ramp (after all, the Raiders wouldn't dare attack the base so directly twice, especially when we're off fighting the kitties, right?), before anyone could even raise a weapon in response after the horrific damage of the explosions.

A whirling maelstrom of blood and dead flesh, much of it from his own troops, slicked deck plating before they gained the bridge in one final push. Panting, excited, yet grieving for those of his troops who would not leave this stinking hellhole, he tapped the command into his comm unit, giving the clear for the remaining vehicles and 'Mechs to rise out of a small arroyo only a kilometer distant and arrive, guns blazing, to finish off the last of the resistance.

He slowly sank down into the captain's seat as Ben entered the bridge, limping, a huge gash over his right eye. Despite everything, despite the urgency that still vibrated through all his men to evacuate before the other kitties' ship could lift off and intercept, they both shared a tired smile. It was over.

At least for now.

28

A pair of aerospace fighters thundered overhead like impending doom waiting to fall. *And I am that doom, come for you, Galaxy Commander.*

Through the forward viewscreen, Kisho made out a towering column of sooty, black smoke off to the far left, wending upwards many kilometers before shearing away under high, upper-atmospheric winds. They would not be escaping through their DropShip.

He remembered the feel, even from afar—sensors jamming all channels and ignoring the demanding, then frantic comm burst from the Spirit Cats—as fighter-borne laser and autocannon fire sliced through heavy armor, shattered the egg-shaped craft, secondary explosions vomiting balls of fire as ammo storage and fuel tanks detonated.

Yes, a good beginning.

The 'Mech jostled particularly hard, dropping slightly into an unseen depression, rattling teeth and bones, snapping his attention back to their rapid forward deployment. The legs of the *Wendigo* stabbed down and rended earth in great gouts of wet, flying chunks of sod and worms and insects, squirming with terrified alarm at the burst of light and movement. A good day for a battle. A very good day.

"Mystic," the voice of Alpha Flight's Point commander effervesced. "Spirits have been cornered. Quadrant forty-three by twenty-seven. Approximately twenty kilometers from your current position."

Fingers flew to switches and keys, toggling the radar and topographical maps, inputting the information. A red triangle—in a circle, for approximate known position—beamed balefully, as though it were an enigmatic eye, pushing back against the furious need of Kisho's revenge.

So close? "Verify, Alpha Flight."

"Verified, Mystic. Twice."

He let the exasperation pass without comment. *Are they turning around to meet us?*

"Mystic, we have them outnumbered. Why are they turning their formation?" That Kopek's words mirrored his thoughts did not surprise anymore. The man will make an excellent leader someday. He knows the questions to ask.

"I do not know." His mind mulled over several different scenarios while he subconsciously guided the *Wendigo* with pedals and slight adjustments to the throttle, as the Nova Cats raced across the rolling prairie, dotted with small lakes like brushes of crystal-clear sky meeting earth and an endless, blanket patchwork's worth of small farming settlements.

"Reinforcements?"

"Perhaps, though I do not think so. We have a clear accounting of their forces."

"It could be wrong, *quiaff*?"

"*Aff*, of course." He paused for a moment, face altering without conscious thought, as he plumbed the depths of his mind before answering further, wondering if the lies were becoming so easy they no longer felt like a lie. "It is not."

"*Aff*, Mystic." The tailored response of a believer, despite the heretic's costume worn for so many long, harsh months in the fires of The Republic.

"Alpha Flight," he said as he changed back to the fighter frequency. "Can you pin them in place?"

"Of course, Mystic. They are pinned. Though fuel levels are reaching critical and return fire has almost relegated my wingman to overflights."

"Understood." Ever conscious, despite the unquenchable thirst for blood that pushed him, Kisho managed to keep the ultimate goals of the Nova Cats within The Republic in mind. "Do not risk either fighter unnecessarily in pinning them down. If they break away, pursue as best able, before returning for refueling. *Quiaff*?"

"*Aff*, Mystic."

Silence descended as the fast-moving vehicles and 'Mechs loped across the ground, hungry felines scenting blood and prey cornered after too long a hunt. The heavy vibrations and the side to side movement as the *Wendigo* pounded along lulled Kisho fully into the moment, dousing the human side and pulling forth the animal locked within through millennia of civilized behavior.

But war is never civilized and mankind excels at it

*like nothing else. And we Clans take it to an art form
unlike any in history.*

Soon the tones of radar recognition at extreme
ranges—still well beyond weapon lock—hummed
through numerous 'Mech and tank cockpits. The fer-
tile ground, previously overflowing with an abundance
of wildflowers, grasses, and trees dotting the landscape
like overzealous mushrooms in a rain forest, even on
the uncultivated farmlands, slowly gave way to more
stunted growth as the ground began to rise sharply,
the water table falling away. Rocky patches appeared
as the malevolent eye of a single, large threat icon on
the screen shattered into multiple blips, like a stone
golem broken, yet reanimated into a host of smaller
demons, all threatening. *Your obakemono, KuritaYori-
san.* He chuckled darkly.

"The time has come, Mystic. We depart."

"Confirmed, Alpha Flight. Your efforts will not be
forgotten."

"Mystic," came the curt reply.

Just as the visual topography of the region began
to make sense, the aerospace fighters thundered back
overhead, on their way to the Nova Cat landing zone.

"This is why they halted."

Kisho nodded in agreement as the entire Nova Cat
contingent ground to a halt at the crest of a ridge. As
though falling from paradise to hell, the land before
them lay shattered, rocky, and dry; an endless expanse
of tortured arroyos, dead-end gorges and coulees,
ghastly steep ravines, and bracken-filled gulches. The
two tracked vehicles of his command were instantly
taken out of the fight, and even the hovercraft would
need to be careful through such terrain. No, he recon-
sidered. Taken completely out of it as well.

"Parak, Bordi . . ." he began, rattling through a half
Star of tank commanders. "You will deploy as pickets

along this line. Parak, you have the command. If possible, move your lines laterally up either side of these badlands, to try and hem them in. They will know our aerospace assets will be airborne once more within the hour to pin in the final fence. This is the hole they have chosen to die in."

The *"affs"* came with resignation, but knowing their duty, the vehicles immediately began to deploy, moving away from the binary of 'Mechs. Looking at the horribly scarred land—as though riven and eaten away by some terrible disease able to afflict soil and rock like perishable flesh—Kisho wondered if they might not get their chance to fight, regardless of their pessimism. *How long will it take us to hunt you down, Galaxy Commander? How long and will you try to make a break for it?*

Of a sudden, he toggled on a broadband frequency, selecting an open channel and deigning to speak to the Spirit Cats for the first time since entering Addicks' atmosphere. "Kev Rosse"—there would be *no* rank and honor given now—"we have tracked you to ground. You have soiled all that you have built with your Spheroid actions. Taking the life of warriors and mystics far above your station as they slept. The cowardice within you rots until the stink befouls the very air. Accept your burden of weakness and step forward to a Trial of Annihilation against you and any offspring that bear your genes, and your warriors will be spared, taken as *isorla*."

A full ten seconds passed before a grainy response came, full of fury and indignation. "*Savashri,* Kisho. What is this about? What are you talking about? Cowardice? Cowardice! You strafe my DropShip without a batchall? You ignore our calls and now dare call me out?"

You coat your voice well, but I know what I would

see if I beheld your face. "Do the lies come so easy? Have the years of your exile so perverted you?"

"I do not know what you speak of! And regardless, I hear the words you speak, Kisho. My warriors will be taken as *isorla,* not bondsmen. What have they done, what have I done that a warrior would take another and relegate him to a lower caste?"

The banked coals of revenge blazed until they towered, eating away at resolve and needed clarity, until breathing came in short gasps. *How dare you. . . . How . . . dare . . . you!* "You know what you have done," he spit through clenched teeth, saliva speckling the forward viewscreen. "If you will not face it, if your warriors will not accept the burden of bringing you to justice, then I announce a Trial of Annihilation against you and your entire command. And pray that I do not find such weakness means all Spirit Cat warrior bloodlines need to be reaved!"

Silence fell like a coffin into a grave at the pronouncement.

"You would dare offer trial to pare down our Bloodnames? All of them? At once?" Incredulity, despite the static snap and wash, flooded over Kisho.

"Aff." The word a hammer blow of bloodlust.

"Have you lost your mind? Have you gone rogue? If this is what a mystic is capable of, then why would we rejoin you? You are the ones who have fallen away!"

Kisho breathed deeply, closing eyes gummed with fatigue. Slowly clicked off the toggle switch to the channel, ignored the steady hum of repeated calls. *He will not listen. He is beyond reason.* Pulling hands away from joysticks, he clenched them together to stop the shaking. Finally he spoke on his command's frequency. "They are become dark caste. Beyond the bounds of *zellbrigen.* Fit only for destruction."

A moment's hesitation, before a subdued benediction and agreement swept back across the channel, sealing the declaration, *"Seyla."*

As his force bridged the crest and began to make its slow way down the steep incline, words tumbled within him like the jumbled and crushed stones bursting into smaller pieces under the heavy impact of fifty-five tons of metal death.

Were you so wrong, old man? Your visions for bringing the Spirit Cats back to the fold. He is corrupt. And by his corruption, he corrupts those who follow him. Will we Reave the Spirit Cats until blood flows as a torrent through The Republic, leaving our mission hollow? A failure?

The death of Hisa, the death of Tanaka; the failure to see this coming . . . for the old man to see it coming. The failure of the old man to see the defilement eating away at the Spirit Cats. Laughter, stark, harsh as solar wind in the depths of space, ripped through the cockpit, unknowingly floating onto airwaves, setting all who heard it on edge, as though the cackle of the ancient dead floated from musty graves, calling for those entering battle to join in the unending misery of the undead.

29

Felldowns, Frankalia
Addicks, Prefecture III
The Republic of the Sphere
30 December 3136

A godlike thunderbolt hammered into the ravine wall, pulverizing rock, sending a treacherous landslide cascading in a river of hard-edged death for the unwary. Another whip of azure energy burst forth from the barrel of the *Wendigo,* thrashing the wall once more, sending another flurry of sliding, bouncing, and jouncing stones down to block the deep gulch. Another two blasts filled the canyon to the point it would take even a 'Mech—provided it did not mount jump jets—precious long minutes to muscle through to freedom.

And you do not have jump jets, do you, Galaxy Commander?

Kisho's laugh sounded as hollow as the hole eating within him. This was the fifth such gap he closed, moving methodically. And, with a scientist-subcaste surgeon's dedication, he would eradicate the infestation of Kev and those who would support such a leader.

Turning away from the savage wound inflicted on the earth—too cold to notice, too focused to care—fingers wrapped throttles and joystick, booted feet connected to pedals, and the BattleMech began wending towards another target.

Before the 'Mech took twenty steps, a foul wind tore into the *Wendigo*'s right side, pitching the machine back. With a deft twist of controls and pedals, Kisho settled the machine back into a half step to regain balance as numerous long-range missiles shattered armor plating. Swiveling the upper torso back around, bringing targeting reticule and weaponry on line with the sudden appearance of an *Arbalest* less than a hundred meters away—stepping halfway out of an almost hidden arroyo branching off from the main trunk of this canyon—Kisho returned in kind.

A shotgun blast from his LB 10-X autocannon scoured away armor like a djinn in a raging sandstorm. Evil strobes of cobalt lighting, as though accompanying the djinn, caressed already damaged armor, sending tendrils of death seeping into gradually widening fissures. Support struts under armor plates across the torso, already pushed beyond survivable stress levels by several previous encounters, softened under the hellish energies of the particle projector cannon, then bent, and finally shore off. As a wash of black exhaust from another volley of twenty missiles leaping hungrily towards him almost obscured the target, Kisho ignored the incoming fire, centering on the newly revealed breach in the *Arbalest*'s defense and lining up another shot from the autocannon, and sent a terrible blast of hypervelocity flechettes straight into the 'Mech's heart.

A testament to the other warrior's acumen, most of the missiles found their mark, shaking the *Wendigo* as though in a heavy storm. However, the *Arbalest* began to dance as though in a palsy, as the gyro, engine, and central processing for myomer musculature all began to disintegrate, jerking the 'Mech in an obscene dance before dropping twenty-five tons of dead metal unceremoniously to the ground.

Kisho sighed with satisfaction, letting out a pent-up breath of adrenaline-choked energy.

And so the battle progressed as Kisho knew it would. In the tortured landscape, battle lines were nonexistent and coordinated attacks impossible. And yet, it seemed right. It *felt* proper. As though Kisho led the Nova Cats here specifically to show the Spirit Cats and their false leader how fallen they truly had become. As though the individual battles, just as that with the *Arbalest*, and the two previous encounters, would bring the Spirit Cats to their knees in awe. Would show them that they might follow the forms and speak the words, but they were as much Clansmen as mercenaries were House troops.

Setting the 'Mech moving once more, he stepped lightly around the smoldering ruin and took a half step into the artery. The arroyo moved erratically back and forth, until it bent out of view to the right, three hundred or so meters from his current position. Rubbing sweat-soaked and tired right-hand fingers and thumb together, he tried to decide which direction to follow.

"Where are you, Galaxy Commander?" he whispered softly, toggling through several secondary screens as he read known topographical maps—woefully inadequate for this region—radar, and other sensor screens. He smiled wryly. Might as well be on a moon. Alone. The smile turned cruel. "But if I am alone, Galaxy Commander, then so are you."

For no reason, he abruptly closed gummy eyes, casting about as though with an invisible will, laughing bitterly at the absurdity. "Where are you, Kev? Where is my great power, old man, to find my prey?"

Hisa!

Like a burning brand of terror, the word sought to unhinge and dislocate. *Not this time. Not this time. This is for you! Even for the* surat *Tanaka.*

Wrenching controls as though to tear them clean from their mountings, he sent the 'Mech forward, almost stumbling, wings of purposefully forgotten nightmares fluttering, until the sound could be heard among the pounding of giant metal-shod feet crushing stone, bouncing back and forth like a harsh oscillation of mocking laughter.

Time distended as he pushed the machine to an extreme of speed in the cramped, interweaving corridors of stone. At times, despite superb abilities, the *Wendigo* shouldered into protuberances, like malignant outgrowths budding and spawning in horrible striations away from the wall; kicked and almost tripped over berms and rocky outcroppings, like stunted, malformed rocks. Like blood dripping from his face, red splotches began to mar the outline of the *Wendigo* on the status display, self-inflicted wounds to scour away a thousand misdeeds, to ignore the crosses behind and the nightmares ahead.

Glorious, all-consuming fire suddenly eclipsed all sight as emerald darts seemed to cleanse, at least for now, the momentary lunacy. Warning sirens shrieked of abrupt enemy proximity and target lock; of harsh damage turning additional sections red, and some even black, on the status display.

Centuries of genetic breeding ran true as, even taken by surprise and lost to his own world, Kisho's body immediately tried to bring the *Wendigo* down to a manageable speed, targeting reticule seeking the golden hue of target lock to unleash a return swipe at its savager. Another double dose of large-pulse-laser energy pounded down at an angle, blistering armor into runnels across a half dozen ulcerous wounds.

Finally fully focused on his situation, Kisho spotted his tormentor and realized with chagrin that the 'Mech actually stood up above the channel of the ravine. *By the Founder, how . . . ?*

Sickly lime-fluorescent light glowed deep within twin over-the-shoulder barrels and another flurry of pulsing energy darts burst armor in scorching rents, before his feet stomped down on pedals, sending the *Wendigo* in an incredibly short arc to the top of the arroyo. Before the machine touched down, twin medium pulse lasers delivered a flowering of jade darts in return, while the deep-throated jugging of the autocannon added to the symphonic crackle of the particle cannon. Most of the weapons unerringly found their mark, and the enemy *Ghost* felt the caress of death waiting in the wings.

For a half eyeblink, Kisho hesitated at the image, as nightmare wings seemed to flutter around once more; beating wings stirring the air currents in the cockpit until the overheated air seemed like a cyclone of sucking warmth. "What have I done?" he yelled, lips peeled back until his face threatened to crack in half under the strain. "What! What do I need to do?!" He yelled not to Hisa, not to the old man, but, for once, to himself.

Something began to unfold within. Something that seemed to blossom as does a seed in the darkness, petals awakening to an unknown energy, unfelt and unseen, unheard before.

The top of the canyon wall proved to be a large plateau, with seemingly unending ditches and humps, as though the swollen and bloated intestines of some

impossibly large creature, baking in the sun, marched
into the distance. An incessant buzz began, of a comm
demanding answers, but Kisho lashed out with killing
indigo energies in response as the *Ghost* used its superior land speed to try to work around the *Wendigo,*
cutting hard to his left.

Kisho struggled, knowing he was the superior pilot,
but it felt like he fought two foes; one without and
one within. As though a ghost rose within—while the
Ghost fought without—and tried to block his every
movement, blurring eyesight and tightening stomach
muscles until he knew his stomach wall would rupture,
splattering fetid and noxious human blasphemy across
the insides of the cockpit.

A god's fist stove in the entire left side of the *Wendigo,* tossing the machine violently to the right. His
head whipped so hard to the left that the neurohelmet
hammered into the control panel and he blacked out,
possibly saving his life as his limp body rode the tumultuous and devastating tumble to the ground. The
force of his ammo exploding forced the machine off
the edge of the arroyo and down through an avalanche
of torn-off rocks to finally land in a disheveled heap.

A voice brought him back.

Hisa?

The voice seemed strident.

Tanaka?

The voice held sincerity.

Old man . . . master.

The voice finally penetrated the webs of uncon-
sciousness binding him down.

"Mystic Kisho. Are you alive?" the voice of Galaxy
Commander Kev Rosse sounded as weary as though
the world hung on his neck, dragging him to oblivion.

As I have felt? As I feel? Moving his head fractionally, pain scorched through every muscle, wrenching a

scream of protest before lips sealed the sound away. With the pain came another sensation . . . the flowering of a seed now sending tendrils out to grasp firmly into the soil of his being.

The soil of his soul.

"Mystic," the voice continued, as though desperate to be heard, regardless of whether Kisho might be beyond the ability to hear it. "I did not do what you accuse me of. I would not strike at a fellow Cat. Not unless you leave me no choice . . . as you have now. Please, call this off. Call your warriors off, before there can never be a great enough *surkai* to forgive what has happened between us."

The surroundings began to take on reality, blood dripping down . . . up to splatter against uncaring metal. *I am almost upside down?* The idea burst a floodgate of knowledge and sensation while, simultaneously, the flowering within persisted relentlessly and a thousand possibilities flooded through him, carried on the current of a voice—a conviction of complete innocence. Violence began to dim under new light.

With the blood rushing to his head threatening to send him once more into oblivion, Kisho slowly raised one arm, until he gripped a handle on the ceiling—now floor—then snapped the release mechanism on the five-point restraining harness. The dead weight of his body almost smashed his head into the ceiling, his arm too wounded to bear the complete weight. Hot, coppery-tasting air hissed through clenched teeth, his skin scraping across unfamiliar metal.

"Mystic. Are you alive? Answer."

Unknowingly, his face bore no semblance of humanity. Through the warring juxtaposition of internal and external sensations, a picture—not a cold, emotionless holovid, but a painting crafted with devoted hands to show a new level of minutia, a new understanding of purest meaning at each viewing—slowly materialized. As with his moments of previous clarity, this burned bright, flowing on the veins of the seedling tendrils now coursing to every part of his body. At such a moment, not even Kisho could lie to himself, despite the acute pain.

Wrong. I am wrong. Whoever has done this, it is not Kev.

A pressure building to the bursting point, a force so pervasive he was not even aware of it until this moment, slowly released, as the truth tore away the obscurants and delusions. Forced him to face the reality of his own situation. He knew he must answer Kev, must face him and accept the consequences . . . but for just a moment, he could finally grieve. Not for Hisa, though that pained him more than he imagined.

But for the pain he caused her.

For faults he wouldn't see.

His own culpability.

She was right.

Lack of Faith.

30

"I come."

The words fell into a chasm, far deeper than the physical one his 'Mech occupied. The sharp blade of a remembered nightmare seemed to pierce through feet, splitting and fissuring ever wider.

With aches, bruises, and pains clogging senses, fingers scrabbled across unfamiliar metal—sweat-slicked, slightly bloody—before locating the egress hatch. He undogged it, only to find a miasma of billowing dirt storming in, causing him to cough until he thought lung blood would surely splatter, joining that already found on hands and a wounded arm.

Eyes watering against the airborne irritants and stark sunlight, a hint of his previous sarcasm peeked out as though from an unused distance. *At least the way is not blocked.*

The sardonic smile died by increments as he made his way out onto the metal cowling and looked around. The *Wendigo* lay almost completely buried under an avalanche of boulders of all sizes: fists to houses. Like a newly created ramp, the 'Mech had collapsed a portion of the plateau, dropping down into the ravine and pulling with it endless thousands of tons of rock.

The last time you will fight for me. He slowly rested his forehead against the metal of his *Wendigo* and found comfort. Found it to be right. As though snipped, his past flowed away, a departing ship leaving him beached on a new shore. Pristine sand marched to a new horizon, waiting for feet to tread a new path. And with the departing history flowed his 'Mech.

Flowed all that went with it.

Better you are buried on the field of battle, than to grow old and have your armor cut away and your engine and gyro and internal components ripped free to save the life of another 'Mech. No, better the honor of death and a lonely memorial on a forgotten world, than disgrace and the ignominies of scavenging.

With a final sigh, avoiding the still-hot metal spots—all too strong a testament of the battle so recently finished—Kisho stepped out onto the rocks and began the tortuous climb to the top. Much to his chagrin, he was forced to stop several times, bending over to catch his breath and control the spots dancing a kaleidoscope across his vision.

How can I be this out of shape? He forged on, each rock edge a nightmare blade to his feet, the loose stones tumbling him about as though he were a 'Mech with a damaged gyro. At some point during that terrible climb he finally faced the need to accept. To accept the need to be completely truthful to himself. The last few weeks had been a torment of the soul and mind. And the body cannot take that type of punishment, regardless of how well honed it might be. He glanced down at the smears of blood marring his fingers. And right now, he was *far* from *honed*.

Finally scrabbling to the top, he bent almost double, head between knees as he coughed and wheezed, vision narrowing down until he knew he would pass out. But he didn't and it passed enough for him to gaze back down the ramp. Vertigo sank gnarled claws into his vision and he wobbled on the edge of capsizing back over the edge: the distance and angle of ascent astonished him.

I came up that? Sweat blurred eyes until he rubbed it away with copper-scented, calloused fingers shaking with the aftereffects of adrenaline. Something pushed and prodded within him; he dodged and twisted until he stopped cold against the rigid reality of his new situation. He began to laugh softly, an unhinged cackle, which he finally subdued before it turned into a scouring wind he would not be able to control.

Long-ago words from Hisa seemed to float and burst into consciousness. *There is nothing so terrifying as standing naked in front of the mirror. Unless it is standing fleshless in front of a soul mirror.*

The clothing of the world seemed abruptly stripped away, until he floated in front of an endless pane of mirrored silver—cruel, cold, and sharp-edged with the reality of his own faults. With all he had done. With the knowledge that he had climbed the avalanche without a care in the world, secretly hoping it would collapse and kill him. Not the honor of *bondsref,* but a terrible, pitiful, cowardly denial of facing his true mettle.

A mettle found wanting in every way.

"Mystic."

The words burst like a laser blast across the cosmos, shattering the mirror into infinite shards, showering down and around, each tickling sound of breakage finally rousing him to the here and now. Slowly standing erect, he took in a lungful of ozone-tinged, hot air and turned to face another mirror.

Sweat-soaked and dirty, Galaxy Commander Kev Rosse stood a short distance away. For an eyeblink, the endless chasm of Kisho's dreams hovered between them, the blade just beginning its bloodletting of feet.

Hisa.

Her memory stirred and the veins growing and flowering within him seemed to take on a greater life as he took a firm step straight into that chasm, across that blade. A half dozen steps and he stopped several feet away from Kev, knelt, and then bowed, holding the position for longer than any previous time in his life. Not even his mentor ever received such. He tried speaking several times, but failed. Scraping flat palms across the dusty, warm rocks until it felt like sandpaper tearing at his skin, he finally found words.

"I ask *surkai*, Galaxy Commander." The words came out a whisper, but with more truth and clarity then any spoken before. "I have been mistaken. There is no *surkai* great enough to atone for what I have done. Not even *bondsref* might wash away my mistakes. Neverthless, I ask it. And by The Founder, and the blood that flows through my veins, I will live to be worthy of your answer."

An eternity seemed to spiral stars through the void, crushing and birthing worlds before Kisho could stand the silence no longer and looked up. Kev, in the silence, had seated in mirrored form, exactly at a distance where their outstretched hands might meet, just finishing his own nod, eyes intent, mouth dropping open to answer . . .

(Kisho jerked backwards, almost spilling from his seated position, mind a violent storm: tears threatened. *I am not worthy; I come, destroying all you know in weakness and error and you honor* me*!*)

. . . and a river of blood violently splattered Kisho all across his body, full in the face, until the wash plugged up nostrils and coated tongue, until Kisho felt it would never end.

The world seemed to hiccup during the splattering of blood, Kisho literally tasting the death of Kev before the large-bore rifle bullet grazed his face so closely that the whip-crack of its passage cut a small, crimson contrail across his cheek, and the spang off the rocks echoed into the distance.

No! he shouted, though whether with lips or within his mind he would never know, and froze. *Kill me. Kill me! Kill ME! KILL ME!*

He yearned for it. Demanded to gush his own blood in place of that of Kev. Knowing the bullet should have taken both their lives, knowing the assassin would be drawing a new bead, his muscles went frigid as a sapling in the harshest arctic winter and he fell away, welcoming the harvester's scythe, knowing he should have died with Hisa, and Tanaka, and now Kev, knowing he had failed, it all had failed.

Interlude IV

And the light of the universe bled;
wails of sorrow, remembrance.
A hundred songs of tears,
a thousand rages of betrayal,
ten thousand trials of retribution.
Blood sings a new path.
The greatest warrior since the Founding,
sacrificing legion,
to safeguard.
First Mystic.
— The Remembrance (Clan Nova Cat),
    Passage 442, Verse 7, Lines 1–10

Ways of Seeing Park, Barcella
Nova Cat Reservation, Irece
Irece Prefecture, Draconis Combine
2 May 3102

His bones hurt.

They always hurt of late. But this night. This meeting. They hurt more than usual. And yet . . . the pain seemed a comfort. A salve against the wall of darkness thrown across this line in life for so long.

Is my birthday so close? With the huge festivities of Homecoming building and exploding yesterday—some activities still ongoing even at this unholy hour; cele-

brations so needed after the last few years—his own
celebration of one more foot towards the grave
slipped his mind.

As it always did.

Who wants to think of how many sunsets are behind
and how few ahead?

And yet, at last, the way forward . . .

At three in the morning, local time, the long corridors of the Nova Cat Genetic Repository held only
shadows and secrets, both jealously guarded this night.
Refusing to show the pain he felt with each step, the
old man moved sedately through frescoed columns,
Corinthian-style archways and alcoves, and endless
flagstones with their buried treasures and memories.

*How many years have I walked these halls? How
many years . . .*

Turning right, then descending a series of stairways,
he continued moving right each time until it seemed
impossible he might still be beneath the tower complex. Yet the old man knew the inside of the building
as though it had been etched upon his retinas. Though
he was deep and in areas only a handful ever traversed, he was still within the shadow of the almost
three-hundred-meter-tall tower at high noon.

His tired chest began to wheeze, compounded by
the stale and arid touch of the artificial air as it rasped
at his lung tissue. This depth was long past the point
when natural air currents might keep a Barcella mole-
rat alive, much less a human. Another dozen steps
and he stood before an iron-bound door. He paused
here, and lightly touched the mahogany.

This extension of the original building existed because of him. This secret chamber was here because
of his own history. Yes. From a lifetime of neglect,
memories surged of an existence before this one, of

other desires and wants and needs. Other responsibilities. No, not that. The responsibilities never changed, regardless of what trappings he wore.

The bas-relief of the door pushed against his calloused fingers, probing, demanding. Incessant. As he'd needed it to be. A lifetime's love of history gave birth to an almost mosaiclike relief on the door, depicting a multitude of scenes. Of Icarus; Caligula; the last samurai in the nineteenth century; the United States of America at the rise of the Western Alliance; the Terran Hegemony at the end of the Star League; ComStar before the schism; the Clans on Strana Mechty at the Great Refusal; the Jihad: almost forty scenes total, each spiraling after the other in a never-ending circle.

The old man smiled slightly, his usually stoic facade cracking at the idea of what it all meant. He might just allow a successor to finally win his post, if he could just find one who could tell him the theme of the door. In a single word. So simple and yet so foreign to so many, especially those in power.

Especially me? He couldn't help the small chuckle, considering the meeting about to unfold.

He shrugged lightly, the coarse cloth of his robes rubbing casually against leathery skin. He pushed against the door and entered.

The chamber within was almost anticlimactic after the marvel of the door's beauty. Spartan to the point of austerity, it contained a simple five-sided table, with two chairs to a side, all with the warm cherry blush of hardwood. A soft glow wreathed the room in familiarity and comfort from a hidden bank of lights in the high-vaulted ceiling. A small raised platform to the right, with a small mat and tea-making apparatus, was the only other oddity in the rather small chamber.

But the simplicity of the chamber belied the expansive technology banking the room completely, enfolding it in a silence as great as resources might allow. His lips twitched once more at the idea of so many years of subduing his previous life for the current, only to draw on it on numerous occasions, when needed. Only when absolutely needed . . . of course.

We always go back to the same drinking hole, don't we, old man?

Lips threatened to twist into a larger grin, but it died unborn, sliding back to a thin line as the other four occupants of the room came into focus. The tall, almost tawny-skinned Khan Ajax Drummond filled a seat with his usual determination and charisma. The dark clouds humped in lines on his forehead could be read by the basest labor castemen, much less one so versed in reading others as he was. *He does not approve of the proposal.* The dark, brooding eyes that met his unflinching grays secured his opinion of the fight to come.

Carefully making his way to the table, the old man seated himself while taking in the other three. Though each sat at a different angle, the deference paid by the two flanking individuals to the third, central, figure was so great as to almost be a physical manifestation he could strum with idle fingers.

Muscles relaxing after the strenuous walk, he let out a pent-up breath, but it didn't bring much relief. After all, the pain in his bones sparked from much more than simply old age and a long walk down darkened stairwells and ghostly hallways.

He nodded respectfully to the guest, ignoring the other two, who'd yet to speak in the months of negotiations that proceded this night. The woman appeared to be of an age with him. Yet where time sat heavily upon his wearied shoulders, the striking beauty of her youth still shone just below the skein of wrinkles and only slightly sagging skin. In white robes that flowed around her like a web of silk spun on the spot, she emanated power and tranquility in equal parts. It was in the way she turned her head, in the look in her eyes, in her posture. A combination he found fascinating, to say the least.

Are you so enfeebled, old man, that you allow your mind to wander at such a delicate time? When all the future unfolds from this night? A pair of pretty eyes to engender regret for decades-long celibacy? He kept himself from shaking his head, but only just. "Abbess Tolonoi, what have you to say?"

Delicate shoulders moved layers of robes imperceptibly, while a smile brought her beauty even more strongly to upturned lips and accepting eyes. "What more is there to say?" She casually pointed towards the holoprojector inset in the tabletop. "My Order has provided all the documentation available. We have withheld nothing. The decision is yours. As it has been for the last three days."

Out of the corner of his eye he saw Khan Drummond open his mouth and moved to forestall an outburst that might cost them. Regardless of the Order of the Five Pillars' seemingly outstretched hand, a devastating war was only recently ended. A war, in fact, that led directly to this place, a war perpetrated by the masters of the very abbess now sitting calmly in their midst.

Ah, the vagaries of fate and the webs of lies and deceit . . . and hope. Yes, hope. The universe must enjoy itself at times. Very much.

"Abbess," he began, "we are well aware of time's stately march. Yet we cannot move into the future you propose without due consideration. I have been on Zane Plateau several times seeking guidance. This may be one of the most pivotal moments in the history of Clan Nova Cat."

She nodded. "I understand. Hence my patience. However, the time comes when decisions must be made. You Clanners must know that even more than any Spheroid. There are times when decisive action is needed."

"As when Warlord Minamoto's mad grab for power sparked another war with Clan Ghost Bear?" Khan Drummond spoke, anger seething in words that filled the chamber with all the hurt and pain and death of the last three years. "When he moved decisively to give action to his hatred of us? To subjugate Clan Nova Cat once and for all to the Dragon, as the Ghost Bear gnawed our flanks?"

The abbess glanced in his direction without moving her head and once more he marveled at the subtle dismissal of his khan's argument. "Warlord Minamoto failed. He has paid for his sins," she responded in soft tones only heard because of the perfect acoustics of the room.

Ajax's hand slapped the table, fury threatening to overcome all the weeks of groundwork. "Perhaps for you, but not for the Nova Cats. Who will atone for the deaths of so many Clansmen? Of so many civilian dead? And you say he failed?" He slapped the table again, voice spinning up even higher. "Then why are we now on reservations on worlds we once owned outright, given to us by Theodore Kurita? Why does Coordinator Hohiro not pull troops from our soil? Why do we not return to the balance of our pledge of loyalty to the Dragon? Or does he not trust us any more than Warlord Minamoto?"

The abbess regarded the khan of all Clan Nova Cats for a few moments, then her eyes flowed towards the old man. He matched her stare, fully aware of the passing of authority implicit in the act. As Khan Ajax began to stand, rage vibrating from his large stance at her affront of dismissing his concerns, the old man spoke.

"Please, my Khan," he began, turning fully to Ajax with the implied blessing of the abbess—he could say things she could not. He must come at this carefully. "Though no ilKhan has been elected since the days of the Jihad and the Wars of Reaving," he began, licking lips to work moisture into his mouth, "by the nature of the position, an ilKhan's hands were ofttimes tied, making it impossible to simply force an issue. Instead, many an ilKhan had to exert pressure elsewhere to achieve a goal. The same applies here. Hohiro is as committed to the Nova Cats as his father. Perhaps more so. Yet he is not all-powerful and his position is precarious. He will support Clan Nova Cat, but the pressure from his warlords currently will not allow him to pull back his troops. To do so risks another Ronin War."

Ajax stood rooted to his spot, turning over both that knowledge and the fact that the words had come from him. What finally convinced the khan, the old man felt sure, was the same reason the abbess did not speak. The same often applied to the khan of a Clan— at times the Clan Council could throw impediments in a khan's way, forcing him to use alternate means. The fact that he avoided mentioning what would be plain between him and Khan Drummond also helped to mollify the khan towards the abbess' actions. At times, even in secrecy and on foreign soil, some words could not be spoken.

"But this?" Ajax continued. "Do we really want to commit ourselves to this course?" Even slightly mollified, the khan's reluctance still rose like heat waves on sun-baked ferrocrete.

The old man lost focus for a moment as glimpses of a possible future gyrated—spurts of technicolor and auditory and tactile sensations slipping through small rents in the blackness of the unknown they now moved through.

The khan may not budge until you hammer it home. Until you destroy the last vestiges of his reluctance. Coming back into focus, he spoke blasphemy.

"Nicholas Kerensky failed."

Ajax jerked back as though pole-axed, the words echoing with power, then falling into a silence so thick with emotions that the old man, for just a moment, felt as though the pumping hearts of those present thrummed along invisible lines . . . lines that might fall apart, but which also might succeed if wound and woven and bound together.

"The Founder failed," he continued, his voice profound—soft, yet powerful as a *Mad Cat* laying waste to enemy 'Mechs on the battlefield. "The Clans failed. As a whole, we did not restore order to the Inner Sphere and reestablish a Star League. Instead, regardless of its sham roots, a Star League formed to stop us. And then someone did bring lasting peace, at least what might be lasting peace, to the Inner Sphere . . . and Devlin Stone had nothing to do with the Clans, nor we him. And he even seduced us with his words, until we Clans joined the Inner Sphere in diminishing the very thing the Founder built us to be. And even Nova Cat visions did not succeed, though perhaps those visions have yet to come to fruition and our current valley of death is a signpost we must pass to reach paradise. . . ." He trailed off, the words spoken almost more for himself than the khan, as eyes once more saw forbidden fruits. The pale, wild-eyed look of his khan finally penetrated his own musings and he wrestled his errant thoughts back to the unfolding battle that must be won, or the seeds of that forbidden fruit would never germinate. He continued, inexorable.

"Though many Clans denigrate Clan Ghost Bear for what it is becoming, it has come closer to achieving the Founder's vision than any other. The Bears rule a combined state, which is the most stable and powerful of any of the occupation zones, and rivals even the Great Houses. Yet they, too, have failed to reach the true, full vision the Founder put forth so many centuries ago."

Though in his peripheral vision he could sense the abbess and her accompanying acolytes locked into immobility at the unfolding display, the world fell away as he used the moment to finally flay away any last objections and open the khan's eyes. Though doing so in front of the abbess was a calculated risk, he believed the very public airing of this dirty secret, which the Clans tried so hard to ignore, might be the final leverage needed to move the khan into a new direction.

"And when you fail?" he continued, voice growing husky at such a long speech for a voice unaccustomed to much speaking. "When you are born and bred across centuries, when an entire society is based upon a single goal and you fail . . . all the Clans must eventually come to grips with this single imperative. "

"The . . . Founder . . . failed." He spoke each word as though they were death blows delivered by a particle projector cannon.

"Does it mean the Clans have no role to play in the future? *Neg.* We Nova Cats, better than any Clan, know the future is malleable and you must flow with the currents or be devoured, as proven by the broken carcasses of fallen Clans.

"Yet the Clans must face this failure and learn to deal with it. The Ghost Bears are doing it. Clan Sea Fox, perhaps the only other Clan to match us for the ease with which they move with the currents, is also making the transition to this new reality. The other Clans can and will deal with it in their own ways as well, or they will perish, rotted and destroyed from within. New philosophies akin to the Warden-Crusader debates will arise. New sects will emerge. And new ways of dealing with the genetics program."

He paused to provide the appropriate emphasis for his next words.

"A program that, like the Founder, failed."

Once again, silence. Though this time Khan Ajax's eyes did not quite bulge, he still seemed frantic, like an animal forced back on its haunches and on the verge of fleeing for safety.

"There is no safety in our current state," he spoke, causing Ajax to jerk as though the old man drew the words from his mind. He hated using such deceptive tactics with his khan—years of observations allowed him to make an excellent guess as to his khan's thoughts—but as the abbess said, there was a time for decisive actions. And this was one.

"The Dragon has been weakened and, though it will grow strong again, it cannot be the ally it once was for us. An ally we must have if we are to survive into the future. We must look for allies elsewhere. Allies where we least expect."

Though Ajax's eyes did not wander, they twitched momentarily towards the abbess.

"We must find a new path for our Clan. A new way of protection." The old man read his khan like a piece of rice paper, tested the air for the right moment, and forged into the minutiae Ajax avoided with distaste.

"The abbess' Order has been attempting to create a

new *Budojin* Neophyte, through extreme new training measures. Neophytes that, in addition to being expert warriors, can under special circumstances think outside of human parameters. That can make deductions and leaps of logic outside regular human experience. That can see what others cannot. Is this not what we Nova Cats strive for as well? To see what others cannot? Visions? *Quiaff?*"

"Aff," the old man forged on, answering his own question, determined to simply bowl over any final objections. "And yet they, too, have ultimately failed in their mission. Though they believe their training to be on the right track, it is the blood of those they train that fails. Our scientists have the capability to produce new blood. And from a combination of this new training and new blood, a new type of warrior will emerge. One that can serve both the Nova Cats and the Order."

"A new phenotype," Khan Drummond finally responded quietly, resignation singing in his voice. "A new caste."

"Perhaps more a new subcaste," the old man responded, trying to mollify. "But *aff*, my Khan. A way to move forward. A new way. The *only* way."

Ajax bowed his head momentarily before meeting the old man's eyes with a hint of his former fiery denial. "And this blood. This first blood?"

For once this night the old man felt on the defensive, as the culmination of what might be his life's work—a culmination of which he was not even aware until presented with the abbess' horrible plans—tunneled down to this single moment in time.

They both knew what was proposed. They had both read the endless bytes of information presented by the Order. The computer modeling and years of research showed those within Clan Nova Cat who demonstrated more talent for visions than any others, those who contained the genetic makeup the Order felt was necessary to begin such training. To *survive* such training. In effect, these individuals were showing latent talent. Talent simply waiting for the proper training to bloom into . . . something new.

A mystic caste.

And of all the people within Clan Nova Cat, the modeling showed a single person to perfectly fit the genetic mold, to contain more latent potential than any other.

Him.

Silence stretched until the universe seemed to bleed from the strain of nothingness. The khan's eyes hammered into his own. *You will force me to say it, won't you, my Khan?* So shaken, his thoughts fell to the vulgarity of his youth in the use of contractions. Finally giving in, knowing his khan felt pushed to the brink and must push back, he parted dry-as-dust lips and spoke the words.

"The blood must come from me."

The khan nodded, as though accepting an offered prize. They knew each other well enough for the khan to realize the pain such an admission must cost. For so many years he'd denied his blood. But to find *his* blood was what might save his Clan from oblivion . . . the bitter irony made him want to weep.

"You will never wear a Bloodname," Ajax spoke, his words steel-hard to instantly cut away all objections.

Though never holding such aspirations, and with no real claim to a Bloodname—no claim to a matrilineal line to one of the original eight hundred Bloodname— he was Clansman enough for such words to burn. Yet he found hope in knowing his khan was finally accepting the necessity of a new reality.

"And no mystic will *ever* wear a Bloodname," Ajax continued, slashing into the old man's already wounded psyche.

"No!" he responded, actually rising halfway out of his chair in protest. "Please do not do this. You have read the material. You know what they will be forced to endure in their training. What they will endure all their lives. What we will ask of them. Do not deny this to them as well. They will be Clan warriors!"

Ajax stood, as though he were an avatar representing the entire Clan, voice emphatic and face the stone of determination. "It is time for my own decisiveness. You talk about new ways, as though it is such a simple thing to cast aside the traditions of centuries. Then this, too, will be cast aside. If your blood is so precious, then it will be used in every mystic sibko . . . as genemother. You have no right to a Bloodname and, through you, no mystic will ever have that right. If this mystic caste is so needed, if the visions you speak of must have outlet, as the Nova Cat khans before me, then so be it. I accept. But all mystics will know their place.

"You have denied your blood. But you say it is through your blood we can find salvation. Then a thousand years from now, the blood you denied will fill the galaxy and your soul shall know a thousand-thousand lives . . . and deaths. So . . . be . . . it.

"Do I have your rede, Oathmaster?"

The silence once more boomed, as his heart thudded in his chest until it threatened to crack open, spewing a torrent of blood across the chamber. His chamber. His blood. His calling.

A hundred-year lifetime. A lifetime drawing to a close, and the opening of a horrific future. Do I consign generations to my blood and the pain they must endure?

He thought of the door through which he'd come to make this abhorrent but unavoidable commitment. Despite the heaviness of the responsibility he carried, the old man almost smiled. Hubris. The door depicted hubris, both personal and universal. The irony was not lost on him.

There really was no choice. There never was. Despite this calling of his blood, he'd spent too long becoming one with his Clan. He was a Nova Cat, and nothing and no one would stand in the way of the Clan. As much as a new way was needed, some ways *could* not change.

All for the Clan.

He nodded, accepting the pain of a future that would shortly kill him, sealing the future of the Clan. "I, Minoru Nova Cat, once known as Minoru Kurita, do accept this rede."

"*Seyla,*" they both said in unison.

31

Felldowns, Frankalia
Addicks, Prefecture III
The Republic of the Sphere
30 December 3136

"**Y**ou have not found him, *quiaff*?" Kisho spoke softly from a sitting position.

The tall, black-skinned Spirit Cat stared hard at Kisho before slowly responding. "*Aff.* Galaxy Co . . . my . . . our . . . forces," he stumbled, unused to the rapid change of circumstances, "have scoured every inch of the region within five kilometers. It is as though nothing ever existed here."

The sound of activity around Kisho continued to swell: numerous booted feet scraping stone, pant legs whispering of ballistic cloth; heavy cough of internal combustion engines of the two vehicles that managed to make it this far into the Felldowns; servos whining and the heavy tread of 'Mech feet that almost swayed them with their impact, bouncing stones and threatening to send another avalanche down the collapsed path, burying his *Wendigo* once and for all—*how appropriate.*

To bury the past.

The hot sun scalded, burning with carelessness. An itch that grew with each moment squirmed across his skin and scalp, until he thought he might go mad from the sensation.

Blood. Kev's blood. Dried and caking. Baking. Into me.

How appropriate. Kisho slowly closed and reopened his eyes, red flecks of dead life cracking off his eyelids and floating down, speckling the ground with dried blood-tears. A mantle seemed to coalesce around him and settle on his shoulders—a mantle of blood. Through Kev's blood he could also feel Hisa and Tanaka's rivers of life smearing and clotting across his skin as well, soaking in.

The understanding was soaking in.

Kisho slowly swiveled thousand-year-old eyes to the warrior, only to find a struggle in muscle, eyes, and cant of head. "What is your name?"

"Star Captain Franks."

"You doubt my telling of events. You wonder if I have assassinated your leader." Not questions. Statements.

The other man gaped for a moment. Then closed his mouth, swallowed several times with eyes that squirmed to retreat, then responded. "I have not spoken it."

"Of course you have. Just not with your lips."

The other man furrowed his forehead, as though trying to understand that statement.

"And I *have* killed him."

The other man jerked at his words, jumping back

278 Randall N. Bills

slightly, then dropping into a fighting stance, surprise and shock warring with animal fury. "What?!"

Kisho's eyes pounded into the Star captain until the other man relaxed into a loose crouch, then finally stood aright again. His fluttering eyelids were the last trace of his frozen flight. "I do not know who has killed him"—*though I can now begin to guess; how could I have been so stupid?*—"but death walks behind me, like a parent to a child, a specter to a warrior. All who come near me suffer. I did not pull the trigger, but I brought death to Galaxy Commander Rosse as surely as though I placed his head in the assassin's sights."

The words ground out like tectonic plates shifting in their inexorable drive to create a world anew. Each word, delivered in dead tones, struck with an almost physical force, until Star Captain Franks took a slight step back.

Kisho saw the superstition rise to the surface in Franks, saw his appraisal of the blood-smeared mess that sat before him, saw the aura of death and violence strip away the warrior's anger and shock, until only one thing remained.

Belief. Belief infused the man's face.

Bitterness poured a torrent of blackness into Kisho, but found no purchase. He was an empty, smooth-bored husk. *So quickly he believes. Believes in me. That I am something that has come to destroy him . . . or save him.* Kisho had been crafted from decanting to believe, his every word and deed designed to instill such belief, but he had found only emptiness. *And yet this warrior believes without knowing anything about me.*

Why?

The word vibrated with such urgency, such need, it seemed a universe unto itself.

Then, somehow, from the void at the bottom of the pit to which Kisho had descended, he sensed something from above. Something waiting. For him. His destiny resting on the simple ability to understand. Or . . .

. . . to accept. *Accept.*

The seedling within began to flourish.

Twenty drum beats echoed across the bruised and broken landscape, now hidden by night's black grip.

Sitting in the same position for almost half a day, Kisho tensed muscles and then released to keep spasms at bay. The acrid smoke and heat of the blazing fire came in waves, as the night wind picked up and brought flashes of heat and cold in intermittent cycles. The small gathering of Nova Cat and Spirit Cat warriors looked as though they huddled around the light, keeping the nightmares from the day at bay.

A slow turn of his head brought the small throng into plain, sharp view, their sweat-streaked faces, bloodied bandages, and combat clothing stark testament of the day's events. Bone-deep regret seeped in at the missing warriors on both sides.

No ceremonial leathers. No white robes or brass instruments for the Ritual of Battle. A slow smile lifted the corners of his lips imperceptibly. Not the ironic twist his face was so accustomed to wearing, but a softer, more knowing smile. A smile that spoke of internal acceptance . . . or at least the attempt.

Why have a Ritual of Battle, when this battle is done? He glanced towards the makeshift drums and found an earnest Spirit Cat warrior, empty fuel drum and wrench in hand. The smile ghosted larger.

You called them fallen, Kisho, yet they follow the forms with as much earnestness as any Nova Cat, regardless of how they might have drifted. Twenty drum-

beats for the twenty original Clans created by The Founder. Even here, on this far-off world, decades separated from us, in the midst of their near annihilation at my own hand . . . and they make do with what they have—belief.

In faith.

Star Captain Franks detached from the main half circle of warriors and stepped forward, then knelt. As with the others, dirt and sweat still streaked his face with careless disregard, yet his eyes shone with fierceness, determination.

"Mystic. You declared a Trial of Annihilation against Galaxy Commander Rosse and all those who would support him."

Only the voracious fire and the wheel of stars overhead initially gave notice to his words. Kisho waited some time before responding, carefully considering every answer he might give.

"Aff." Keep it simple.

The other man nodded and straightened even further, as though preparing to ask a more difficult question and readying himself for the answer. "We supported our Galaxy commander, Mystic. Do we not fall under the rules of the Trial?"

Another pause, as Kisho once more mulled over an answer. Yet, despite the importance of the situation, his mind was drawn into consideration of two other questions. Who killed Kev, Tanaka, and Hisa (the hurt had lessened a bit), and what is this new inner understanding?

First, the murders. Who had access to all three of them? He scorched with shame over the obviousness of the connection linking Tanaka and Hisa: the ISF. Small detachments of ISF were assigned to each Dragon's Fury unit, placing them in a position to murder

Tanaka and then Hisa. Though it made no sense—the Nova Cats were there to forward the aims of the Fury and, ultimately, House Kurita—the memory of the Cats being caught in internal Combine machinations before stung deeply, felt all too real. For whatever reason, the ISF must have killed them, to pull away Nova Cat support from Warlord Tormark. To make her fail at resurrecting the Dieron Military District? The questions were never ending.

But for Kev? How could the ISF possibly have followed them through such erratic jumps? How could they know the fighting would occur in these wastelands, far from any population centers?

And the other overarching question; what was this strange, new understanding slowly infusing Kisho and what did it mean for the future?

Smoke, along with the human stench of fear, blood, and sweat, and the dryness of the downs snagged his attention back to the moment. He met the unflinching gaze of Franks. The man's entire carriage spoke of supreme acceptance. He was simply waiting to know what the mystic would have of him.

As the endless stream of questions continued to batter for attention, nightmares fluttered for a moment. Images of an endless sword, of dragons and spirit cats eating nova cats, and slowly, softly, looking at Franks, he knew. Not with the hammer blows of his previous epiphanies, the strange visions that seemed to blanket out all sensations with their proclamations, but from a soft voice within.

Of a sudden he came to a decision of the path to take, trying to finally, fully, set aside his arrogance. "I lost the Trial."

Franks managed to constrain his reaction to a startled widening of eyes, but the rest of the gathered warriors moved and whispered as though a swift wind blew through a wheat field. After several attempts to find his tongue, Franks spoke. "You lost the Trial?"

"*Aff.* Galaxy Commander Rosse defeated me in honorable combat. Neither you, nor any bearing his seed, nor any of your warriors, will perish under my hand."

The gathering seemed to hold its breath, taking in the words, before a smile swept Franks' face. A smile not of relief, but of vindication. As though he had known what Kisho would say.

"Mystic. You came bearing a declaration of open arms. You proclaimed that the Spirit Cats and any with Nova Cat blood in their veins in The Republic could return to the fold. Does that still stand?"

Sudden humbleness infused Kisho in such an overwhelming rush that he struggled to breathe. The look on Franks' face, the direction of his questions—there could be no doubt where it would lead. *And after all I have done and yet you still accept. You still believe.*

Kisho nodded numbly.

"Then my warriors would accept your welcome. We would cast aside our Spirit Cat trappings and pull on the mantle of Nova Cats."

Even though he had known what was coming, the statement deprived Kisho of speech for long heartbeats as eyes roved away from Franks to take in the other Spirit Cats, identical determination painting shadowed faces in the lambent light.

Because of me? This came about because of me? A long look into Franks' eyes once more and a new level of understanding emerged. *You knew this all along, did you not, Master? But you never told me. You knew my destiny, knew that I was playing at a role. Yet you knew a greater role awaited.* He waited for bitterness to surface, but instead further knowledge embraced him. *I was not ready. I would not have understood such a simple concept.* Once more, he mentally set aside another layer of arrogance, chipping away at the layers that kept him separate—a task he knew would take years and decades to accomplish.

This has nothing to do with me. I am simply the messenger. They do it for themselves. They do it because they desire. They believe.

And do I desire? Do I believe?

He slowly nodded; whether to Franks or in answer to his own question, he did not yet know.

With abrupt movement he stood over the kneeling man and, ignoring the screaming muscles and pulling wounds, he tore strips from his undershirt. He then settled into a crouch, where he quickly tied the scrap to the man's wrist in a cloth cord.

Franks glanced down at the bondcord, accepting his absorption into the Nova Cat Clan. Suddenly, like a snake striking for its target, Kisho pulled the other man's knife free from his belt and slashed the bondcord. He slowly stood, ignoring the disbelief twisting Franks' face—mirrored on all those present—and moved to the fire, where he cast in the cord.

"You are *abtakha*," he said, voice strident, filling the night to bursting with firm resolve. "Fully adopted into the warrior caste of Clan Nova Cat."

"But, you cannot—"

Kisho simply glanced at Franks, the power of his visage shearing the man's words instantly. "I, Mystic Kisho of Clan Nova Cat, make it so."

The group hesitated for a moment, then the word *seyla* seemed to come simultaneously from all present. He nodded.

"There is much work to do. You have proven your worth a thousand times over: in your trials since the collapse of the HPG system, in the keeping of our traditions in the face of Spheroid contamination for decades . . . even in your fight against us." He gestured towards the fire already consuming the makeshift bondcord. "And so our recent history is cleansed and forgotten. You are Nova Cat warriors."

Franks stood, holding his wrist as though unable to believe no cord bound it. Then he nodded acceptance.

"There is much to be done, still. Our forces fight for Warlord Tormark, a mission we must return to with haste. And you will be a guiding light to other Spirit Cats—to accept, to believe. To return to us."

The other man hesitated, then spoke despite visible discomfort. "Not all will follow you. Some will denounce us as traitors. They will call you a murderer of Galaxy Commander Rosse."

"Aff," Kisho said, face falling into inhumanity as he put together the bits and pieces. "But that is my *surkai* to accept. Some will not follow and will continue in their hollow quest to find a haven. But many, many will come to our banner. They will fight at our side, or will pass back into the Nova Cats lands in the Combine. And the Nova Cats will be strong again. There is much work still to be done. Let us be about it."

The other Spirit Cats hesitantly moved forward, still in shock over the bondcords Kisho fashioned from his own clothing, which he then cut and tossed to the flames.

As he performed the rite, questions still raced through Kisho's mind. *Do I believe for Hisa? Perhaps not. Do I believe for me? Perhaps . . .*

But rising through it all, he felt the comfort of that small voice, telling him it all stemmed from a single idea. A single seed. One so simple that bitterness, anger and, most of all, arrogance had not let him see it.

He had a *desire* to believe.

He felt he could now come to know the powers his mystic caste had laid at his feet. And now he would ask the right questions. A long path still lay ahead. A lifetime path. But it was one he now *chose* to take— not one forced on him by others, or dictated by his conditioning. Now he took this path because he desired it. For himself. He could finally start to forgive and understand. The pain of his upbringing slowly slid into context . . . and acceptance.

That was the big picture, the *vision* for his path. But more immediately, he would hunt down the parties responsible for the latest carnage. Not for revenge. But for justice. He was wrong to divert from the task of aiding Warlord Tormark. Wrong to be sidetracked from the task of strengthening the Clan, even if that meant strengthening the Dragon as well. But he would not needlessly divert again. *I will hunt down those who murdered the mystics and Galaxy Commander Rosse.* Lines of Kev's glory that Kisho would add to The Remembrance were already flowing.

And by The Founder, they will pay.

Epilogue

Unity Palace, Imperial City
Luthien, Kagoshima Prefecture
Pesht Military District, Draconis Combine
9 February 3137

The calm of the room caressed senses with silky confidence.

Ramadeep Bhatia opened his eyes and placed the cold sake cup back on the bamboo tray to his left, while right-hand fingers once more nestled rice paper into a reading position. The cool bioluminescence coating the room allowed his coal black eyes to absorb all the information once more.

The geisha makes progress. He grunted at the idea, but marginally dipped his head once more, as though a salute across a field of battle to an unexpectedly talented foe. Not equal. *Iie.* Not that. More a devious geisha, using her wiles to snag a samurai lord above her station.

He knew it was time to put the paper aside. He had already dedicated more time this day to the geisha concern then he had anticipated. But the chagrin of her continued successes in The Republic—four more worlds pacified?—coupled with the realization of one of his own pawn moves, along with a very surprising development . . . it warranted extra time. Albeit *only* a little.

Galaxy Commander Rosse dead. *Go* stone placed, enemy removed. His lips quirked with pleasure. *I doubt even the Maskirovka would have the delicacy to subvert a Clanner into killing one of his own. How did the agent manage that?* The smile slipped momentarily at the knowledge that even his Internal Security Force might not have managed it either, as the deed actually originated through the Order of the Five Pillars. The smile tugged his mouth into a crescent once more, knowing he pulled strings within the Keeper of the House Honor's own organization to execute the deed.

With the leader of the Spirit Cats out of the equation, that cult of personality would likely evaporate. At the very least, most of them would be in no great hurry to join the Nova Cats in any form.

Just what I need, more strength to their numbers. He scanned the last few lines of the missive. *But this. This is interesting.*

Nova Cat Mystic Tanaka murdered. Nova Cat Mystic Hisa murdered. Bodies brutalized. Agent(s) unknown. Reasons unknown.

The textured feel of the paper slid from his fingers as he placed it on the smaller of the two piles, fingers twitching to pick up the next and continue the night's reading. His eyes lost focus as possibilities unfolded.

Who would kill those mystics? Even safeguarded by the best the Nova Cats could provide—their Watch a travesty, even with O5P meddling, mere decades old compared to over a half millennium of ISF diligence in safeguarding the Dragon from enemies without, as well as within—he knew well the perversion of Kurita blood into the Nova Cats new mystic caste. Seers? Prophets? Visions? Ha. He knew of the O5P's experimentations into systemic, hyperanalytical conjecture, with quasi-quantum mathematical sequencing and genegineered superlative observance acuity and blah, blah, blah.

He'd read the report, but found most of it to be either meaningless or preposterous. It appeared they were trying to create someone who could predict the future based on observations. From that report, he knew of years of horrible failures. Further, he knew that some of that might have spilled into the O5P–Nova Cat relationship. Though that continuing bond bothered him, he was more than willing to allow the O5P to divert time and precious resources into such ridiculousness.

Yet, despite his own distaste concerning the mystics' blood, or their O5P links, striking there would prove to have . . . troublesome consequences. Might as well attack their genetic repository. No better way to turn tenuous allies into the most fanatical of enemies. Especially pressed so near our heart here on Luthien.

No. That was a bed he had refused to make, yet now someone turned down the sheets, laying a mint on the pillow. Who?

He straightened marginally, the taut move at odds with the calm of the room, disrupting the harmony of his refuge. His lost pupil? The fake Bounty Hunter? Kappa? He tongued his teeth, while questions tumbled. But he apparently stood with the geisha now. Why would he seek to undermine her like this? It simply didn't make sense. And yet, of all the people who might act in such a manner, damned be the consequences . . . that, *that* fit Kappa like a glove.

But it was an ill-fitting glove, overall. Was he truly behind it, or was something, or someone else behind it? Ramadeep filed a mental note to pull on the threads of his hidden empire slightly concerning Kappa, the mystics, and the geisha. See if any of the pieces fell into a recognizable pattern.

With that, his mind closed off that chapter for the day, another rice paper sheet already in hand, black eyes drinking in new knowledge of actions unfolding elsewhere.

About the Author

Randall N. Bills began his writing career in the adventure gaming industry, where he has worked full-time for the last ten years. His hobbies include music, gaming (from electronic to RPGs to miniatures to all those wonderful German board games), reading (of course) and, when he can, traveling.

He currently lives in the Pacific Northwest where, in addition to his more-than-full-time gaming work, he pursues his writing career. Randall has published five novels and two Star Trek novellas. This is his sixth novel.

He lives with his wife Tara Suzanne, children Bryn Kevin, Ryana Nikol, and Kenyon Aleksandr, as well as an eight-foot red-tailed boa called Jak o' the Shadows.

MECHWARRIOR: DARK AGE

A BATTLETECH® SERIES

R020

Enter the realm of

Carol Berg
SON OF AVONAR

BOOK ONE OF THE
BRIDGE OF D'ARNATH TRILOGY

Magic is forbidden throughout the Four Realms. For decades sorcerers and those associated with them were hunted to near extinction.

But Seri, a Leiran noblewoman living in exile, is no stranger to defying the unjust laws of her land. She is sheltering a wanted fugitive who possesses unusual abilities—a fugitive with the fate of the realms in his hands.

0-451-45962-8

Also available:
Book Two of the *Bridge D'Arnath* trilogy:
Guardians of the Keep

Book Three of the *Bridge D'Arnath* trilogy:
The Soul Weaver

**Available wherever books are sold or at
penguin.com**

The Stardoc Novels
by
S.L. Viehl

STARDOC
0-451-45773-0

BEYOND VARALLAN
0-451-45793-5

SHOCKBALL
0-451-45855-9

ETERNITY ROW
0-451-45891-5

Available wherever books are sold or at
penguin.com

N230/Viehl